BANKING ON MURDER

J.D. WHITELAW

RED DOG
UK

Published by RED DOG PRESS 2020

First Edition

Paperback ISBN 978-1-913331-96-2
Ebook ISBN 978-1-913331-97-9

www.reddogpress.co.uk

To Anne-Marie as always. And baby who makes three.

One

THE FRONT DOOR opened with a creak. The noise seemed to wake everything up. Early morning light seeped in, chasing away the shadows. Martha Parker stood perfectly still in the doorway and looked about her kingdom.

The office was hers, the business was hers. This was where she made her money, but more than that, it was where she helped others. She liked to think that in her own small way she was making a difference. Even if it came in bad circumstances.

Parkers Investigations was her own little empire. She had played with the name, thinking she was clever getting a nod to the P.I. in there. As it turned out, they were mostly known as the Nosey Parkers, and not always positively.

Still, it was all hers, and it was hopefully growing. Sure her offices were little more than the garage attached to her house. And yes, more often than not her clients wanted her to spy on their cheating partners, but to Martha it was her life, her way of giving back. And that's what made her open the doors every day.

This morning though, she wasn't her normal enthusiastic self. Normally she'd be able to see the good in any situation. The sun shone from her cheery smile, laughter would flow and everyone would feel alright. Not today, however. Today, she was fatigued, bogged down—dog tired.

The festive cheer was starting to get to her. If she heard *Fairytale of New York* once more, she thought she might scream. She didn't mind Christmas, she loved it in fact. But when the whole machine cranked into gear six weeks before the big day, she felt a bit Christmassed out.

That's why she was standing in the doorway. That's why she hadn't rushed to her desk and started up the computer. That's why the kettle was still quiet and the biscuits hadn't been divvied up amongst the three of them. That's why... there was something wrong.

"Hold on," she said, watching her breath float away in front of her. "What's gone on here?"

She looked about the place. Three desks were spread out across the room—as normal. The computers were off and the phones were all silent—as normal. If she didn't know better she would have thought the place was exactly the same as she'd left it the night before. Only she *did* know better.

"Right," she said, rolling up the sleeves of her cardigan. "What have you done this time?"

Slowly, she stepped into the office. The door closed gently behind her, plunging the whole place into darkness again. Letting her eyes adjust, she began stalking around the room like a lion hunting its prey.

She passed by her desk and let her fingers trundle along the top. She tapped the surface. Tap. Tap. Tap.

"I know you're in here," she said. "I can tell, I can *always* tell. Call yourself a professional, ha! I've got your number, pally."

There was no answer. The office was still and silent. Martha reached the far side of the room. She stopped, scanning the place for any sign of movement. If he were to leave, she'd surely see him. The first rule of detective work, she'd read somewhere, always cover your exits.

This was why she did what she did. She loved a challenge and she loved her talent for detection getting a good old test.

Then she spied something moving out the corner of her eye. He was quick, very quick, almost too quick. Easing her way around the chair, past the bin, around the old printer and the filing cabinet with the broken lock, she got ready to pounce.

"This is your last chance," she said firmly. "Come out and there won't be any trouble. Stay in hiding and, well, I don't know what I'll do…"

Nothing. She got ready, hunching on the balls of her feet, ready to explode like a coiled spring. One more moment, just an extra second, wait for the right time and…

Martha leapt forward. She dived over Helen's desk and grabbed the invader, holding on as tightly as she could. Lurching back, she pulled with all of her might until she was back on her feet.

"Got you!" she said, triumphantly. "Thought you could get away from me, eh? Well no such luck."

The chubby face of a large, ginger tomcat stared back at Martha. Ears and whiskers twitching, he looked neither interested or intimidated. A cable from one of the computers dangled from his mouth. Martha pulled it out and examined the chewed wires.

"How many times have I told you Toby, you're to stay out of here at night," she said, shaking him lightly. "And you should lay off the cables, you'll give yourself a terrible shock."

The cat said and did nothing. He didn't even purr. Instead he looked about beneath him, already fed up of Martha's antics.

"I know what you're thinking. 'How did she catch me? I was so careful this time.' But that's where you're wrong, Toby. You repeat offenders, you're all the same. You get too used to a life of crime that's why you come back for more over and over again. Shame on you."

Toby *still* wasn't interested. In fact, Martha thought he looked bored. But she wouldn't be a proper detective unless she lectured her criminal. That's what they did on TV so that was good enough for her.

"I'll bet you thought you'd get away with it this time," she said, smiling at Toby. "But you should have been more careful covering your tracks. A master criminal, Toby, never ever leaves clues lying around. Take exhibit A for example."

She spun him around and walked him over to Geri's desk. Pointing down at a water bottle left on its side, Martha smirked.

"Too easy," she said. "You should know by now my sister, messy though she is, isn't so bad she'd leave a bottle of water tipped over on its side. She knows I'd go through her like a dose of salt. But, there's more."

Martha darted back across the room, Toby still in her arms.

"Exhibit B," she declared. "An empty plate beside Helen's computer. Now I know what you're thinking; 'So what? That could have been empty for ages.' But no, it wasn't. I happen to know that when we left here last night there were three, yes *three*, gingerbread men with little Santa hats on. And now look. Nothing but crumbs. Dear oh dear, Toby, you have been sloppy this time buddy. I don't know what to do with you."

She gave the cat a big hug. Toby purred with delight before springing from her hands and landing on the floor. He strutted his way across the room and scratched at the door.

"Ah, I see," she said, joining him. "Get out before the victims arrive and leave me to take the blame. Very clever Mr Toby, maybe you *are* a master criminal after all. Although I don't know what Helen is going to say when she realises her biscuits are gone. In fact, no, I know *exactly* what she's going to say. She's going to hit the roof."

The sound of an engine distracted Martha. She peered out the window of the door and saw two headlights pulling into her driveway. She opened the door and let Toby waddle out, watching him as he vanished into the hedge beside the garage.

"Great," she said. "The victim, right on time. As usual."

An old Mini Cooper chugged its way almost to her feet. A plume of dark smoke puffed from its back end as the engine gurgled to a halt. The engine died and the door opened, a head of unkempt frizzy hair appearing immediately.

"You better not have eaten my biscuits," came a hoarse voice, followed by a sneeze.

"Good morning to you too, Helen," said Martha. "No 'how's my favourite big sister?' No 'How's Geoff? The kids?' Nothing. Your cup just overflows with kindness."

"Forget the kindness," said Helen, shuffling out of her battered old car. "You're in first, you're *always* in first. That means I'll have no biscuits left. You've always been the same."

"Now that's not fair," said Martha. "And anyway, you don't even know the biscuits are gone."

"Oh I know," said Helen.

She juggled two bags, several books and an old handkerchief in her hands. Moving like a scruffy tornado she went to head in the office. Martha blocked her way.

"Hold on," said the older sister. "Now just hold on, wait a minute would you. Before you go in there I have a confession to make."

"A confession, right," said Helen, her eyes closed suspiciously to slits. "Here it comes."

"Your biscuits are gone," said Martha.

"I *knew* it!" Helen shouted. "You've eaten my biscuits! Those were from the Christmas market Martha! The *Christmas market!*"

"I know, I know," Martha struggled to keep a smile from her face.

"God," Helen groaned. "I was really looking forward to those today too. I feel terrible with this cold, I've got a heap of marking to do and I was really, *really* building myself up to those biscuits. They were from the Christmas market Martha. Did I tell you that? The *Christmas* market."

"Yes you did," Martha said, giggling into her sleeve.

"What's so funny?"

"Nothing," she said. "Nothing at all."

"Are you… are you laughing at me?"

"No."

"You are."

"I'm not."

"You bloody are!"

"I'm not, honestly," said Martha, drawing herself together. "I'm just laughing at the fact you're so bothered by three little gingerbread biscuits. Remind me again how many degrees you've got? Remind me also what you do for a living?"

"I hardly think my higher education has anything to do with anything really," said Helen pompously. "And the fact I help you catch cheating partners behind their wives and husbands' backs really doesn't change the fact my bloody biscuits are gone!"

Martha sighed loudly and turned back into the office. Thankfully the phone started ringing.

"For the record, the cat ate them," she said.

"Oh yeah, that old excuse," said Helen, shuffling with her bags and books towards her desk. "The cat ate them, nonsense."

"He did. I caught him this morning. He almost electrocuted himself chewing on the cables beneath your desk."

"Then where is he?" asked Helen. "Come on Miss Marple? Where's the man of the moment?"

"He's gone, obviously."

"A likely story."

"Are you going to get the phone?" Martha asked.

"Forget the phone," said Helen, lifting the empty plate on her desk. "What about my biscuits?"

"I'll get it then," said Martha, ignoring her.

She picked up the receiver while Helen grumbled loudly.

"Good morning," she said, surprising herself at how chirpy she'd become. "Parkers Investigations, Martha Parker speaking, how can I help you?"

"Hello… yes…" came a nervous voice on the other end of the line. "I'm… I'm not sure if I should be calling but… I saw your ad and… well… I need your help."

"Biscuits," Helen shouted from across the room. "Bloody gone, friggin' typical."

"Yes, of course," said Martha, waving her sister away. "Well we're always happy to help. Why don't you let me know what we can do and we can take it from there?"

"Yes… thank you…"

The woman on the other end of the phone began to sob uncontrollably. Martha sat down and pulled a pad and pen from her drawer. The doors were open, another busy day was ahead.

Two

"HOW MUCH DO you reckon a place like this goes for then?" Helen said, squinting in the sunlight. "I mean, look at the size of it. It's not so much a house as a bloomin' castle."

Martha couldn't disagree with her sister. The massive mansion standing before them was probably one of the biggest homes she'd ever seen. Three storeys high, the estate was ringed with massive hedges, hiding it away from the rest of the world.

Two elegant looking Rolls Royce cars sat brooding in the driveway. A mighty Christmas tree guarded the front door, although it didn't seem very jolly. It was beautifully dressed, but Martha sensed something was amiss. Much like the rest of the place, the house, the cars, there was a loneliness about them. Martha could feel it.

"Don't get snippy now," she said, walking up to the front door. "I don't want this turning into one of your lectures."

"Lectures?" Helen coughed. "When do I lecture? I mean, I'd *love* to lecture, but that's not happening any time soon. I've got enough degrees to start my own flippin' university, but here I am."

"Yes, here you are. So no lecturing."

"Fine," she huffed. "Are you going to tell me what this is all about anyway? A clue even?"

"It's a job, that's all," said Martha.

"Very cryptic," said Helen.

"That's all I know. The woman was in tears when I answered the phone. She gave us her address, said she needed our help and that we were to come around straight away."

"Mysterious," said Helen, rubbing her chin. "She didn't sound… you know, like she had a screw loose or anything?"

"I didn't think so," said Martha, suddenly concerned. "Although she was crying an awful lot. Why do you ask?"

"No reason," she said. "I just like to know what we're walking into."

Martha hesitated then rang the doorbell. Somewhere beyond the giant oak door a gong sounded. The Parker sisters looked at each other and tried not to laugh.

"You rang?" they both said together, before bursting into a fit of giggles.

"Stop it," said Martha. "Let's try to at least appear professional. Especially in front of the money."

"Professional?" Helen scoffed. "Us? Since when? We're already a man down and we're not even in the door yet."

"Have you heard from Geri?"

"No, I phoned her and left a message," said Helen. "You know what she's like. She'll probably be asleep behind a bin somewhere."

"God forgive you," said Martha. "That's a terrible thing to say."

"Terrible but *true*!"

"It isn't."

"It bloody is," said Helen. "I tell you what, I didn't behave like that when I was her age."

"Oh shut up, you're barely away from her age now."

"I'm thirty Martha, thirty years old. Or don't you like admitting that?"

"I'm well aware of what age you are Helen. I was around at your birth, remember?"

"Hold on, if I'm thirty, that must make you…"

The door swung open. The flushed, red face of an older woman appeared on the other side. She mopped her brow and let out a long gasp.

"Can I help you?" she wheezed.

"Hello, hi, yes, we're here to see Mrs Coulthard," said Martha. "She's expecting us."

"Oh, right, I see," said the red-faced woman. "Are you sure?"

Martha looked at Helen, who shrugged back. Martha shuffled a little on her feet, feeling awkward. She hated being out of place. She hated even more when a schedule didn't run to plan.

"Yes, she called us this morning, about an hour ago. My name is Martha Parker, this is my sister Helen. We're… investigators."

The red-faced woman took a nervous gulp. She looked across the driveway, as if checking to see if anybody was about. Then, leaning in to the sisters, she pulled them in the door.

"Quick, quick, before anybody sees," she said.

Martha and Helen were hustled into the lobby. The red-faced woman closed the door and wiped her sweaty brow with a handkerchief.

"I'm sorry, awfully sorry," she said. "I don't think Mrs Coulthard wants anybody to know about you. She told me you were coming in the back door. She told me to make sure nobody saw you arrive."

"Charming," mumbled Helen.

"That's quite alright," said Martha, nudging her sister. "We're very discreet, it comes with the territory. Are you the housekeeper?"

"Yes," she said. "May, I've worked for Mrs and Mr... Mrs Coulthard for a decade. Watched this house grow up from a tiny wee bungalow to this. And my joints know all about it, cleaning the place."

"I'll bet," said Helen, looking about the airy lobby. "What exactly does Mrs Coulthard do to afford a house like this?"

"Nothing," said May. "Mr Coulthard is an investment banker though. Very successful too."

"I'd say so," said Helen. "I don't imagine marble staircases buy themselves."

"They don't clean themselves either," May said.

"You'll be a busy woman then May?" asked Martha.

"Cleaner, housekeeper, washer-woman, you name it. I even pick up the dog mess in the garden."

"Dedicated then," laughed Helen. "More dedicated than I'd ever be."

"Well, they look after me," she said. "Or Mrs Coulthard does anyway."

"And what about Mr Coulthard?" asked Martha.

May's face soured a little. Her puffy cheeks drew in, lips puckered. It was involuntary, but Martha and Helen both noticed. Immediately, May corrected herself, as though remembering who she was speaking to.

"Mr Coulthard gave me this job when I was desperate," said May. "And I'll always be thankful for that."

Martha nudged her sister again. She was building up a profile of her new client. In her experience, it was always so much easier when there was a housekeeper or a cleaner. Usually they let slip all the dirty secrets the client wanted to keep hidden for as long as possible. And more often than not they were happy to do so.

"Well we won't keep you any longer than we have to," she said. "Can we speak with Mrs Coulthard, she sounded a bit upset on the phone."

"Yes," said May. "Yes, she's in a terrible state, a terrible state."

"What's wrong with her?" asked Helen.

"It's not for me to say," said May.

"Of course," said Martha, nodding.

"Follow me," said May.

She started up the large marble staircase, groaning with every step. Martha and Helen stayed at a safe distance behind her, scared she might topple backwards. When they reached the first landing, all three women sighed with relief.

The house was impressive. Even more spacious than it appeared from the outside, May led the sisters down the long hallway. Everything seemed new, and there was a faint smell of paint about the place. She leaned closer in to Helen, making sure May couldn't hear her.

"What do you think?" she whispered. "New carpets, new coats of paint, a renovation process? Covering something up?"

"Or they could just be doing their house up, Martha," said Helen. "It does happen you know."

"Vanity project maybe, keep the wifey busy while he's out gallivanting about all over town. Cut and dried, isn't it?"

"You do this every single time," said Helen, shaking her head. "We haven't even met the woman yet, and already you've condemned the husband as a cheat."

"And how often am I wrong?" she asked.

Helen didn't answer. May came to a stop at a set of double doors. She mumbled something and crossed herself. Looking to the others, she mopped her forehead again.

"Can you help her?" she asked. "Will you help Mrs Coulthard? Is that why you're here?"

There was a desperation in the woman's voice. Her eyes were glassy, appealing to Martha and Helen for something much more than they could offer. The Parker sisters were quiet.

"She's been good to me," May continued. "Too good, for a long time. I can't stand to see her like this, I really can't. Your ad, in the paper, I saw it. It says you can help. You have to help her, please *help* her."

"We'll try," said Martha. "We always try May, honestly we do."

"Thank you," she said sadly.

The housekeeper knocked on the door. Martha glanced at her sister. Helen's eyebrows were arched, the look she always got when she was confused.

"What's going on here?" she whispered. "Have we stepped into a Dickens novel or something?"

"Enough," said Martha curtly.

"Because I'm no Little Dorrit and you're *certainly* not Oliver Twist."

A muffled voice came from behind the double doors. May slowly turned the handle and opened them.

Inside was a large bedroom lined with giant, panoramic windows. They looked out over the tall hedge that guarded the mansion and gave a sweeping view of the city in the distance.

The view, however, wasn't enough to distract the sisters from the mess the room was in. Clothes, food and broken furniture were strewn about the floor. The carpets were stained with spilled drinks and in the corner was a large, shattered mirror.

The bedclothes were cast all over the place and in the centre of the mattress was a little bump. Martha peered over and saw that it was moving. May immediately began tidying up the debris closest to the door, hurrying like she was embarrassed.

"She's gone on a rampage again," she tutted quietly. "We only just had this room done up and now look at it. She's so upset, the poor little toot. You have to help her, please."

Martha treaded carefully into the huge bedroom, Helen close by her side. She could feel her sister's apprehension. Martha could always tell when Helen wasn't comfortable. She went quiet.

"Hello," she said. "Mrs Coulthard?"

The lump on the bed didn't budge. Martha cleared her throat, May busied herself behind her.

"I'm Martha, Martha Parker. We spoke on the phone earlier. I was... we were just wondering what we could do to help?"

The lump moved a little. Pushing back the sheet, a head appeared, followed by two, bony shoulders. Mrs Coulthard, presumably. She pushed her long, black hair out of her eyes, revealing a gaunt, pale white face. Her red eyes stared out at Martha and Helen, who tried not to look at her bare chest.

"You're the detectives," she said in a hoarse voice. "You're the ones I spoke to. Your advert in the paper, I saw it. You say you can help me with my problem."

"That's right," said Martha, trying to sound chirpy. "Well, I suppose it depends on what the problem is."

She nudged Helen. Her sister rummaged around in her bag. She pulled out a dog-eared notepad and a pen.

Mrs Coulthard's face changed in an instant. In a flash, the quivering, frail woman with the red raw eyes vanished. In her place was a screaming banshee, teeth bared like fangs.

"The problem," she yelled. "The problem is *him*!"

She reached over to the bedside table and pulled an alarm clock from its socket. In a lightning quick swoop she launched it at Martha and Helen. The sisters ducked out of the way just in time to see it smash into pieces against the wall behind them.

"Bloody hell," Helen shouted. "That almost took my head off."

"I'm sorry, I'm sorry," said May, rushing over to the weeping Mrs Coulthard's side. "She's just so upset. Now you see, don't you? You have to help her."

Martha could feel her stomach churning. Of all the clients she had worked with before, this, by far was the strangest introduction. The wrecked room, the lavish mansion, the weeping wife in the middle of the bed. She felt like she was dreaming.

Only it wasn't a dream. It definitely wasn't. The discomfort in the pit of her belly was enough to remind her of that. While the woman in front of her was quite clearly unstable, she was also deeply upset. And Martha, being Martha, couldn't help but feel the greatest of pity for her.

"Bloody hell," she said quietly, echoing her sister. "What have we gotten ourselves into here?"

Three

"OKAY, WHY DON'T you start at the beginning, that's always a good starting point," said Martha.

She was beginning to sound like a primary school teacher. She nodded with every word, hoping Mrs Coulthard would understand her. Such was her client's annoyance; she could very well have been an eight-year-old girl again. The opulence of the house, the flash cars in the driveway, they were a long way away from the quivering, snivelling mess in front of Martha.

She prided herself on being approachable and calm. Every client deserved her respect. That was the agency's mantra. Anyone who walked through their door would be given an equal chance, no prejudices. Martha was certain that was why they were still in business. Surely there couldn't be *that* many people in the city who were unhappy with their partners.

"My name's Martha," she said, offering her hand. "And this is my sister Helen. From Parkers Investigations. We're here to help."

The sobbing woman was hunched over. May had dressed her in a towel and had shoved a mug of warm tea beneath her running nose. She sat rocking gently, staring into the space between her feet. She looked like she was hypnotised, stuck in a trance. The whole world could have fallen about her shoulders and Martha reckoned she wouldn't flinch.

At least she wasn't screaming and throwing things anymore. Ducking and diving out of the way of debris wasn't good for the blood pressure. And she didn't want that rising. Not after what had happened last year.

"Mrs Coulthard? Can you hear me?" she said.

She looked at May. The housekeeper was gently rubbing Mrs Coulthard's shoulders. Like a mother hen, she watched over her employer, careful not to let anything else upset her.

"I don't really know what else we can do," said Martha. "If she won't speak to us, we don't have anything to go on. I'm sorry."

She didn't want to go. She wanted to help. Glancing over at Helen, she could tell her sister was spooked.

"Mrs Coulthard," said May. "Tracey, please tell these women. You phoned them, you must want to tell them something. They've said they can help. Please, just talk to them."

Tracey Coulthard's head twitched. She placed her mug down on the floor and pushed the hair from her face. She looked at Martha, then at Helen and back to Martha. She was still an attractive woman, despite her state. Martha could see the natural beauty in her face, her slender figure, her delicacy. Her bloodshot eyes were clearer now, like a fever had been lifted from them. She was determined, focussed.

"Do you have any idea what it feels like to be humiliated?" she asked, her voice low and collected. "Do you?"

Martha swallowed. She shook her head. Helen did the same, taking the lead from her older sister.

"What Gordon Coulthard, has done to me for the past fifteen years is beyond humiliation," said Tracey. "He's made me crawl on all fours and beg, like a dog, for this sham of a life. I've been a prisoner in my own home, a slave to his whims. He's a monster, do you understand me? A control freak, a manipulator, a man so twisted and bad, he'll say and do *anything* to get his way. With me, with you, anybody—*everybody*! Do you have any idea what it's like to be married to a man like that? Do you?"

Helen cleared her throat. She shifted restlessly in her chair.

"Well, actually, I'm not married… so…" she said.

"And what about you?" said Tracey. "What about you Martha Parker? Do you know what I'm talking about?"

Martha didn't answer. She had a feeling that no matter what she said, it wouldn't be good enough. Instead she sat confidently, her back straight, meeting Tracey Coulthard's glare.

"Mrs Coulthard, please—" Martha said, but was promptly cut off.

"Tracey," snapped the woman. "Tracey, don't use his name around me. I want nothing to do with him."

"Fine, Tracey," said Martha. "You called us, you asked us to come here, which means you must want our help. We're not here to be lectured by you though. We want to help you in any way we can. But to do that you've got to talk to us."

"They're right. Listen to them," said May, rubbing her boss's shoulders again. "Please, just listen to them."

Tracey sat back in her chair. She tightened the towel about her, her nostrils flaring. Martha kept her peripheral vision on the mug of warm tea on the floor. It was dangerously close to being launched.

"I want you to uncover my husband's latest affair," she said flatly.

"Okay," said Helen. "We can look into that. Sure, no problem. We can find out if he's seeing somebody else."

"No!" Tracey snapped. "That's not what I said!"

"It isn't?" Helen bleated.

"I said I want you to *uncover* my husband's affair. I know he's having one, I need to know who it's with. Or, rather, who the current one is with. I'm not stupid, ladies. I might be a housewife in the wealthiest postcode in Scotland, but I'm not an idiot."

"Alright, cool," said Helen, holding her hands up. "Whatever you say boss."

"So you know your husband is having an affair?" asked Martha. "Pardon me Tracey but what do you need us for then? I mean, we normally try to establish *if* a partner is cheating, that's why we're hired. But it sounds to me like you already have a good idea."

Tracey sucked on her teeth, her sneer turning to a snarl, her knuckles going white as she clenched her fists. Martha eased her way to the edge of the chair, ready to leap out of the way, but Mrs Coulthard was able to control herself.

"I read your ad, I'm not blind," she said. "I know Gordon is playing away. I want you to find out *who* he's with, what they do, where they live, everything. I want you to do those things for me and I want you to bring the details back here and give them to me. Is that understood?"

"Eh…" said Martha.

She had a sudden sense of unease. Her pity was still there for Tracey Coulthard. But it was being pressed hard by a feeling of dread. The woman in front of her didn't seem so frail anymore. Instead she appeared more like a maniac.

"But, Tracey, if you don't mind me asking, what are you going to *do* with that information?" she asked. "I mean, we don't normally ask these things but I feel I should—"

"If you don't normally ask, then *don't ask*," Tracey smirked. "You'll be paid upfront. Cash. I assume that suits?"

"Well, we don't normally discuss fees until the work is done. That way…"

"Twenty thousand," she said. "Plus expenses."

"We'll do it," blurted Helen. "We're yours. We'll have a USB with pictures, files, addresses, names, numbers, the whole works. We'll even deliver it personally with a big red bow for that price."

Martha tried to intervene but Helen was in full flow. She reached out and offered her hand. Tracey Coulthard took it and the pair shook.

Martha looked at May, the old housekeeper's face still flushed red. She wasn't happy, Martha could tell. She looked exactly how Martha was feeling.

"May will show you out," said Tracey. "I want it as soon as possible. No messing about, no excuses. Quick, clean, I'm in a hurry."

"Yes, of course Mrs Coul... Tracey," said Helen, standing up. "We'll put our best minds to it straight away. Won't we Martha?"

"What... yes, of course," she said, in a daze.

Tracey waved a lazy finger at May who sprang into action. The housekeeper led the sisters through the strewn debris of the room and back to the door. They said their goodbyes while Tracey ignored them. The trio weren't two steps down the hallway when they heard the shatter of the glass and another angry, painful howl.

May guided them back through the house and out the front door. As they were leaving, she pulled a thick brown envelope out of her pocket.

"Here's your money," she said. "You don't need to count it, it's all there."

"Thanks," said Helen, snatching it greedily.

"I've put a picture of Mr Coulthard in there too, and an address of his office. I don't know what you need, we've never done anything like this before."

"Thank you," said Martha. "That's very helpful. Helen here has been taking notes, we should have all that we need. Isn't that right Helen?"

"Hmm... what?"

Helen was thumbing the cash in the envelope. Martha thought her eyes were about to pop out of her head. Another quick nudge and Helen righted herself.

"Will Tracey be okay?" Martha asked the housekeeper. "I mean, she doesn't seem very... stable."

May sighed loudly. She began busying herself with the lights wrapped around the huge Christmas tree beside the door. Her brow wrinkled. She was fighting back tears.

"She wouldn't have called you if she didn't think you could help," she said. "If you can, then do it, please, for her. She's not well, she needs help. Please, just do this for her."

"We will, won't we Martha?" said Helen.

But Martha wasn't so convinced. Helen pulled gently at her arm, dragging her away from the door, the house, May and the weird world of the Coulthards.

"We'll be in touch," Helen shouted.

She didn't stop pulling until they reached the street. Jumping into her old Mini, she opened the envelope and let out a happy squeal.

"Can you believe this?" she shouted. "Twenty grand. Just like that. Look! It's all here, fifty-pound notes. It smells. Can you smell it? It smells like money, do you know what I mean? It smells like wealth. Here, have a sniff."

She shoved a handful of notes into Martha's face. The older sister swatted her away.

"Don't. Stop it," she said. "Come on, let's get out of here."

"What's wrong with you?" asked Helen, starting the engine. "We've just made more in an hour than we have all year. You should be jumping for joy."

"It's not the money," she replied. "It's never about the money. Why do you think we've not made any this year?"

"Because you're a terrible businesswoman Martha. Oprah you ain't."

Martha couldn't see anything to be happy about. She kept thinking of Tracey Coulthard, shouting and screaming and tearing up her bedroom.

"Money is only a tool," started Helen. "It will take you wherever you wish, but it will not replace you as the driver. Ayn Rand said that."

"And?" said Martha, watching the bare trees of the plush suburb roll past the window.

"And, money isn't everything, but it sure makes being a poor, unemployed graduate student a little bit easier. If you know what I mean."

Martha made a low grumbling noise of agreement. They pulled out onto a main road and started back towards the office.

"And speaking of students, you better give Geri a call," she said. "Make sure she's woken up from behind the bins."

"Can I tell her about the job?" asked Helen excitedly.

"You can tell her whatever you like," said Martha. "We've got work to do and I've got a feeling we'll *all* need to be firing on all cylinders for this one. Something tells me Mrs Tracey Coulthard isn't one for hanging around."

Four

THERE WAS NO denying it, Martha was having a crisis. She'd tried her hardest to ignore that horrible gnawing feeling in the back of her mind. She'd closed her eyes, boiled the kettle, even tried knitting. But it wasn't going away. No matter how hard she tried.

Two thirds of the Parker sister partnership had returned to the office, and immediately began sulking. They should have been happy, there was an envelope of money sitting on the main table. Martha knew how important that cash was. She knew it was going to keep them in business for at least another six months.

But that was the problem. It was dirty money, blood money. They were taking it, knowing that the information they provided would be used maliciously. If she'd opened the envelope and found pieces of silver she wouldn't have been surprised. While funds were important to the running of the business, there was always a moral judgement. And she wasn't sure if taking the payment was in any way, shape or form moral. Mind you, what was moral about cheating on your wife. Maybe he deserved it. But did the woman he was seeing?

"What's wrong with your face?" asked Helen, chewing on a piece of liquorice. "You've got a look on you like a burst couch."

"Thanks," said Martha, running her hands through her tangled, curly hair. "That makes me feel a *whole* lot better."

"Oh come on, what's the matter?" said Helen. "You should be over the moon. You should be dancing on the ceiling. We should be having a party, not moping about in your garage."

"It's an office Helen. *Our* office," Martha said, curtly. "And I know we should. I just... I don't know."

"No, you *do* know, you're just not saying."

Helen rounded her desk. Martha watched her sister carefully. Her bright eyes shone behind her thick spectacles. Helen was an academic, a born student. Ever since they were children she had kept her nose in the books. Ask her anything about particle physics, the universe, even how tectonic plates worked and she'd answer you quicker than a flash. And, like most students, when it came to money, she was a shark. She'd fight to the death for a torn fiver. With that she could live on dehydrated noodles and expiring yoghurts for a year.

Martha, on the other hand, was a little more sophisticated when it came to cold, hard cash. She knew its value, sure, but she didn't ever want to feel guilty about it. There might have been a day, not that long ago, where she cared much more for it. But not now. Never again. She wasn't going back there.

"Look, it's simple," said Helen, dropping into a chair in front of Martha. "We take the money, scope out this Gordon Coulthard guy, take a few snaps and we're done. We don't need to know anything about what that woman's going to do. It's none of our business, is it? She's employed us, we're her employees. Simple."

Martha stared at her sister. Helen puckered her lips.

"Don't look at me like that," Helen said.

"Like what?" asked Martha.

"Like you know exactly what."

"What?"

"That bloody look Martha. You know the one I mean. The one you learned from Dad. The one he pulled every time he wanted us to figure something out on our own. I bloody hated that look. He *always* gave me that look."

"Well maybe you should have learned from it then," said Martha, folding her arms.

"Obviously I didn't. We're still talking about it."

"Obviously."

"Obviously."

"Fine."

"Fine."

"Fine."

"Enough," said Helen. "Just pull yourself together, woman. There's nothing wrong with this, it's just another job."

"But it's not, is it?" asked Martha. "You saw Mrs Coulthard."

"Tracey," Helen wagged her liquorice. "She doesn't like to be called Mrs Coulthard remember."

"Tracey then," Martha dismissed. "You saw her Helen. She's not a well woman. She's trashed that lovely house of hers. That's probably why it smelled of paint and had new carpets. I'd bet she's wrecked the whole place at least once before. We can't in good conscience, take that money. It would be... wrong."

"What's wrong with it?" blurted Helen. "*She* called *us*, we're just providing a service. She wants us to track her husband, find out who he's sleeping with and tell her. That's no different to what we normally do. You don't usually have a problem with it, do you?"

"But what is she going to do *afterwards?*" asked Martha. "That's what worries me. She needs help."

"She needs a divorce," said Helen. "And quick. We're merely helping that along. Simple."

Martha wasn't sure. She stared at the fat envelope sitting on the desk. She thought she could hear it thumping on the wood, like it had a pulse. Any moment it was going to leap up, call the police and report her for not being a sensible, diligent human being.

Or it wasn't going to do that at all. Maybe Helen was right. Maybe it was just money for work. All they had to do was take the job, do it to the best of their ability, like they always did, and move on. The rest would be out of their hands. What Tracey Coulthard did with the information was up to her. She was a grown woman. She knew what was right and what was wrong. So why did Martha still feel terrible?

"Oh god," she said, leaning forward and rubbing her eyes. "Why couldn't it just have been another heartbroken wife with a husband playing around with his secretary."

"How clichéd," said Helen. "And besides, that'd be boring."

"Do you two ever stop talking?"

Martha and Helen jumped, both turning to see Geri casually leaning in the doorway.

"You almost gave me a heart attack," gasped Martha.

"Calm down, would you," said Geri, sauntering into the office. "You're old, but you're not *that* old. Give me a break."

The youngest of the three Parker sisters collapsed into her chair and propped her big, muddy boots up on her desk. She let her head loll backwards as she stared at the ceiling through her sunglasses.

Martha could smell drink from her, and smoke. She didn't care much for her sister's dress sense either.

"Please tell me you didn't go out dressed like that," she said.

Geri tipped her head forward. She peered over her sunglasses.

"Pardon me?" she asked.

"You look like you've just been kicked out of a 1980s punk bar," Martha went on. "After being dragged through a hedge backwards."

"Thank you sister," said Geri sarcastically. "Coming from a woman who wears a knitted cardigan to work, I'll stick with my wardrobe choices thank you."

"She's got you there Marth," said Helen.

Martha went to answer. She poked a finger through a hole in her cardigan then stopped herself. There was no use arguing. She didn't have a leg to stand on.

"Nice of you to join us at…" she checked her watch. "Lunchtime. Where have you been?"

"Christmas night out," said Geri. "It became a Christmas morning out then a Christmas elevenses out. Then it was just out."

"Ah the old undergraduate student night out," said Helen. "I remember them fondly."

"Of course you would," said Geri. "You've been a student for about a hundred years. To you it must have been like a birthday, coming every year."

"Very funny."

"I was being serious!"

"Alright, knock it off you two, I'm not in the mood," said Martha.

The sisters sat in silence for a moment. Then Geri spied the envelope in the middle of the desks.

"Hey," she said, taking off her sunglasses. "What's that? Is it… is that money?"

She went to grab it but Helen was quicker. She snatched it up and raced towards the door.

"Hey," shouted Geri. "Where'd all that cash come from? Have you two robbed a bank or something? Hey! Did mum die in her sleep?"

"What? No!" Martha blurted.

"It'd explain the used notes Martha," said Geri. "She keeps a whole stack of them under her bed."

"You shouldn't be looking under her bed," said Martha. "And Helen, come back in here. Stop behaving like a bloody six-year-old. Sit down."

"Go on, ask Geri," said Helen, slowly edging back into the room, holding the envelope tight to her chest. "Ask Geri what she thinks of it all. Ask her what we should do."

"Ask me what?"

Martha took a deep breath. She didn't want to talk about it, didn't want to even think about her dilemma. Every time she did it seemed to hurt her that little bit more. But here was a chance to make it all go away. The casting vote, the decider, the one who'd split the difference. She didn't have much faith in her youngest sister's moral compass. But it was better than nothing.

"Geri... we've—"

A hard rattling sound interrupted her. Her mobile danced across the surface of her desk, vibrating hard on the old scratched wood. She reached over and picked it up, seeing a number she didn't recognise on the screen.

"Who's that?" asked Helen.

"I don't know," said Martha. "Don't know the number."

"Well answer it then," said Geri. "Honestly, you two, you're so bloody dramatic."

Swiping her finger across the screen, she answered it. She held the device to her ear and spoke softly.

"Hello? Martha Parker here."

"Have you found him yet?" came a screeching, high-pitched scream from the other end.

Martha winced. She pulled the phone away from her ear and blinked hard. Helen and Geri watched her, confused.

"Bloody hell," she said. "I think I'm deaf."

"Hello! Hello!" the voice echoed out the phone. "Parker! Where are you? Parker! Answer me! Where the hell are you! Parker!"

"Is that?" Helen nodded.

"Yes, I think so," said Martha. "I think she wants to know how we're getting on."

"You think?" said Helen.

"Who the hell are you two talking about?" said Geri. "And who's that screaming idiot on the phone?"

"It's a long story," said Martha.

"If you'd been in work on time this morning you'd know," darted Helen.

"I see," said Geri.

She dashed across the room and grabbed the phone from Martha's hand. Keeping it at a safe distance, she cleared her throat.

"Hello? Can you hear me? Right, good. Shut up you maniac."

"Geri!" Martha and Helen both said in unison.

"What's that? No I *can* hear you, which is no surprise given the amount of shouting you're doing. Get a grip of yourself. You don't phone people up and start screaming. Who do you think you are? Learn some manners you self-absorbed git!"

"Geri!" Martha whispered, her fists in balls up to her mouth.

"Geri, you idiot," Helen did the same and waved the envelope around. "That's... that's who gave us this!"

"What's that?" Geri silenced her sisters with one finger. "I'll tell you who I am, I'm the sister of Martha Parker, the one who's eardrum you just burst. And if I catch you doing it again, I'll personally come round and stamp on your throat. Got that?"

The line went dead. Geri looked at the phone then shrugged. She handed it back to Martha, like nothing had happened.

"Oh Geri," said Helen. "Why did you do that?"

"Hey, that was out of order," she said. "You don't come on the phone screaming and shouting like a spoiled little brat. She should learn some manners, whoever it is. Who was it anyway?"

Martha had buried her face in her hands. Like it or not, her mind had been made up. There was no way they could refuse Tracey Coulthard now. Even if she asked for her money back, a polite gesture of doing what she wanted was the least they could do. Especially after one of her employees offered to stand on her throat.

"Geri..." she said.

"What?" said the young woman. "I'm not allowed to defend my sister now, is that it? Come on. I might not like you two very much but I won't have you getting pushed around."

"Aww," bleated Helen. "That's about the nicest thing you've ever said when I've been in the room."

"And patter like that is exactly *why* that's the nicest thing I've said around you. Enough. E-bloody-nough."

Geri nodded confidently. Martha shook her head. Helen looked about ready to cry. The Parker sisters.

"So you want to tell me where all that dosh came from? Or do I have to guess?" asked Geri.

Martha took a long, deep breath and felt her bones and muscles ache. It was going to be a long day.

"Yeah," she said. "Looks like we've got a new case. And you've already pissed the client off enough that she hung up on us. Great start, don't you think?"

Five

"THERE ARE NO spaces! Why are there never any spaces!"

Helen punched the steering wheel. She was always like this when she had to drive in big cities. Her knuckles white, her back hunched over, her face grey with worry.

"Why would you let so many cars in, if you didn't have enough room for them to park?"

"Would you please calm down?" asked Martha, gently tapping her arm. "One will appear, you'll see. Go round the block again."

"Again," Helen blurted. "We've been around six times already. And we've almost been run off the road twice. I thought we were going to be car-jacked another time. And you want me to go round *again*?"

"Don't be such a drama queen," said Geri, lounging in the back. "We're only parking up, it's not the high seas."

"Says the girl who can't drive," darted Helen, looking in the rear-view mirror.

"Hey, I've got my provisional," said Geri, hurt. "And when I can scrape together enough cash, I'm buying a motorbike."

"No you bloody aren't!" said Martha. "Those things are death traps."

"I'll buy what I want," said the youngest sister, petulantly. "Speaking of money, when do I get my share of the payment for this job? I'd like it now."

"Yeah, she has a point," said Helen, suddenly calm. "When do we get paid?"

"You get paid when the job's done," said Martha flatly. "And not a moment before. This is serious business, I don't think you two have quite grasped that yet."

"All I've grasped is that we're sitting on twenty grand and you haven't given us a penny," said Helen, darting into a gap in the traffic.

"Yeah," said Geri.

"Oh look," said Martha, a little relieved. "There's a space!"

"Oh good," said Geri.

"Oh god," droned Helen.

The middle Parker sister pushed the little Mini on through the traffic. Darting across three lanes, she managed to squeeze the car into the spot between two much bigger, fancier motors. With a sigh of relief, she turned off the engine.

"Bloody hell," she wheezed. "I don't think I could have gone round again. That was murder."

Something twanged in the back of Martha's mind. She didn't know what it was. It felt like somebody pulling on a rubber band, echoing in her ears. She ignored it and clambered out of the car.

The air was cold and crisp. Light sprinkles of snow peppered the pavement and people in suits and long coats huddled against the chill, passing by the three sisters without looking up.

The financial district, in the heart of Glasgow. Buzzing with people, but no soul about it. Tall buildings reached up to touch the clouds but they were just as cold as the weather. There had to be around twenty thousand people in a five-block radius alone. Yet the whole place felt empty and soulless.

Martha felt out of place. Suddenly her old cardigan, battered jeans and trainers seemed very shabby. She disliked not dressing for the occasion. Although she didn't know what this occasion was. Everything had been such a hurry today. And with the prospect of Tracey Coulthard phoning up for another screaming match at any moment, she didn't want to dally.

"Right," she said, fishing her mittens out of her pocket. "Let's get down to business shall we."

"Yes, let's," said Helen, stamping her feet. "I don't know about you Geri, but I'm freezing. Aren't you cold in that skirt?"

Geri ignored her sister. She was looking around the street, her face etched with concentration, like she was searching for something.

"You okay, love?" asked Martha.

"Yes, yeah, sure," said the youngest sister. "Yeah."

"What's the matter?" asked Helen.

"Nothing, no, nothing at all," she answered. "It's just, I don't know, I sort of feel like I've been here before, although I know I haven't."

"What do you mean?" asked Martha.

"I don't know," she laughed. "I mean why the hell would I ever come to the offices of banks and building societies. I'm not dull as dishwater. And there are no pubs around here, so it's a no go. But it feels strangely familiar. Like I've dreamed it all up."

"You need to lay off the cider," said Helen, teeth chattering. "Can we *please* get moving. I think my hair is freezing solid."

"Yes, okay, let's get going," said Martha, starting down the street. "Usual rules apply. We have a look about, see if we can spot Mr Coulthard's car, scope out his place of work and even, if we're lucky, see if we can get a sight of the man himself. We've just missed lunchtime so it might be hard, but it's worth having a bit of recon. Agreed?"

"Anything to keep that screaming harpy off our backs," said Geri.

"Banshee," said Helen. "Banshees scream, harpies don't."

"Whatever," Geri tutted. "I don't much fancy putting Martha through another call with that mad tart."

"Language," said Martha. "But you're right. Let's see if we can find a spot that we can claim for our own too. We'll probably have to stakeout the building at some point. You know what these bankers are like, coming and going at all hours. It'd be good to know we can sit and watch all the doors without missing anything."

The others nodded. Martha felt a warm glow inside of her. She always did when her plans weren't questioned. She took it as a sign that they were good, that she knew what she was doing. While she always prided herself in her detective work, it was nice to get a backhanded compliment from time to time.

"Now let's see where we're going. It's around here somewhere."

She opened the envelope May the housekeeper had given her. The money was gone, locked away in the company safe. There were several sheets of paper with Gordon Coulthard's contact numbers, addresses and schedules. There was a photo too. Martha took it out and passed it to the others.

"He's hot," said Geri, lifting her sunglasses. "You didn't tell us he was such a looker."

"Oh please," said Martha snatching the picture away. "We're professionals."

She looked down at the photo. A bronzed, bare-chested man stared back at her. He was in his late thirties, with a full head of straight, glistening black hair. He was broad-shouldered and athletic, a sign he'd played rugby before and still went to the gym. He was posing on a sunny beach somewhere, obviously loving the attention.

"He's not *that* bad I suppose," she said.

"See, I told you," laughed Geri. "If he bought you a drink at the bar, opened the door to his flash car and said 'I want you to run away with me' you'd be on him like a shot."

"That's not the point... no, I wouldn't... enough," said Martha flustered.

Her sisters laughed at her. She stuffed the photo back in the envelope and waved them up the street.

"Come on, it's up here."

They marched through the mid-afternoon traffic on the pavement, bashing into bags full of Christmas shopping. Finally, they came to a halt across the street from Gordon Coulthard's office.

It was the biggest building on the road. A clear ten storeys bigger than anything else. The glass was curved, making the whole thing look like a sideways wave.

"Impressive," said Helen, adjusting her glasses. "I mean, for an office block. You don't see many buildings in these parts like that one."

"And you're familiar with architecture now are you?" snarled Geri.

"I dabble," said Helen proudly. "See, that's where you let yourself down as a detective Geri. You just look at this place, all glass, steel and cool office stuff and think 'oh, that's just another office'. Whereas me, I see something else."

"Go on," said Martha, watching her sister intently.

"I see a business doing well. I see expensive plans, expensive materials, money from top to bottom, built at a cost, planning permission, great location in a city centre, and a heap of staff coming in and out all the time."

She nodded towards the door. Dozens of similarly dressed men and women were pouring in and out of the revolving glass doors. They whizzed around like worker ants entering and leaving the nest.

"Which makes me think that whoever this Gordon Coulthard is, he's doing well," continued Helen. "Nice big house in the suburbs, flash motors in the drive and a workplace gleaming and new. He's got everything a man could want. Which in turn makes me wonder why he's playing away from home."

Helen folded her arms. She smiled smugly, looking at her sisters for praise. Martha nodded in agreement.

"All valid points," she said. "But maybe he just wants a bit of excitement."

"Excitement?" Helen blurted. "How do you figure?"

"Well, like you say, he's got everything he could ever want. The house, the cars, the job, the good-looking size four wife. So maybe he's bored."

"She has a point," said Geri. "Blokes love to be stupid, it's like a hobby. Maybe he wants a bit of rough now and then. Keeps things lively, doesn't it?"

Helen frowned. She wasn't convinced, Martha could tell. But that was okay. She was the brains of their operation, not the common sense.

"Maybe so," she said. "But I'll tell you one other thing you lot missed. There's a rather snazzy car park hidden underneath the building."

She pointed around the side of the office block. The road dipped and a long, narrow ramp dropped into the ground. Martha made a mental map of the street and the car park. She was already working out where they would be best placed to sit and wait for Mr Coulthard.

"Okay," she said. "I think we've gotten everything we need, don't you? Quite simple really. Main doors there, car park to the side and a one-way street outside. Perfect. Now all we need to do is draw up a rota on who's going to wait for him to appear."

"No need," said Geri, skipping out on the street. "I've found him already."

Before Martha and Helen could react, their sister was darting across the road. Cars honked and drivers screamed at her as she narrowly avoided them all. Martha could barely watch. Finally, she reached the other side.

That's when Martha's stomach really dropped a few inches. Geri was running along the opposite side of the street, chasing after two men in dark coats. As she squinted, she could see that one of them was Gordon Coulthard. A little paler and fatter than his picture, his shock of dark hair was most definitely him.

"Oh no," said Martha. "What is she *doing*?"

"Come on," shouted Helen, grabbing her hand.

They sprinted across the road. The beeping and honking followed them. They weren't as graceful as Geri, and by the time they reached the other side, they were both panting.

Martha pushed her racing heart and burning lungs from her mind—she needed to do something about her fitness, but not now. She could see Geri up ahead. She'd stopped Gordon Coulthard and his companion.

"What is she doing?" she asked again.

Geri stood with her hip cocked, her head to one side, a devilish smile on her face. The two men had stopped, watching her closely. Martha and Helen shuffled up behind them.

"Hello Geri, what are you doing disturbing these nice gentlemen?" said Martha through gritted teeth. "Come on."

"Oh, hi," said Gordon Coulthard, a smile of bright, perfect teeth stretched across his face. "Are you her mum?"

Somehow, some way, Martha managed to contain herself. She could feel her blood boiling in her veins and she thought she felt steam coming from her ears. When it came to first impressions, Gordon Coulthard wasn't the best at making them.

"No, she's my *sister*," she said, forcing a smile.

"Oh right, well, you can tell your sister she's a real flirt, eh Mal?"

Coulthard's companion laughed. He looked the same as Gordon, only a little taller and leaner. He wore the same coat, the same type of suit and silk tie. Martha had to blink a few times to make sure she didn't have double vision.

"Eh, I'm standing right here, you know," laughed Geri. "You guys, what are you like?"

"Yes, right, well, sorry about that. Come on, Geri," she tried to pull her away.

"So do you always just stop random guys in the street and ask for their numbers?" asked Mal. "Or are we something special?"

Martha's toes curled up in her boots. This was cringe-worthy beyond anything she'd ever known. Her days of chatting up men were long behind her. Was this what young people did nowadays? If so she had never been happier to be forty.

"Only the good-looking ones," Geri winked at them both.

Coulthard and Mal snorted like schoolboys. They exchanged a strange handshake and bumped knuckles.

"Tell me Geri," said Coulthard. "Do you like to party?"

"Does she like to party?" Helen laughed awkwardly. "She's only just *in* from one, aren't you Geri."

She guffawed loudly, nudging her younger sister. This was about as close to flirting as Helen ever really got. Martha could forgive her for being a little off-putting.

"Yeah, right, well, cool," said Coulthard.

He looked at Mal who smirked. A knowing look passed between them.

"Listen we're going to a party tonight, a big soirée our company is hosting to celebrate Christmas. We're bankers, by the way, the good kind, not those losers you hear about on the news. Why don't you come along?"

He reached into his coat pocket and produced a business card. He handed it to Geri and winked.

"You some sort of big shot then?" she asked.

"Oh yeah, the biggest," said Mal. "We both are. In fact, we're the guests of honour."

"I am, he isn't," scoffed Coulthard. "It's at The Square hotel, up town, nice and fancy, plush, you'll love it. Just tell them Gordon Coulthard invited you, you'll get in no problems."

"Alright," said Geri, taking the card and shoving it down her top. "Maybe I will then. We'll see, I might be busy tonight."

"Busy? Love, do you know who we are?"

"Yeah, you just said," said Helen, still smiling fecklessly. "You're David Coulthard... sorry Gordon Coulthard, *Gordon* Coulthard."

Coulthard and Mal ignored her. They eased their way past Geri, brushing up against her as they went. Clicking their fingers, they waved as they sauntered off down the street.

"See you there, starts at nine, tell them Gordon Coulthard sent you," he shouted. "And wear something sexy!"

"You should be so lucky!" Geri called back.

When the two men were far enough away, she uncocked her hip. Letting out an infuriated groan, she shivered all over.

"Man, talk about a creep," she said, rolling her head. "I reckon if he'd stared any harder, his eyeballs would have dropped out his head. Same for the other one. Mal was it? I mean, get a life would you."

She reached into her top and pulled out the business card. Handing it over to Martha, she clicked her tongue.

"Piece of cake," she said. "Had to make sure it was him and not a bunch of dud information the banshee gave us. Numbers, name, phone number and e-mail address should match."

Martha had been ready to go through her sister like a dose of salts. However, she couldn't argue with the results.

"You know you were hugely irresponsible there," she said, taking the card and tapping it against her knuckles. "I mean, what if he'd just ignored you. Our anonymity would have been blown."

"Yeah, I know," said Geri confidently. "But unlike you two, I know how to flirt. And when I flirt, ladies, you better make sure all wives and girlfriends are a long way away. Because… boom!"

She shouted. She held her hands up for high fives. None were coming so she shrugged.

"Anyway, we're in with them now, right? We're going to a Christmas party."

"We?" asked Helen. "You don't think he meant, like, all of us do you?"

"Of course he didn't," said Martha. "And I'm most certainly *not* going."

"What? But you have to," pleaded Geri. "I can't go on my own, I need, you know back up. Although you guys should probably wear something that came out *after* 1999. And Helen, for God's sake, keep your flirting to a bare minimum. It also helps when you get the guy's name right."

"Right," said Helen, making a mental note. "I'll try."

"So what do you say, Martha? We ready to go deep undercover and maybe get a free drink or two while we're at it?"

This was all highly irregular. Martha wasn't sure what to think. It wasn't how she'd approach the case, in fact it was about the total opposite of what she'd do. Normally they kept their distance, Martha liked it that way. Keeping away from their targets, their clients' partners, meant they could stay anonymous, like shadows.

Thanks to Geri, they had gone full-blown spy—undercover agents at cocktail parties with glamorous people. The only thing glamorous about Martha was that she could spell it in scrabble.

She blamed Gordon Coulthard, of course. If he'd been like all the rest of the folk she'd tracked this wouldn't be an issue. But he was roguishly handsome, in a scoundrel sort of way. She could hardly blame Geri for throwing herself at him in the way she did.

Then she remembered his poor wife Tracey, in her room, naked, shouting and screaming. She was no ordinary client, either. Maybe the ordinary approach wasn't going to work, not this time.

"Fine," she said. "But I'm not dancing."

"Oh yes you are," said Geri. "And you'll enjoy it. Shake off some of the cobwebs, get the old motor going again."

"Oh god," said Martha. "What have you gotten us into, Geri?"

Geri gave them both a big smile. She linked her arms through theirs and began skipping down the street. The long day was getting worse. And now it was extending into the night time.

Six

WAS THIS THE right dress? Martha hadn't been to a party in such a long time. She hadn't been to a grown-up party in even longer. The last time she was invited to something, there had been cake and juice and a clown entertainer. The days of pithy jokes and fine wine were a long distant memory now.

Instead she'd settled into the tedium of her rapidly approaching middle-age. Although it wasn't called that anymore. What was it her birthday cards had said? Life begins at forty? She wasn't so sure about that. If she'd known she would have prepared.

That's why she was standing in front of the mirror now, unsure what to expect. She barely recognised the woman staring back at her. It was refreshingly nice to see herself out of her usual uniform of cardigan, jeans and trainers. In fact, she was quite pleased.

"Not bad," she said, doing a little twirl. "I'll just keep it to myself that this dress is about twenty years old."

She had been relieved when she pulled it out of the cupboard. She'd been even happier when she found that it still fitted. Sure the zip was a little harder to pull up and there were one or two more bulges here and there that hadn't been there before. But those were details. They could be hidden.

It didn't really answer her question though. Was this appropriate? Did people still wear the Little Black Dress anymore? Was it even a thing? Too many questions. And that was before she even started thinking about why she was going to this party.

She shivered. The thought of Gordon Coulthard was starting to do that to her. In the five minutes she'd spent in his company, he'd evidently left a lasting impression. Much like his wife. Although they were hardly a perfect match.

While she couldn't be sure, Martha wasn't expecting to see Tracey at the party tonight. Somehow she didn't suspect the Coulthards as the happy couple type. Especially after seeing the way he leered at Geri.

Martha rubbed her arms, feeling her goosebumps. She suddenly wasn't so happy with the way she looked. She checked her watch, there wasn't enough time to start rummaging through the wardrobe again. Instead she grabbed a cardigan, lighter than her usual one, and threw it on.

Right on cue there was a toot from outside. Helen was here, her sister electing to drive for the evening.

"Bugger," she said. "Bugger, bugger, bugger."

In a rush, she snatched her bag, coat and shoes and ran downstairs. She caught a quick glimpse of herself in the mirror by the front door and let out a sigh.

"I'm off!" she shouted back into the house. "Don't know how long I'll be, don't wait up."

Martha hopped along the path, slipping into her heels. Almost immediately her calves began to hurt. But she ploughed on. It was for work, she kept telling herself, she was a professional.

She climbed into the Mini and shut the door. Helen stared.

"Wow," she said. "Who are you and what have you done with my sister?"

"Oh shut up," said Martha. "Come on, drive."

"No I'm serious Mart. You look... well, you look like a woman."

Martha pulled the sun visor down and flashed her teeth in the mirror. She didn't want any lipstick on there. She was self-conscious enough.

"Would you please drive," she said, rubbing her teeth with her fingertip. "Otherwise we'll be late. And I want this over and done with as soon as possible."

"I mean, like sorry, I'm just a bit taken aback is all," said Helen, leaning on the steering wheel. "You know, I don't think I can remember the last time I saw you with make-up on. And have you... have you *straightened* your hair?"

She reached out and stroked Martha's head. Martha batted her away. She was embarrassed and Helen wasn't helping. Although she did appreciate her sister noticing.

"Helen Primrose Parker, if you don't start driving this minute, I'm going to box your ears. Now go!"

Helen laughed. She threw the Mini into gear and pulled out of the driveway. They started off into town in silence.

"Where's Geri?" asked Martha, trying to think of anything but the way her shoes were pinching her little toes.

"She said she's meeting us there," answered Helen. "Something about how she didn't want to be around when we got our corsets on or something, I don't know. You know how cruel she can be."

"Yes," smiled Martha. "But she doesn't mean it. She's got a heart of gold."

"And a liver that glows."

"Don't say that."

"Well it's true. Her intake of cocktails is frankly heroic and appalling. When I was a student I didn't drink nearly as much."

"When you were a student Helen, they barely had the internet."

"Meow," she purred. "Anyway, not that it matters a jot. It's thanks to our younger sister that we're getting so close to Mr Coulthard."

"Gordon," said Martha. "Try to at least remember his name this evening."

"Yeah, bugger, I know, I know."

Martha patted down her dress. Her mind was working overtime, turning over everything that had happened so far. It had been a strange case from the start, the people, the setting, the motive, everything. And they weren't even out of the first day yet.

But still something else was bugging her. Something she couldn't put her finger on. Was it the money? Was it Tracey's obvious breakdown? Was it how confident and obviously horrible Gordon was? Or was it their unorthodox approach to the whole thing?

She didn't feel right getting so close to the mark. It just seemed so unnatural, so dishonest. The lying and cheating were what her clients did. Not her. Not Martha Parker and Parkers Investigations. Everything about this case was challenging her morals.

There was very little she could do now though. The snowball had been sent down the mountainside. And it was picking up speed the further it went.

"Here we are," said Helen, snapping Martha from her daydream. "Swanky, why am I not surprised."

The Square was one of a new breed of hotels sweeping through the city. Plush, over-priced, and gaudy; doors open to anybody with more money than sense. Tonight was no different.

As Helen panic-attacked her way into a space across the street from the entrance, Martha couldn't help but notice the number of people flocking to the door. They all looked the same. Young men in expensive suits with identical haircuts. Women tottering in wearing similar dresses, only the colours and height of their heels changing.

And to Martha's surprise, they were all—men and women— an identical colour. Fake tan, it seemed, wasn't just for the holiday-starved girl wanting to look good anymore. The guys could get in on the act too.

"I'm getting old," she said, getting out of the car. "I remember when mum and dad used to throw parties. Do you remember Helen? You could tell people apart from how they looked. Some wore jumpers, others wore shirts and ties. Now, everybody looks the same."

"You're right," said Helen. "You *are* getting old. But who isn't? So hey-ho, what are you going to do?"

"Not sure I like your casual attitude, Helen," grumbled Martha. "But I suppose you're right."

The sisters started across the street. Helen slipped her arm into Martha's. It was comfortable and warm, and made Martha feel a little better. She really wasn't comfortable with all of this, for many reasons. Knowing Helen was with her though, and in turn Geri, would help her through it all.

"Oi, oi, here they come, a couple of maneaters," laughed Geri, leaning against a lamppost, smoking.

"Good to see you too," scoffed Helen. "Give us a fag would you?"

"Neither of you should be smoking," said Martha. "What would mother think?"

"Newsflash Martha," said Geri, offering Helen a smoke. "Mum ain't here and you're most certainly *not* her."

Martha mumbled quietly to herself. Geri was right of course, she wasn't their mother. She still felt she had a duty to protect her younger sisters though. Sure they were grown adults and able to look after themselves. But they were still kids in Martha's eyes.

"Well I must say Martha, you do scrub up well," said Geri.

"You know, I was saying the exact same thing in the car," agreed Helen. "Doesn't she look totally different with a bit of slap on and a pair of heels?"

"Totally," said Geri. "You too Helen. Nice to see you've gone for that 'I'm still a student but don't judge me' look. Seriously, sandals? Come on, this is practically a black-tie event."

Helen took a step back. She wriggled her toes that poked out from beneath her long skirt. She let out a breath of smoke and batted her own head of messy, curly hair.

"I thought I looked alright," she said, sounding a little hurt. "It's better than that skirt you've got on. Bloody hell, I've seen belts thicker!"

"Hey, if you've got it, flaunt it," darted Geri. "Keep your big nose out of my fashion sense. Alright?"

"You keep yours out of mine then!"

"I will!"

"Fine!"

"I'm glad it's fine!"

"Would you two pull yourselves together?" said Martha, stepping in between them. "You're like a pair of bratty school girls. Honestly, act your age, both of you."

"She started it," said Helen, crushing out her cigarette.

"I don't care," said Martha. "Let's not forget why we're here tonight ladies, okay? We're working. We're here to glean as much information as we can on our benefactor Mr Coulthard.

Now if I'm right, I reckon this mysterious mistress Tracey Coulthard is so convinced exists will be here tonight. In which case, we get all the details we can on her. And if she's not, then we ask questions, talk to people, circulate. As far as I'm concerned, we're in and out tonight. Take care of business, put this case to bed early and enjoy that pile of money sitting in our safe. Is that understood?"

Helen and Geri didn't speak. Instead they exchanged awkward glances. Martha crossed her arms.

"Are we all on the same page here?" she asked.

"Yes," said Helen.

"I guess so," said Geri.

"Good," said Martha. "Now let's go. My feet are already killing me."

She turned and limped towards the main entrance of the hotel. Helen and Geri followed behind, sulking.

THE DOORS LOOMED large, bright light pouring out onto the street from the huge chandeliers in the foyer. A large, square-shaped bouncer stood guard at the door. His tuxedo looked three sizes too small for him. Martha still reckoned it could have doubled as a family-sized tent.

He stopped people as they approached, checking their names on his list. Martha was suddenly overcome with nerves. She began to question everything again. Was she dressed for the occasion? Was she too old for this place? What if the bouncer knew, somehow, that they were investigating someone on his watch? What would he do then? Would they even be let in? That was the biggest question.

Martha climbed the stairs. She felt her stomach churning. She'd never been good at getting past bouncers. She had always been a little scared of them.

"Erm... hello," she said, feeling totally out of place. "We're here... we're here for the party. There's a party tonight, yes?"

The bouncer didn't say anything. His flat face was empty, eyes dead. The more he stood there like a brick wall, the worse Martha felt. And the worse she felt the more nervous she became.

"See we were... we were invited by... we were invited earlier today. It's a funny story actually, you'll never guess it. But we bumped into... we bumped into..."

"Oh for god sake," said Geri, pushing past her sister. "Here, we were invited by Gordan Coulthard. That okay?"

She handed over Coulthard's business card. The bouncer examined it, his brow twitching. He stood to one side and tipped his head towards the foyer.

"Upstairs," he grunted, handing the card back. "Second room on the right. They're waiting for you."

"Waiting for us?" blurted Helen. "Waiting for us to do what?"

The bouncer didn't say anything. He was already waving on the people approaching behind the sisters. Geri shoved Martha and Helen into the hotel.

"Don't ask questions now," she said under her breath. "We're in aren't we. First rule of parties, you don't question the bouncer. If they've given you the go ahead, you just smile and move on. Bloody hell, have you two never gone out before?"

"Yes we have Geri, we have," said Helen, tripping a little as she was forced up the stairs. "But we don't all go out with our bits and pieces on show to distract gorillas like that one at the front door."

"What did I just say out there?" said Martha. "Knock it off."

"It's knocked off, it's knocked off," said Helen. "I'm just saying is all."

"Well don't," Martha and Geri said together.

The Parker sisters made their way along the hallway until they reached the second door. Loud thumping music was coming from inside. They stood for a second.

"Right, this is it," said Martha. "Are we ready? Do we know what we're doing?"

"Yes, yes, yes," said Geri. "You've told us enough. Let's get on with it, I'm dying for a drink here."

"Okay," said Martha. "In, out, job done. Got that? And good luck."

"Aye, aye captain. Come on!"

Geri pushed the door open and the wave of noise came crashing down on Martha. Bright lights flashed, loud music wailed and bodies moved around like shadows in the semi-darkness. Increasing feelings of decrepitude notwithstanding, she was in the thick of it now.

Seven

IT HADN'T TAKEN long for Martha to become isolated. A room full of new people who looked younger than the latest round of police recruits made sure of that. Being on the fringes of the party was one thing, but being physically blocked out by the partygoers was a new one on her.

Thankfully, she'd found a cubbyhole to hide in—a little corner of a much quieter room just off the main function suite. She had taken solace for a moment, to catch her breath or stop the ringing in her ears. She was sticking to the soft drinks now. One expensive glass of foul-tasting red wine quashed any urge to drink more.

She'd stopped looking at her watch. There were only so many times she could be disappointed by how early it was. Instead, she was willing away the seconds until she could leave. Or her target appeared.

There had been no sign of the infamous Gordon Coulthard. A quick sweep of the function suite, with its DJ, dance floor and hundreds of guests had yielded nothing. Either the banker wasn't coming to his own bash or he was fashionably late.

Martha had dispatched Helen and Geri to circulate around the party. The mood for her investigation had even left her now. Pain was welling up from her feet and she could swear she'd gone deaf in one ear from all the noise. In short, having some peace and quiet, on her own was just what she needed.

Not that her sisters had needed much coaxing. Geri had practically needed to be restrained when they first hit the lavish party. She was hopping up and down like a puppy as soon as she entered the big room. Even Helen seemed keen once she was in.

Around her fortress, very few people had come and gone and the barman had eventually left in search of some actual drinkers. Martha sat with her chin in her hand, staring at the pattern in the carpet.

Suddenly, the door flung open. In staggered a tall, leggy brunette woman in a tight-fitting dress. She was grumbling to herself and swearing. When she saw Martha sitting in the corner she straightened herself defensively.

"Oh!" she shouted. "What are you doing here?"

"Sorry," said Martha standing up. "I didn't mean to frighten you. I just had to get away from the noise, that's all."

Martha smiled at the young woman.

"I know what you mean."

The woman looked at her, her blood-red lips twisting into a half-pucker, half-frown, like she didn't know what she was supposed to do now.

"I'm Martha," she said.

"Estelle," she replied.

"Oh, wow, that's a lovely name," said Martha.

"Thank you," said Estelle, her heavily made-up face twitching into a smile. "My mum named me after Estelle Lauder."

"Estelle Lauder?"

"Aye, you know, Estelle Lauder. They make the face cream and that."

"Don't you mean…"

Martha trailed off. Estelle looked at her, long lashes flapping.

"Mean what?" she asked in a thick Glaswegian accent. "Oh, no, don't worry, my surname's not Lauder. That would be really dumb." And she cackled a cheap laugh.

"It would, indeed," said Martha.

Estelle snorted loudly. In one quick, well-practised movement, she opened her handbag, pulled out a mirror, adjusted her lipstick and put it all away again. It was over so quickly, Martha was unsure of what she'd just done.

"So what are you doing in here on your own?" asked the young woman. "You drunk already?"

"Drunk? No, no not at all," said Martha. "I was just having a sit down. I'm not used to big parties like this. It's all a bit much."

"Oh aye, a lightweight are you?" Estelle laughed. "You're like my mum. She cannae hack it anymore. Two bottles of wine and she's on the floor, bless. Me though, I can go all night."

"I'm sure you can," said Martha, politely.

"In fact I'm in here looking for a drink. The bar's ten deep out there. Full of screaming wee lassies who don't know how to act."

Martha kept her mouth shut. Estelle looked barely out of her teens, even with the makeup and six-inch heels.

"There's a bar over there but I think the barman's gone home," said Martha.

"Oh aye," said Estelle, spying the bar. "Doesn't matter, I'll help myself."

"I don't think you should, I mean—"

"Och aye, sure, come on. You want something?"

"No I'm… okay."

Estelle strutted her way to the annex's bar. Letting herself in behind it, she immediately began pouring out drinks. Martha counted the three shots she took in quick succession before she broke into the vodka. Propping herself up on the bar, the young woman focussed her attention on Martha.

"So," she said, her face drawn. "Who are you here with?"

Martha thought quickly. She didn't want to give too much away, she didn't know who was listening. And she certainly didn't want to let a stranger know why they were there. That would have been madness. She was glad she wasn't drinking. All this deception was hard work.

"My sisters," she said eventually. "The three of us, we were invited earlier today."

"I see," said Estelle, pouring another vodka. "And who are you anyway? Do you work for the bank?"

"Not exactly," said Martha. "What about you?"

"I'm guest of honour," she laughed. "Well, my man is anyway."

"Guest of honour?" Martha asked.

Her mind raced back to the street, to meeting Coulthard for the first time. The conversation, the flirting, everything came rushing back.

"Gordon Coulthard?" Martha said.

Estelle suddenly became defensive. It was a little change at first, but Martha had studied body language and this young woman was screaming at her. Folded arms, sharpened eyes, she brandished her glass like a weapon.

"Yeah," she said suspiciously. "You know him?"

"Erm… yes, sort of," said Martha, trying to be careful. "Yes it was him who invited us actually."

"Did he now?" said Estelle. "Well, let me tell you something."

"Pardon me?"

Estelle rounded the bar. She drained her glass and slammed it down hard. Martha stood her ground as the young woman towered over her.

"Gordon Coulthard is mine," she said aggressively. "Do you catch me?"

"Erm… hold on a second I think you might be getting mixed up…"

"No, it's *you* that's getting mixed up, hen," she poked a sharp nail into Martha's chest. "He's mine and don't you forget it. You hear me? I don't know what you think you're going to get from him tonight. As if he'd look at you anyway, I mean, what age are you, fifty or something? You're older than my mum."

"Look, I don't know what you think of me," started Martha. "But I can assure you I'm not after Gordon Coulthard."

"Liar," Estelle snapped.

"I'm not a liar. I think you've had too much to drink."

"Don't tell me what to do," the young woman sneered. "Who the hell are you anyway?"

Martha could feel herself getting angry. She started breathing through her nose, trying to keep herself calm. The young woman in front of her was clearly misguided. If only she knew what Martha knew. She thought about telling her. But something kept her mouth firmly shut.

"Okay," she said. "I'm going to leave you alone, thank you."

"Don't walk away from me," Estelle screeched. "Hey! I'm talking to you. Come back here, you scrawny old cow."

Martha felt something pull at her hair. The next thing she knew she was being pulled backwards. The force was so hard, one of her shoes came off.

"Snooty cow," Estelle shouted. "You stay away from my man."

Martha winced with every pull of her hair. She shielded herself from the weak blows raining down on her from the drunk Estelle. Against her better judgement, she was about to throw her first punch when somebody shouted from across the room.

"Estelle!"

Immediately the grip on Martha's hair was released. She straightened up and spotted Gordon Coulthard standing at the door, a magnum of champagne and two flutes in his hands.

"What the hell are you doing?"

The man Martha had met in the street, the one she was spying on, now dashed over and took her by the shoulders. He pushed stray hair from her face and looked into her eyes.

"Are you alright?" he said. "Are you hurt?"

He actually sounded concerned though Martha was having a hard time believing that. She rubbed her scalp.

"I'm fine," she said.

"Estelle, baby, you can't go about attacking people," he coughed. "What the hell is wrong with you?"

"She started it," Estelle pouted.

"Just a misunderstanding, that's all," said Martha.

The young woman stood fuming by the bar. She grabbed a bottle and refilled her glass.

"Okay, okay, right, good," he said relieved. "I'm glad… I'm glad you're not hurt."

He set the champagne and flutes down on the bar. Reaching into his pocket, he pulled out his wallet.

"Look, can I give you something," he said, looking around furtively. "Just as a little sorry."

"What?" said Martha.

She watched as he pulled out a handful of fifty-pound notes. He began peeling them out of the ball but Martha stopped him.

"No, please, it's alright," she said. "I don't want any money, I'm fine."

"No, please take it, please, just as a sorry for my girlfriend."

"Eh, excuse me?" said Estelle. "What do you call this?"

She held up her left hand. Sparkling on her fourth finger was a massive diamond ring. Martha could feel her skin turning ice cold. She was shocked and angered all at once.

This woman, the one who had attacked her, the one who looked like she wasn't old enough to tie her own shoelaces, was engaged to Gordon Coulthard? The same Gordon Coulthard who was already married—to Martha's employer.

Martha didn't know what to say or what to do. So she said nothing and simply nodded.

"Sorry. Fiancée," Coulthard corrected himself quickly. "Please, take it, buy yourself a drink, please."

He pushed the notes into Martha's trembling hands. He closed them around the money and shook them.

"Thank you," he said, winking confidently. "Come on, Estelle."

The young woman finished her drink. She handed him the champagne and flutes and pushed past Martha, sneering back at her over her shoulder. The pair disappeared through a door on the opposite side of the annex, away from the party still raging in the next room.

"Holy Hell's Bells," said Martha, gasping for air. "Wow, wow, this is big, this is very big. This is huge! This is huge!"

Martha stumbled over to her table. She steadied herself, trying to catch her breath. In all of her time investigating cheating other halves, there had been plenty of scandal and outrage. In fact, she thought she'd seen almost anything and everything partners would do behind their wives and husbands' backs.

But this was massive. She'd never come across a polygamist before. And that was before she even thought about Tracey Coulthard's reaction. She broke out in a cold sweat.

"Hey, there you are," came Geri's voice from behind her. "I've been looking all over for you."

At the sight of her younger sister, Martha felt tears well up in her eyes. She darted over and hugged Geri tightly.

"What's the matter?" Geri asked. "You alright?"

"No," said Martha. "No I'm not. We're in a bit of bother here, or rather, a big bit of trouble. This case, it's bigger than we thought. Much bigger."

She pulled away. Geri offered her the sleeve of her top as a makeshift handkerchief. Martha rubbed her nose and wiped her cheeks.

"Yeah, well, we might have to put a hold on that for a minute," she said. "Hey, where'd you get all that money?"

She pointed at the notes Martha was still holding tightly onto.

"What? These, no, these, that's what I'm talking about Geri. It's Coulthard, Gordon Coulthard. I've met him. I met him again, he was just here, a minute ago. And I've met the other woman. She almost pulled all my hair out! Look!"

"Right, okay, cool, you're right Martha, that is big, but we really need to get back in there," said Geri.

"No, no, it's even bigger than that Geri, so much bigger."

"Right, okay, I get it but you need to listen to me. We need to get back into the party, like right now."

"What? Why?" said Martha. "We need to go, right away. Wait, where's Helen?"

Geri sighed. She pointed out the door towards the party.

"She's in there," she said. "And it doesn't look good."

"Doesn't look good? What do you mean?"

"Have you ever seen somebody riding one of those mechanical bulls?" she asked.

"What?" Martha's mind was like scrambled eggs.

"Yeah, it isn't pretty. And *this* is even worse."

She took Martha by the hand and led her towards the door. The Parker sisters went back into the party, ready to get their sibling.

Eight

GERI LED MARTHA through the sea of bodies in the main room of the party. People danced and drank, boogied and bopped all around them. It was hot and stuffy and the smell of sweat mixed with potent aftershave and perfume.

Martha was desperate to leave. The run-in with Coulthard and Estelle had been the final straw that broke her particular camel's back. What had started as a difficult day had matured into a dreadful one. And now she wanted nothing more than a cup of tea and a biscuit. Only there weren't any left—the bloody cat had eaten them.

"Where is she?" she shouted over the din of the music. "Where's Helen?"

"What?" asked Geri, leaning close.

"Where's Helen, you said there was something wrong with Helen!"

"Yeah she's just over here," Geri shouted back.

"We need to go Geri!" Martha's throat rasped. "We have to get out of here and think. This case isn't as straightforward as we hoped."

"Enough!" Geri shouted. "I can't hear a word you're saying. Come on!"

She pulled Martha more urgently now. Weaving in and out of the other partygoers, they made their way into the centre of the room. There, a large collection of people had gathered.

Even before she saw what was going on Martha had a bad feeling.

"Oh god," she said to herself.

Geri pushed a path for them through the others. They were all cheering, shouting, leering towards a central point. As Martha made her way through, she began to put two and two together. And when she got to the front her worst fears were confirmed.

"There you go," shouted Geri. "Our sister, Helen Primrose Parker."

"Oh god, oh god, oh god," shouted Martha.

The crowd around her were cheering, and in the centre of it all was Helen. She was standing on a low table, gyrating her hips, shaking her rear end and moving like a woman possessed. With every beat blasting out from the speakers, Helen did some terrible dance move.

The look on her face was of total concentration. Her long, straggly, curly hair was plastered to her sweaty cheeks and forehead. Her sandals sloshed through empty glasses, kicking them wildly into the roaring crowd.

Martha couldn't tell if she was in agony or ecstasy. She moved like a mad thing, a slave to the rhythm and beat of the DJ's tunes.

"Oh god!" shouted Martha. "Didn't you look after her? How much has she had to drink?"

"I don't know!" yelled Geri. "But the way she's dancing, I don't reckon any amount of looking after would have stopped her. At least she's not doing her Tina Turner impression… oh wait."

Geri trailed off as Helen began stomping up and down the table. Her lips were puckered, her arms jolting up and down like she'd been plugged into the mains. As the lights danced around her, she looked almost like a robot.

"Tina Turner she isn't," said Martha. "Come on, let's get her down."

"Good luck with that," said Geri. "I don't think her audience will let you get near her."

"They're laughing at her. That's cruel. Come on, we need to get out of here."

Martha beckoned to Helen. It was useless though, she was hypnotised by the music.

"Helen," Martha shouted. "Get down from there. Come on. We're leaving."

"Leaving? No way man, no way," Helen shouted back. "I'm just getting started!"

"Helen. Come down from there before you break your neck."

Helen stuck out her tongue. She looked like she was about to strut all the way down the length of the table again when she obviously spied somebody more interesting than Martha, who had just reached up to grab her.

Helen's outreached hand found Mal, Coulthard's friend, and he was pulled from the crowd by his tie. Encouraged by the cheering group, he clambered up onto the table and began dancing with Helen. They tangoed and shuffled, throwing each other about the place. In her inimitable fashion, or lack thereof, Helen managed to incorporate bopping, boogying and breakdancing into her routine, and all before the song was finished. And as the final note rang out, Helen planted a huge kiss right on Mal's lips.

The audience went berserk—hollering, hooting and showing their appreciation for the performance. Martha had to look away. This type of thing upset her stomach.

The dancing couple were helped off the table as the music moved on. The crowd slowly started to dissipate, back to the party. Martha slowly turned back to her sister who was now draped around Mal.

"She's quite the dancer," he said, his face flushed red.

"Yes, she is," said Martha. "But it's past her bedtime."

"No," Helen said, with a hiccup. "I'm staying up all night. I'm going to a nightclub, a disco. Take me to the hottest place in town!"

"You're going nowhere Helen," said Martha sternly. "Come on, we have to go home."

"Can't she stay out for a little while longer?" asked Mal. "She's having so much fun. I'll see she gets home safely."

He propped Helen's drooping body up. While Martha didn't want to interfere in Helen's social life, it was clear she was in no fit state to do anything. She could barely stand.

"No, not tonight," she said, throwing Helen's arm over her shoulder. "And while I'm sure you're perfectly nice and all, I don't really think I could live with myself if I let a complete stranger look after my sister. Not in this state anyway."

"Ah," nodded Mal. "I can't really argue with that."

"You can take *me* home if you like," said Geri, stepping forward.

"You're coming with us," Martha shouted. "Come on, help me out to the car with her."

Martha and Mal led Helen out through the crowd and into the street. It was cold now, and Geri collected their coats. The lightest flickering of snow was beginning to drop from the late-night sky.

They walked down the street towards the car. Helen was singing now, her head bobbing up and down with every word. Her feet dragged along the pavement as the others helped her.

When they got to the car, Mal and Martha dumped her in the back seat. She was asleep before her head hit the cushions.

"Thank you," said Martha. "I can only apologise for her. She doesn't get out all that often. And when she does, well, you can see she gets a bit carried away."

"Oh don't be so stuck up," said Geri. "Let the poor girl enjoy herself. She doesn't need you saying sorry for her all the time."

"Geri!"

"That's quite alright," said Mal. "Believe me, I've seen a lot worse. Hell, I've been a lot worse. It's just a party, no harm done. Just make sure she has lots of water when she gets home. I reckon she'll have a really bad headache when she wakes up."

Martha was immediately struck by how genuine this young man seemed. He had a warm face with kind eyes that shone through the bravado and gaudy taste of his outfit and appearance. As a friend of Gordon Coulthard, she had been expecting him to be just as obnoxious. But he appeared to be genuinely concerned for Helen's wellbeing.

"We'll take care of her," said Martha. "But thank you. And please pass on our thanks to Gordon for the invite. It was very nice of him, of you both. I saw him earlier, but I didn't get the chance to say so. His fiancée Estelle interrupted us."

"Fiancée!" blurted Geri. "Did you say fiancée?"

"Yes," Martha nudged her in the ribs.

"Yeah, Estelle. She's a bit of a handful," said Mal, shaking his head. "But she's a lovely girl, really nice. A hairdresser or a stylist or something. Gordon's been helping her with her new salon, money wise that is, I don't think he could cut hair to save himself. But, I you never know... he has many hidden talents."

Mal trailed off, staring at the ground. Martha sensed something was wrong. There was something in the tone of his voice, the way he spoke. *Who wouldn't want to be more like Gordon Coulthard*, Martha realised.

"You two work together, right?" asked Geri. "You're both bankers."

"What? Oh yeah," he said, straightening up. "Yeah we've been partners on the international investment team for about five years now."

"Do you enjoy it? Your work?"

"Yeah it's great. You get to do a lot of this—late night parties, flash motors, plenty of cash," he said. "Gordon is heading to the top. And he acts that way, all the time. He deserves to, I guess. He's going places, you know? He won't stop until he's at the top."

"And he'll take you with him?" asked Martha suspiciously.

"Yeah," Mal droned, a sly smirk on his face. "Yeah I'll go with him. I'm his partner, his number two guy. I reap as much success as he does, and all the benefits. So I can't complain."

Mal ran a hand through his thick hair. He straightened his tie and fixed his cuffs.

"Anyway, sorry ladies, sorry, I didn't mean to bore you," he said, as if remembering where he was. "Look, make sure she gets home safe and when she wakes up, could you pass on my number?"

He handed Martha his business card. It was the same as Gordon's, complete with corporate logo and information. Mal turned back towards the hotel and waved.

"Tell her to call me when her hangover clears up."

He dropped into a jog towards the entrance. Martha and Geri watched him disappear back into the hotel.

"I'll take that," said Geri, snatching the business card. "I like to keep my collection up to date."

"What a nice guy," said Martha.

"You think?" said Geri.

"What do you mean?"

"You don't think he was trying a bit too hard? You don't think he was playing up that false modesty a bit too much?"

"No," said Martha flatly. "I don't think that at all. I think he sounded like a nice young man who's quite clearly too good for all of this rubbish."

She waved towards the sprawling hotel and fleet of fancy cars. Turning back to the Mini, she peered into the back at Helen sprawled across the seats.

"And *we're* certainly too good for this place. Get in," she said.

Martha found the keys in Helen's coat and climbed in. Geri reluctantly joined her sister in the front of the Mini.

"That's my night over then, I take it," she said. "And look at that, it's not even half-twelve yet."

"Do you want dropping off at your flat?" asked Martha, starting the car and pulling out into the street.

"No," said Geri.

"No?" asked Martha, surprised.

"No. I think I'd much rather come home with you two. You won't be dropping her off at her place, will you? I'll stay in your spare room, I'll sleep on the floor. Somebody's got to make sure the Dancing Queen here doesn't do anything stupid like choke to death in her sleep."

Martha smiled warmly. She reached over and squeezed Geri's hand tightly.

"You know something kiddo," she said. "That's about the nicest thing I've heard all day."

"I don't doubt it Martha," yawned Geri. "I don't doubt that for a second."

Nine

"OH GOD," GROANED Helen. "Why does my head feel like an imploded star? That can't be right can it? Should I still be able to hear the music from last night?"

Martha placed a plate down in front of her. A bacon sandwich, perfectly sliced and ready to be eaten. Helen's stomach gurgled at the sight and she pushed it to one side.

"Listen, the amount of drink you shoved down your neck last night, I'm surprised you're even upright at all," said Geri.

The youngest Parker sister leaned over and grabbed the sandwich. She began eating it loudly, licking the sauce from her fingers. Helen let out a loud groan and pulled her dressing gown about her shoulders.

"I'm just glad you're still with us," said Martha, busying herself at the sink. "The way you were acting I had every reason to think we'd find you dead in your bed this morning."

"Believe me, I may be here biologically, but my soul has long expired," Helen said. "I mean, I know I'm a lightweight and all, but surely somebody slipped something into one of my drinks last night. This can't be natural."

"You're just getting old," said Geri. "That's what happens when you get old, your body can't handle the rock and roll lifestyle. And believe me Hel, you were rocking and rolling all *over* the place last night."

Martha laughed. Helen's face turned an odd shade of grey. Any colour that had been in it was now gone.

"What are you talking about?" she said.

"You don't remember?" asked Martha.

"No way," Geri laughed loudly. "You mean you don't have a clue what you got up to last night?"

"Look at me," said Helen. "I'm a husk, I can barely remember my name let alone anything that happened twelve hours ago. Tell me, what happened? I wasn't… I wasn't rude or anything?"

Geri clapped her hands together with joy. She let out a long, loud whoop of excitement.

"No way! No *way!*" she shouted. "Hold on, wait a minute, wait a minute, I want to get this straight so I can properly enjoy myself."

"Geri," Martha chided.

"You're telling me you don't remember *anything* from last night. Not one iota."

"Geri, please," said Helen. "Do me two things. First, stop shouting because I think my skull might crumble. And secondly, No, I have no recollection of what I did last night. It's totally blank. So just tell me."

"Fan-bloody-tastic!" she hopped up and down on her seat. "Oh I am going to *enjoy* this so much. Far too much!"

"Alright, settle down you two."

Martha handed Helen some painkillers and a mug of warm tea. She sat down at the kitchen table and steepled her fingers.

"You can fill Helen in on her 'performance' later. In case you've forgotten we've got a job to do."

Geri kicked back in her seat. She put her feet on the table while Helen buried her face in her dressing gown. Hardly the most professional meeting Martha had held but at least they seemed keen to listen.

"Right, as I was trying to say last night, before Helen's interruption…"

"Oh God, Hel, you should've seen yourself," Geri laughed.

"Later," Martha chided again. "Anyway, while you were centre stage, I met Gordon Coulthard's mysterious mistress. And she's a piece of work, let me tell you."

"Hold on, I meant to question that last night," said Geri. "Didn't that Mal bloke say Coulthard was *engaged*?"

"Engaged?" Helen croaked. "How can he be engaged? He's already married."

"Calm down," said Martha. "I know. Yes, Geri, he is engaged and yes, Helen, he *is* married. But as we all know we're not dealing with normal people here, are we? Something stinks here, and I'll be perfectly frank, the quicker we're rid of this lot the better."

"So what's the next move?" asked Geri.

Martha took a long, deep breath. She'd been up all night asking that very question. What was already a difficult case was becoming more nightmarish by the minute.

"To be honest with you, I don't know," she said.

Geri and Helen both sat up. They stared at her and then at each other.

"Eh?" asked Geri. "What do you mean you don't know? You *always* know Martha. That's why, well, that's why you're the oldest."

"That doesn't make sense you idiot," said Helen. "I think, Mart, what our dim-witted sister is trying to tell you is that you *always* know what to do."

"That's what I just said!" Geri shouted. "Or can't you hear me all the way back in the eighties? Tina Turner?"

"Tina Turner?"

"Okay," Martha yelled. "Stop. I get it. I'm just not sure what we should do next. There's something going on here that doesn't make any sense. And quite frankly I'm not at all sure how Tracey Coulthard will react to finding out her husband is already engaged to another woman."

"I know how she'd react," said Helen, slurping her tea. "She'd go through the bloomin' roof. And probably take us with her."

"Yeah," said Martha. "That's what worries me."

"What about Mal?" asked Geri. "He seemed a bit unsure of the whole engagement thing last night. Didn't you think it was a bit odd the way he spoke about this Estelle character? Do you think he fancies her?"

"I don't know about that either," said Martha. "What I *do* know is that this whole thing is a mess."

"Wait, Mal?" asked Helen. "Mal? That's Coulthard's mate isn't it?"

"Oh yes," said Geri. "And your new best friend."

"Eh?"

"The fact remains, we're in a very delicate position here," said Martha. "And it's one we've never come across before. I mean, there have been some real scoundrels in the past, but none like this. We've *never* had a bigamist before."

"It's not Coulthard that bothers me, though," said Geri.

"No?"

"No, it's the two women in his life. I mean the wife is totally nuts, a real fruitcake. But the other one, this Estelle, she's completely bonkers too. Look."

She slid her phone across the table. Martha and Helen both leaned over to see what was on the screen. A social media profile had appeared. There were thousands of photos and comments on screen, most of which Martha didn't understand.

"That's her alright," she said. "I'd recognise that trout pout anywhere. And you don't tend to forget the person who tries to pull your hair out from the roots."

"Jesus," said Helen. "Who is this? Barbie and Ken's lovechild?"

Geri sniggered. Martha wasn't so amused.

"Yeah, a real plastic fantastic if ever there was one," said Geri, taking her phone back. "I reckon we just tell Tracey Coulthard, take our money and let them tear each other apart when she finds out how far it's gone."

"As much as I hate doing it, I agree with Geri," said Helen. "If things are so bad that he's got engaged to somebody else, then what the hell are we supposed to do? I mean, we were asked to find out who the mistress was. That's it, we've done it. Whack that profile onto a USB stick, drop it over, and be done with it."

Martha knew Helen and Geri were right. She'd known all along. She just needed them to tell her, that was all. She had to be sure that her thoughts of simply handing over the information and forgetting about the consequences were right. That's what they had been employed to do, nothing else. They weren't marriage counsellors or therapists. They were investigators. And they'd investigated.

Yet, with all of that considered, Martha still didn't feel right. Maybe she cared too much. Maybe she wasn't satisfied that the whole thing had been so clean cut and final. After all, they'd only been working on the case for a day. And maybe she felt bad about getting twenty-thousand pounds for not a lot of effort.

"It just doesn't seem right," she said. "I mean, isn't it all a bit too easy?"

"Easy will do," said Geri.

"Especially if we've got the cash in the bank," said Helen.

"I think I'd still feel better if we had some actual evidence of them together to give her," said Martha, trying hard to justify her fee. "I mean, all we've got is what we've heard. Shouldn't we give her some evidence that they are actually engaged?"

"She already knows," groaned Geri. "I thought our jobs were to find out *who*, not why. Let's just tell her and be done with it. Or better yet, let's tell her and spend some of that cash."

"No, no it doesn't feel right," said Martha. "We should at least get a photo of them together."

"And how do we do that?" asked Helen.

"You're a private investigator Helen, use your imagination," she snapped.

Martha got up and went to a drawer beside the fridge. She pulled out the envelope that May, the housekeeper, had given her the day before, emptying out the contents onto the kitchen table.

"There was another address in here somewhere, I saw it," said Martha. "It was for a flat, in town."

"Penthouse," said Helen.

"Excuse me?" said Martha.

"It's a penthouse," she said again.

"How do you know that?" asked Geri.

"Mal told me."

Immediately, Helen's face stiffened. She quickly tapped her temples.

"I remember, wait I remember. Oh God, I remember last night," she said. "There was music, lots of music, and dancing, lots and lots of dancing. And I was dancing... I was dancing with him. He tried to get me to go to his penthouse."

"Bloody hell," said Geri. "It's like listening to the love life of a goldfish."

"Shut up Geri," Helen spat. "You're right Mart, it's in the middle of town. They both use it, you know, for things."

"Things?" asked Martha. "What kind of things?"

Helen and Geri both pulled silly faces at their older sister. Martha felt immediately embarrassed.

"Oh, right," she said. "Wait a minute, I think this is it. George Square, bloody hell. Talk about the centre of town."

"And you think that's where lover boy and the bimbo will be?" asked Geri.

"It's a Saturday morning," Martha shrugged. "They were both at the party last night. And he's certainly not going to have gone home, is he?"

They were all in agreement. Martha folded the paper with the address on it and shoved it into her pocket. She tidied up the mess and clapped her hands.

"Right, we ready to roll?" she said. "Let's get a snap of these two and deliver that to Tracey. Then I'll feel better about taking her money. Although I'm not looking forward to that meeting."

A loud buzzing interrupted her. Her phone rattled on the kitchen table. She spied the name on the screen.

"Oh shit," she said. "Speak of the devil and she'll appear."

She picked up the phone. Answering, Martha winced in preparation for a screaming match. To her pleasant surprise the soft voice of May the housekeeper spoke.

"Martha? Martha Parker?" she said.

"May, yes, hello," replied Martha.

"Oh, thank God. Thank God I got through to you."

She sounded scared and breathless. Martha could feel her legs going weak. A sense of terror started to well up, all the way from her toes.

"May, what's wrong?" she said, her voice catching in her throat.

"Martha, please," she began to cry. "Please, can you come over here? It's Mrs Coulthard. She's…"

"May?" said Martha. "May!"

But the line had gone dead.

Ten

"I KNEW WE shouldn't have taken this case, I bloody knew it!"

Martha was panicking. She could feel herself tingling all over. She hadn't dipped below forty miles per hour the whole drive. At last count she'd almost crashed the Mini six times.

"Would you do two things for me Martha?" asked Geri, holding tightly to the handle on her door. "Would you please calm down and would you please, please, *please* slow down for God's sake. You're going to kill us!"

"I feel sick," moaned Helen in the back.

"Shut up Helen!" Martha and Geri shouted at the same time.

"I'm sorry," said Martha. "But we need to get to the Coulthard's place as quick as possible. I've got a bad feeling about what we're going to find there."

"Then what's the rush?" asked Geri.

"The rush is… well… we just need to get there, okay?"

The roads were empty. It was a Saturday morning but there were still plenty of hazards to dodge. A bus here, a bin lorry there, somehow they always seemed to pull out just as Martha was racing past them.

When they screeched to a halt outside the Coulthard mansion in the suburbs, everybody let out a sigh of relief. Peeling her fingers from the wheel, Martha raced out the door, leaving the others behind.

"Hold up," shouted Geri. "I'm trying to help the invalid here. She smells like a brewery."

"Hey," Helen darted back. "I can still hear you, you know."

"Hurry up," Martha barked.

She reached the front door and rang the bell. There was no answer. Waiting microseconds, she began pounding on the hard oak, hurting her hands.

"May?" she shouted. "Tracey? Anyone? Hello?"

In truth, she wasn't sure what to expect. Now that she was here, she supposed there could be anything waiting on the other side of the door. There was something about this case that had got under her skin. She felt a bizarre compulsion, a sort of inherent responsibility for Tracey Coulthard's welfare. And when a teary housekeeper phones urgently, red alert sirens had gone off in Martha's mind.

The door opened. May stood on the other side, her face as flushed as ever, eyes like red wool. She was sniffing, blowing her nose. When she saw it was Martha, she began to bawl.

"Oh you came," she said loudly.

"Yes, we came May, what's the matter. What's happened?"

"You came. You came," she reached out and pulled Martha tightly into her.

The old housekeeper smelled of bleach and smoke. Martha hugged her, rubbing her back. The others arrived behind them and Martha motioned for them to go inside.

"Come on, May," she said. "What's going on? Where's Tracey?"

"She's gone," said May. "She's vanished. Disappeared. I went to bring her breakfast in bed like I do every morning. And... and when I went into her room she was... she was..."

"She wasn't there," said Geri glibly.

"She wasn't there," May bawled. "I don't know where she is. She's in danger, I can just feel it. I can tell. I know about these things you know? It's sort of spooky. I can always tell when somebody is in trouble. And I can feel it, Martha. I can feel it in my water."

Martha's panic began to subside. She was still feeling edgy but she realised they were getting nowhere quickly. She straightened up and decided to take charge.

"Okay, come on, let's get you sat down with a cup of tea," she said, rubbing May's shoulders. "We're all going to calm down, take things one step at a time and work out a solution for this. Okay? Nice and calm, nice and calm."

"Calm blue ocean," mumbled Geri. "Up and down, up and down on the Seven Seas."

"Oh God," Helen clamped her hand to her mouth. "Bathroom. Where's the bathroom?"

She darted back out the door. Martha winced. As far as she was concerned, their professional integrity had taken enough of a beating this morning. If her speeding hadn't done the trick, Helen's hangover might be the last straw.

"Right, come on, where's the kitchen, May?" she asked. "Let's get to the bottom of this. Geri, check on your sister, and then meet us in the kitchen."

She leaned in a little closer to her sister, sensing she was about to protest.

"And have a look around on the way, okay?"

"I see," said Geri. "Gotcha."

She winked and went out to help Helen.

"Oh Helen, how can I help you sister dear?" she called, closing the door behind her.

"Okay, let's go May," said Martha.

She took the housekeeper's arm in hers. May shuffled along the hall, staring at the floor, wiping tears from her cheeks.

They reached the kitchen and Martha sat May down at the long, glass table. Martha had to choke back her astonishment.

The kitchen, much like the rest of the mansion, was massive. So big, in fact, the panoramic windows that overlooked the gardens seemed to vanish into the distance.

When she'd steadied herself, Martha found the kettle. At least that never changed from house to house. She prowled around the cupboards until she found some mugs and teabags. The kettle finished boiling and she poured four cups full.

"So," she said, handing May a cup. "Do you want to start at the beginning."

"You have to find her," said the housekeeper. "She's a danger to herself. She could be in a lot of trouble."

"Have you called the police?" asked Martha.

"The police?" May almost yelped. "Oh no, no, no I couldn't do that. No, I wouldn't... I wouldn't want to bother them you see. No, no, we can't have the police involved."

"Why not? If Tracey's in trouble, they'll have a better chance of finding her than we will. We should call them."

"No, no police!" May snapped. "Think what the neighbours will say."

She had grabbed Martha by the arm, a serious look on her flushed face. When she realised she had shouted, she quickly retreated, blowing her nose.

"I'm sorry," she said. "I'm on edge. I don't know if I'm coming or going. It's just been... it's just been a terrible few weeks, that's all. Ever since... ever since..."

She trailed off. Martha watched her intently. Every move, every twitch of the housekeeper's body screamed secrets. There was much more to what was going on in this house. There was more to it than an off-the-wall housewife and her cheating husband. The whole situation was off and Martha felt herself sinking further and further into the middle of it.

"Okay," she said calmly. "We won't call the police. But we have to find Tracey, okay? If she's in some sort of trouble then you have to tell me everything you know, May. It might help us to figure out where she's going to be."

"Yes, yes, of course," she said. "Let me see."

"When did you last see her?"

"Last night," she said, drinking some tea. "I was locking up. It would have been around half-seven, my train is at twenty-to and it takes me ten minutes to walk down the road. I left her with her dinner. She was in her room, she'd been quiet all day, barely spoke to me, barely ate anything."

"And then what?"

"I came in this morning, I'm always a little later on a Saturday. My Jim takes the dogs for a long walk up the park on a Saturday morning and I wait until he's home before I cook him some breakfast."

"You don't get weekends off?" asked Martha.

"You've seen the state she's in," said May strongly. "Would *you* leave her for two days on her own? Or worse, with that man? No. I like to come in and check on her. But... this morning... I walked into her bedroom and... nothing."

She began to sob again. Martha comforted her.

Geri and Helen arrived. Martha shrugged at them as she rubbed May's back while she cried.

"She's still a wreck I see," said Geri.

"She's very upset Geri, cut her some slack," croaked Helen.

"Did you find anything?" asked Martha.

"Nothing unusual," said Helen. "No smashed windows, no sign of breaking and entering. The whole place is secure. Except one of the Bentleys is gone. But that makes sense if Tracey has legged it somewhere."

"Was there anything out of the ordinary about her room?" Martha asked May. "I mean, any *more* out of the ordinary."

"Her dinner," said the housekeeper, drying her eyes. "It'd been thrown against the wall. She's never done anything like that before. That was new."

"I see," said Martha thinking.

"Does that mean something?" asked the housekeeper.

"Maybe not," said Helen. "But if she's thrown her dinner against the wall and she's never done it before then maybe she got some news, or heard something she really didn't like."

"A phone call maybe?" asked Geri. "From Gordon?"

"Possibly," said Helen. "New behaviour is usually the result of new stimulus, a reaction, good or bad, to a whole new set of variables. In fact sociology studies have shown—"

"Okay, thank you Helen," said Martha interrupting. "So we think Tracey might have had some news last night, after you left, May. Now, think very carefully, would there be anywhere she would go to? Anywhere at all, maybe to get away from it all. Family? Sisters or brothers? Her parents?"

"No," said May. "As far as I know the only family she has is Mr Coulthard. And that's no family at all if you ask me."

"Bloody hell," said Geri. "If that's all she's got I pity her, poor cow."

Martha got up from the table, shooting Geri a stern look. She tugged on the bottom of her comfortable cardigan, needing to think. As if this case wasn't trying enough, the most trying person in it was now a missing one.

"Okay, here's what we do," she said. "May, we're going to go out and look for Tracey. If we don't find her within the hour I'm going to call the police."

"No, you can't!" said May. "Please don't call the police, I'm begging you."

"Why not?" asked Geri. "Is this house knocked off or something?"

"What would the neighbours say if they saw police cars outside the house?" said May.

The Parker sisters all groaned collectively. While they were all different in so many ways, none of them were the least bit interested in appearances.

"No May, we don't know what the neighbours will say," said Martha. "But Tracey could be in a bit of trouble. I'm compromising here, give us an hour and then we go to the cops. You called us for help, that's what we're giving you. Okay?"

May didn't say anything. She looked sour now, her mind already busy fending off the impending gossip. Martha didn't care. There was more at stake here than some twitching curtains.

"In the meantime let us drop you off at your house," she said. "I think you should be with your husband. He'll look after you, yes?"

"I suppose so," sighed May. "Oh please find her Martha, please find her. I'm sick with worry. She doesn't deserve this, she deserves so much more, so much better than him. She's better than all of this, please help her, please."

"We'll try," she said. "Now get your coat, our car's out the front."

May got up and tottered out of the kitchen. When she was out of earshot, she brought Helen and Geri in close about her in a huddle.

"What the hell's going on here?" asked Helen. "I mean, I know I'm hungover and all the rest of it but this is really strange. Tracey going missing, the housekeeper worried about what the neighbours will say. Us getting called willy-nilly, it's bogus man."

"That's what twenty-grand gets you," said Geri mournfully. "Beck-and-call, day and night. More money, more problems."

"We should *definitely* have asked for more money," said Helen ruefully. "Anything more is worth this running around."

"Can I remind you two that a woman is missing here," said Martha. "Now I agree, I don't reckon she's *really* missing but we don't know that yet. And she's a client, we owe it to her to be a bit more respectful."

"Fine," said Geri.

"Yes, you're right," nodded Helen. "So where do you think she's gone to?"

"I have a feeling she might have gone into town," said Martha. "To a certain playboy husband's penthouse."

"Why?" asked Geri. "I mean, if she knows about him and his antics, why now?"

"I don't know, yet," said Martha. "What was that you were saying earlier Helen, about new information?"

"If she's been told something new she might act differently. Depends on what it is right enough. I mean, it has to have some sort of emotional connection to her."

"I've got a bad feeling that somebody might have told Mrs Coulthard about Mr Coulthard's lover," said Martha.

"Oh Christ," said Geri. "Then we *are* in trouble."

"She might ask for the money back," panicked Helen.

"Pull yourself together, Helen," chided Martha. "Anyway, let's get moving. We get rid of the housekeeper and get to that penthouse. I have a feeling there'll be a familiar looking Bentley parked outside."

May returned, buttoning up her duffle coat. She fastened her scarf tightly about her neck and stood looking at the Parker sisters.

"I'm ready," she said. "If you get me home now, I'll be able to make the bingo."

"Great," muttered Martha. "Nice prioritising there."

Eleven

"SO WHAT DO we do now?" asked Helen.

"Why are you asking me?" said Martha. "You're an equal partner in this company. You decide for a change."

"Oh come on, Mart," laughed Geri. "Everybody in this car knows you're the boss. And we also know that's exactly how you like it."

Martha smirked. She drummed her hands on the steering wheel of the Mini. They were parked, illegally, up an alleyway in the centre of Glasgow. Beyond the lane, there were people walking by with brightly coloured shopping bags, filled with Christmas gifts, completely unaware the sisters were there.

Martha tried to shut the shoppers out of her mind. She still had plenty of shopping left to do. A husband and two grown up kids would still be expecting a visit from Santa. They weren't interested in the seedy double-lives of the rich and infamous.

Besides, the sisters were there for a reason. To her surprise when they arrived at the address of Coulthard's penthouse suite, there was no Bentley outside. Martha was disappointed. She had been quite sure that Tracey would have been there already. So sure was Martha, that they were still sitting outside, waiting for her to turn up.

"She's not coming," said Geri, as if reading her sister's mind. "This is a waste of time, we could be out trying to find her."

"And where would we look?" asked Helen. "She could be anywhere, quite literally. At least Martha's idea that she might come looking for her no-good husband makes sense."

"Thank you Helen," said Martha. "How long have we got left?"

"About twenty minutes," said Geri. "Are you going to call the cops if she doesn't show up?"

"I think we have to," said Martha. "She's not been seen since last night. She's fairly unstable, there's every chance she could be… well we won't go there."

She sat back. She was starting to get nervous. Suddenly she thought twenty minutes was a very long time. The idea of just calling the police and letting them deal with it was very appealing. It would wash their hands of the whole affair.

But she'd given her word to May. And while she didn't approve of the housekeeper's motives, she was reluctant to disobey them for the sake of another twenty minutes.

"You really think she's unstable?" asked Geri.

The others looked at her. She was messing around on her phone, scrolling through social media.

"How do you mean?" asked Helen.

"She seemed pretty unstable to me," said Martha. "The dinner throwing, the state of the house. When Helen and I first met her she wasn't wearing anything and was shouting and screaming at us. Do you think that's normal behaviour?"

"Obviously not," said Geri, reclining in her seat. "I don't know, it just… it just seems a bit too put on for me."

"I don't follow," said Helen. "The woman's quite clearly upset about the deterioration of her marriage. And she's not handling it at all well."

"Yeah, yeah I get that, it's just… I don't know. Don't you think it's more of a cry for attention than anything else? I mean, she must have known the kind of guy she was marrying."

"A cry for attention in what way?" asked Martha, her interest piqued.

"Well, look at it this way. She's super rich, wife of a really good, hotshot banker who's going straight to the top. But what does she do all day? Sits at home, smashes up her lovely house and employs us to dig up dirt on her no-good man."

"That doesn't sound normal to me Geri," said Helen.

"No, that's the point," she said. "Like, it's deliberately *not* normal. Anybody I know would have divorced Coulthard, just like that."

She snapped her fingers. Martha blinked.

"She gets half of his money, half of the estate and, most importantly, gets shot of the sleazeball for good. But instead she's going about the houses, showing us how upset she is, hiring investigators, pulling a vanishing act. I don't know, I reckon there are easier ways to go about things."

She folded her arms. Martha could feel her head starting to hurt. Everything with this case was complicated. Now she had Geri, whose judgement she trusted, throwing in curve balls.

"I'm no psychiatrist, obviously," Geri said. "But all of this makes you wonder just what's really going on?"

"She has a point, Mart," said Helen. "I mean, what if we're just part of a big game?"

"No… stop it," said Martha. "Look, we're investigators right, all we can do is go with what's presented in front of us. If Tracey Coulthard is playing us all for a bunch of patsies then so be it. But until then we have to assume she's telling the truth and that she is, in fact, missing."

They sat in silence. Staring out of the alleyway, they could see the entrance to Coulthard's building. Martha could feel her eyelids growing heavy. She hadn't slept at all well. How could she? Her every waking moment was being taken up by this case. Now, with the heat of the car and the comfy cardigan about her, she felt like she could just doze off.

"Bloody hell," whistled Geri, waking her up. "Would you look at the state of that. Like I don't profess to have an up-to-the-minute fashion sense but even *I* can tell she's trying too hard."

"Oi, that's not what you said yesterday," protested Helen.

"What?" said Martha, groggily. "What are you talking about…"

She peered through the shoppers to the far side of the road. There, standing at the entrance of the building was Estelle. Still dressed in the same skin-tight shiny dress and six-inch heels from the night before, she lit up a cigarette and puffed away.

"That's… that's Estelle," said Martha.

"You know that woman?" laughed Helen. "How the hell do you know a bimbo like that?"

"Estelle?" said Geri. "You mean? Coulthard's fiancée Estelle? From the party?"

"That's her," said Martha. "I'd recognise that face, that outfit even, a million miles away. That's the one who almost yanked my head off last night when I met Coulthard at the party."

"Hell's Bells," wheezed Helen. "Talk about a looker. Mr Coulthard sure knows how to pick 'em. She's even worse in real life than online. I didn't think that was even possible!"

Martha and Helen both peered at the young woman standing smoking. People were staring at her as they walked past, men whistling, women gossiping. Estelle did and said nothing. Instead she looked like she was enjoying the attention, flicking her peroxide blonde hair back and forth over her shoulders between puffs.

"Eh guys…" said Geri

Geri grabbed at Martha and Helen but they were fascinated by Estelle.

"How does she even walk in those heels?" asked Helen.

"She can walk in them alright, she can fight in them too, trust me," said Martha.

"Guys," Geri repeated.

"I mean, she's like those women you see on comedy shows, sitcoms, you know, like the one who's always after the men."

"Tarts," said Martha. "Well she's not nearly as funny and she's certainly more unpleasant."

"Hey!" Geri shouted, frightening the other two. "Are you listening to me? I think we have a situation here!"

"What is it?" asked Martha.

"Our pal Tracey Coulthard, she drives a Bentley right?" asked Geri.

"Yeah, so?"

"And I take it its registration plate is something along the lines of T4 CEY? Yeah?"

"I don't know, maybe, makes sense I suppose," said Martha. "Why?"

"Because a Bentley with that very reg has just pulled up along the street. And there's a dark-haired woman with a face like thunder getting out. And now she's running towards Estelle."

"Oh God," Martha exclaimed. "Quick! Do something."

"Do something? What?" Geri replied.

"I don't know, anything. Oh God, why is this happening?"

"What? The spurned wife attacking the new lover. God knows," said Geri sarcastically. "Who'd have thought?"

Martha threw open the door and clambered out. She untangled herself from the seatbelt and bolted out of the alleyway, pushing past some Christmas shoppers and narrowly avoiding the traffic. But she was too late. Tracey Coulthard had reached Estelle first. And now the two were going at it in the middle of the street.

Martha found herself rooted to the spot. It couldn't have been for any more than a few seconds but it felt so much longer. With every scratch, swipe and sneer of Tracey and Estelle, the worse she felt. It was only when they tumbled to the ground in a heap did everything whizz back into action.

"Bitch!"

"Cow!"

"Tart!"

"Slag!"

Back and forth the insults went, stopped only for screaming. The two women lashed at each other, their manicured fingernails being put to good use as talons. Martha shook herself into action. She raced forward and attempted to get in the middle of them.

"Enough!" she shouted. "Enough, stop it! Stop fighting! You're not schoolgirls. Pull yourselves together!"

Being in the middle of two fighting women had its hazards. And Martha certainly felt their wrath. She took a scrape, a scratch and a pull of her hair as she fought to split them up. Only when Geri and Helen arrived were they properly separated.

Martha caught her breath. A small crowd had gathered around them. People stared, unsure just what was going on. Martha felt embarrassed, although she didn't know why. She'd been there to break it up, not take part.

"Alright folks, nothing to see here," said Geri. "Go on, toddle back to your shopping. This is Glasgow isn't it? Can't two... erm... women have a dust up in the middle of the street? Get outta here."

There was some quiet laughter before the crowd began to disperse. Tracey and Estelle weren't quiet. Instead they seemed to be trying to outdo each other in a screaming match.

"You!" shouted Tracey. "I knew it was you. I bloody knew it. You've hung around him like a bad smell for years."

"You've got the cheek to talk," Estelle fired back. "At least I treat him like a real man, at least I've given him what he wants."

"Okay you two, just calm down," Martha shouted. "Shouting and bawling like this in the street, get a grip of yourselves would you?"

Tracey and Estelle stood snarling at each other. Martha was between them, acting like a referee. Helen and Geri were her linesmen, keeping a watchful eye for any sudden movements.

"Now I think we should go somewhere and talk this through, calmly, like adults. Okay?"

"There's nothing to discuss," spat Tracey. "She's a hussy, plain and simple."

"Eh, excuse me? I think we both know what choice Gordon's made and it ain't you honey!"

Estelle flashed her huge engagement ring. Martha swore she could feel the heat of Tracey's white-hot rage radiating onto her. It seemed every pair of eyes were now on Mrs Coulthard.

Tracey's eyes were wide as plates as she scowled at Estelle's finger. Her fists were clenched so tightly they were shaking. Her naturally beautiful face had contorted into the nastiest, most hate-filled scowl that Martha had ever seen. She looked like a volcano about to erupt.

"That's... that's... an engagement ring!"

She screamed so loudly even the buildings seemed to shake. Pigeons scattered from George Square across the street and the whole city felt like it was brought to a stop.

Martha, Helen and Geri all winced. Estelle clamped her hands to her ears. When she'd ran out of energy, Tracey walked slowly towards them.

"Where is he?" she said, calmly. "Where is that bastard?"

"He's... he's upstairs," said Estelle, terrified by the woman standing in front of her.

"I'm going to kill him.," said Tracey.

Before any of them could react, she was gone. She was lithe, agile, darting away from Martha and the others with ease.

"No," Martha shouted. "No! Wait! Hold on, come back. Tracey"

But she was gone. Martha panicked, she turned to the others.

"We've got to stop her," she shouted. "Before she does something stupid."

The Parker sisters raced into the building after Tracey, with Estelle in tow. Mrs Coulthard had reached the only lift first and they saw it climb through the numbers towards the penthouse.

"The stairs," shouted Martha. "Hurry up!"

Twelve

MARTHA, HELEN, GERI and Estelle wheezed their way to the top of the staircase, all four women desperately trying to catch their breath. Martha could feel her lungs burning and her cheeks flushed. She mopped her brow and sucked air in through her nose. There was no time to dally; they had to stop Tracey from doing something she'd regret.

She opened the door and stepped out onto the top corridor. A landing opened up in front of her, with a balcony that overlooked an enclosed garden. She could hear the hustle and bustle of Glasgow filtering over the tops of the building. But it was strangely peaceful up here.

Fighting the distraction she remembered why she was there. To her left was a door. It was sitting ajar. The others came staggering in behind her.

"That the penthouse?" she asked Estelle.

The young woman coughed and spluttered, nodding as she clutched her chest.

"Right," said Martha.

She darted over to the door. Pushing her way in, she climbed the wide steps that led to the rest of the roomy apartment.

"Tracey," she called. "Gordon? Hello?"

There was no answer. Helen and Geri followed her, Estelle close behind.

"Tracey," she shouted again. "Tracey, we know you're in here. Come on, let's talk this over. We don't want you to do anything stupid now. Tracey—"

Martha stopped, her ears pricking up. She looked about at the others.

"Do you hear that?" she asked.

"Water?" said Helen. "Running water."

"The shower," said Geri. "Where's the bathroom?"

"Through there," said Estelle, shoving past Helen and Geri. Martha tried to grab her but she slid by. They followed Estelle as she ran in her six-inch heels, galloping through the untidy penthouse with remarkable speed.

She vanished around a corner. Martha and the others followed her as quickly as they could. But they were stopped in their tracks by the sound of a blood-curdling, scream.

"Holy hell," said Helen. "What was that?"

"Quick," said Martha. "The bathroom. In there."

When she pushed the door open her breath vanished, sucked out of her lungs in an instant. There, in the bathroom, were Estelle, Tracey and Gordon Coulthard.

Only Mr Coulthard was face down in the bath, his body limp. His wife was perched by his side, her face ashen with shock. And Estelle cowering in the corner, shaking uncontrollably.

"Oh God," gasped Helen. "What's happened?"

"Is he... is he dead?" asked Geri.

Something twanged in the back of Martha's mind. The mention of death was like a starter gun. Maybe it was maternal, maybe it was just terror. But she vaulted over the others and pulled Gordon Coulthard from the bath.

"Help me," she shouted. "Quickly, does anybody know CPR?"

The banker's body hit the tiles with a thud. Water splashed everywhere, making Martha's hands slippery. She quickly checked for a pulse. There was nothing.

"Quickly," Martha urged. "CPR? Anyone? Call an ambulance."

"Right... right... an ambulance, right," said Helen. "An ambulance, yeah, an ambulance, nine-nine-nine, yeah."

"Just do it, Helen!" Geri yelled.

Helen pulled out her phone from her jeans. Geri snatched it from her and dialled the emergency number.

Martha bent down and tried to resuscitate Coulthard. The banker was unresponsive. She tried pumping his chest but still nothing.

"Please wake up," she said. "Gordon. Gordon please!"

"He's dead," spat Tracey. "He's already dead."

"No! Helen, where's that bloody ambulance?"

"It's... it's..."

"It's on its way!" Geri said.

"Oh god this is awful!" said Helen, bursting into tears.

Martha wasn't giving up. She continued pumping his chest, remembering her emergency responder skills which told her mouth-to-mouth was pretty futile in the community, best just trying to keep blood pumping until the ambulance arrived. Nothing happened. When she checked the pulse in his neck there was still nothing. It was the same in his wrist.

"Oh no," she said, her bottom lip trembling. "Oh no."

She kept going. Gordon Coulthard's body was sprawled out on the bathroom floor. Martha tried to catch her breath but it was hard. She could feel tears welling up in her eyes. What had been a bad case already had now spiralled out of all control.

"He's dead," she said, quietly. Martha looked down, the man below her hands was cold to touch and his face and torso dusky from being face down. She knew they were too late, she knew he was long gone. She sat back on her haunches, defeated. Her resolve to keep up the CPR had dwindled with each passing moment. He'd been dead when they found him.

Estelle stifled another scream. The five women sat silently, the body separating them. Martha's hands were trembling. She looked at them, the fingers twitching and quivering of their own volition. She was terrified, there was a dead body just there. She was in deep.

"Martha," said Geri, tugging at her sleeve. "Martha, come away, he's dead."

"I couldn't save him," she whispered.

"There's nothing you could have done. Now come away, we have to be careful," she said.

"Careful?" Martha replied. "He's already dead, Geri. It's a bit late to be careful."

"Yes, I know, I know," she said. "But we have to be *careful*, if you *know* what I *mean*?"

Martha blinked. She didn't know what Geri was talking about. But the look on her sister's face was serious enough that she knew she had to listen.

"I'm making a phone call," she said. "And I think you and Helen should come with me, right now."

"Who are you calling?"

"The cops."

"The police?" said Tracey.

"The polis!" Estelle gasped. "No, no, no you can't call the polis."

She stormed across the bathroom, stepping over Coulthard like he wasn't even there. The mascara running down her face made her look like a Native American smeared in war paint.

"You can't call the polis. I'm serious," she hissed.

"And why not?" Geri fired back. "This man is dead."

"You just can't," Estelle was getting more aggressive.

Martha was wary. She'd seen how quickly Estelle could get violent. She curled her fists into a ball, just in case.

"Look at what's gone on," Geri continued. "We've got a dead body here, a big shot banker drowned in his bath. His wife, his mistress, and us three punters are all standing about. So before anything—and I mean *anything*—else happens, I'm calling the police to clean this mess up. Because I'm *not* going to jail."

"You can't!"

"And why not?" Geri darted. "Have you got something to hide Barbie?"

"What?"

"Geri," said Martha. "Stop."

"What? No," Geri spat. "She's not wanting the cops called, makes me think she's got something to hide. Am I right?"

"You're mental."

"No Barbie, I've got the phone. And I'm the only one amongst you idiots who's thinking straight."

"Give me that phone."

"No."

"Give it!"

Estelle lashed out at Geri. She tried to grab the mobile but she missed. She wobbled and tripped, crashing forward into the bath. A huge splash went up and Estelle let out another scream.

Geri burst out laughing. Martha was appalled. As if this situation wasn't bad enough it was being turned into a circus.

"Right, enough," she said, leaping into action. "This is getting out of control."

"Don't look at me," said Geri, still laughing. "I didn't start it. It was Moby Dick over there."

"Enough," Martha said. "A man has died here. Have some respect."

"She's right," said Helen, her face now a terrible grey colour. "This is awful, just awful."

"Right, okay," said Martha. "Before you lose it again, Helen can you please take Mrs Coulthard into the kitchen, make her and yourself a cup of tea."

Helen nodded. Martha knew that her sister needed instruction. She didn't work well without a structure. And Martha was more than happy to start dishing out the orders.

Helen walked over to Tracey who hadn't moved since they discovered her with the body. She gently took her by the arm. When she felt Helen's touch, she twitched her head. Martha thought it looked like she'd woken up from a trance. She was a little disoriented, her face slack and pale.

"Could you go with my sister please, Tracey," she said. "We'll get the police over."

"Yes," she said. "Of course."

Helen led her around Gordon's corpse. They were just about to leave when Tracey stopped short of Martha. She looked down at her, her eyes sharp and focussed behind her long, dark hair.

"I didn't kill him," she said firmly. "He was like that when I found him. I didn't kill him, you know? He has a lump on the back of his head. That wasn't me."

"Okay," said Martha. "Please, go with Helen, she'll make you some tea. You're in shock Tracey, we'll sort all of this out."

Tracey held her gaze a moment longer, then let herself be led out of the bathroom.

"Lump on the back of his head?" asked Geri. "Did she say lump on the back of his head?"

"Not now, Geri," said Martha, pinching the bridge of her nose. "Come on, help me with this one."

Estelle was sitting in the bath crying. Martha and Geri helped her out. She was the picture of misery, pathetic and lame, she limped her way out of the bathroom. They sat her down on the sofa.

"Geri, fetch her a towel," said Martha.

"Fine, then I'm calling the police."

Estelle let out a loud moan of unhappiness. Geri left them, smirking.

"What's the matter Estelle?" asked Martha. "Is there something you want to tell us?"

"I can't have another run in with the polis," she said, between sniffs. "I just can't."

"Why, what have you done?"

"Nothing, I swear," she said. "They just, they just have it in for my family. My brother, they're always hanging around his garage, looking for trouble. Then there's my mum, she's still on parole from the last time."

"Parole? What did she do?"

"Nothing… just a bit of shoplifting. Once they see me they'll lift me, they'll think I did that to Gordon. Oh god, Gordon, look what's happened to him."

She sank her face into her hands and sobbed loudly. Martha rubbed her back.

"It's okay," she said. "We don't know that *anything* happened to him. He could have just… you know, drowned accidentally."

"Yeah, right," said Geri, returning with the towel. "Wake up and smell what's going on here, Mart."

She threw the towel at Estelle, then dialled the emergency services again. She smiled with glee as she asked for the police, explaining what had happened.

There was a thud at the door. Two paramedics appeared lugging with them their equipment.

"In there, in the bathroom," said Martha. "But you're too late."

One of the medics rushed into the bathroom. The other headed straight for Martha.

"Okay, are you feeling alright there?" asked the medic.

"What? Yes, of course I am, why?"

"Martha," said Geri. "You're holding your chest."

Martha hadn't realised it but she was clinging tightly onto her chest. Her knuckles were white she was holding so hard. Only then did she admit that she was in pain.

A stabbing ache darted through her chest. She leaned on the edge of the couch, suddenly feeling very weak and uneasy.

The medic produced a large, silver blanket from her equipment bag and wrapped it about her shoulders.

"Okay, what's your name?" she asked.

"Martha, Martha Parker. I'm a private investigator."

"Okay Martha, you're going to come with me now, alright? Can you walk?"

"What? Of course I can walk. No, I can't come with you, there's… there's been an accident."

"Okay, that's alright, we'll sort it out, it'll be fine. But you need to come with me."

"What? No…"

"Are you in pain Martha?"

"What? Yes."

"In your chest?"

"Yes, but it doesn't matter, it's just… it's just…"

The paramedic led Martha away from the others. She looked over her shoulder as Geri and Estelle watched her go from the lounge. She passed Helen and Tracey in the kitchen, the pair huddled over large mugs of tea. Then she was taken out of the apartment and down to the waiting ambulance.

Thirteen

MARTHA LOOKED ABOUT the cubicle. She felt like she'd been stuck there for days, but it had actually only been a few hours. The curtains were drawn around the bed but she could hear the busy accident and emergency room beyond. There was crying, shouting, talking, laughing, everything in between.

Occasionally there would be what sounded like a mass panic. A lot of footsteps would rush past the curtain. Then it would all go quiet for a while, before the regular hubbub would start up again.

She hadn't been to A&E for a long while—not since Margo was very young. The times she had raced through the night streets to get emergency help when her baby couldn't breathe properly all came flooding back. The panic, the sheer terror at hearing the wheezing and grating sounds coming from such a tiny little body. It had reduced her to tears then and almost did the same now.

Then there were all the visits when she herself was younger. Helen and Geri were forever getting themselves into scrapes. Broken arms, broken ankles, anything that *would* break invariably did with those two. If she'd signed her name on one plaster cast she'd done it a hundred times.

It was strange what came flooding back when there was nothing else to do. The cold, sterile smell of the hospital reminded her of when Geri had been born. She couldn't recall Helen's birth but Geri was different. She was older then, nineteen, old enough to remember seeing her mother with the newborn baby in her arms.

Even then Martha had felt an over-protectiveness over her baby sister. Their father had looked exhausted already, the prospect of raising yet another child so late after the last one had obviously taken it out of him. Only Martha had relished the opportunity to care for and about Geri.

That had been twenty-one years ago now. How the time had flown by. She'd had and raised her own child in that time too. Now she was getting to work with her sisters every single day. She was blessed.

At least, she thought she had been. Today hadn't been the best of days. In fact, it had ranked down there with some of the worst she had ever experienced. When she had pulled herself out of bed, the last thing she had expected to find was Gordon Coulthard dead.

And he was dead. He'd been dead when Martha found him. That image of him face down in the bath, his arms floating in the water was always going to stay with her. Even now, hours later, when she closed her eyes she could still see him, just there.

The curtain was pulled back. A young doctor appeared, fresh faced and bright eyed. He smiled warmly, peering over his little round glasses.

"Hello Martha," he said. "I'm Brian, I'll be your doctor for this evening."

"You make it sound like we're in a restaurant," she smiled. "Are you going to take my order?"

"Yes, well, we're not that kind of place I'm afraid. The only thing I can offer you are some soggy sandwiches I should have eaten about six hours ago. And trust me, you don't want them. I'm here to make you better, not feel worse."

He examined Martha's chart that hung from the end of her bed. He scratched the back of his head and looked at her.

"Okay Martha, so you've been brought in with chest pains, is that right?"

"Yes," she said.

"Do you have any family history of this sort of thing? Heart attacks, that sort of thing?"

"Well... my mum had one about five years ago."

"Ah, right," said the doctor. "Well that means we're going to have to be extra careful with you then. Family history and chest pains are a no-no to us medics."

"No, I get it," she said sadly. "I don't think I want to be going through what my mum did. I'm only forty."

"Exactly. We'll get your bloods done soon by one of the nurses. In the meantime we're going to get you hooked up to this clever little machine called an ECG. Just to get a tracing of your heart, make sure there isn't anything sinister going on."

"Sinister?" asked Martha. "You don't know how right you are."

He smiled uncomfortably. The medic attached sticky patches to Martha's chest. Wiggly lines flashed up on the screen and Brian nodded. When he was satisfied, he unhooked her from the device and tore off the print-out.

"Okay, do you want the good news, the bad news or a bit of both?" he asked.

"Bad news Brian, bad news," she said, sitting a little tensely. "Today has just been one bit of bad news after another. You may as well pile it on, on top of everything else."

"Okay, well, first and foremost, your ECG looks ok. But the bad news is we're going to keep you in under observation."

"Keep me in?" she said. "Oh no I couldn't possibly."

"Believe me, Martha I wish I could let you walk out of here and free up a bed, but that would be incredibly negligent of me," he laughed. "No, we'll move you to an observation ward just to keep an eye on you for the next twelve hours or so. We'll get a blood test in twelve hours, to check for any underlying damage to your heart muscle and if it's ok then you'll be allowed to go home."

Martha lay back down on her bed. She rubbed her forehead and ran her hand through her tangled hair. Of all the things that had happened, being kept in hospital was really the last thing she needed.

Then again maybe it wouldn't be that bad. Maybe being kept in a safe, secure ward for a few hours while she pulled herself together would do her the world of good. No running around, worrying about Tracey Coulthard, worrying about Helen and Geri, or anyone else for that matter, could be a blessing in disguise.

"Okay Martha, I'll get the nurses to take your bloods and have you taken up to the ward," said the medic. "We'll get you sorted. Okay?"

"Thank you, doctor," she said. "Sorry about all this."

"Don't be daft," he laughed. "Compared to some of my other patients today, you're a total joy. Take care."

As Brian left, a nurse came and wheeled Martha out of the cubicle and through the A&E department. She tried not to look at her fellow patients, but curiosity got the better of her.

They were all in various states of disrepair. Men, women, old, young, children, everybody. The casualty ward was a meeting ground for all who lived in the city. It was the great leveller, Martha thought. Although she suspected she was the only one there today who'd come from such a bizarre set of circumstances.

The nurse left her off in a quiet corner of the observation ward. She took a blood sample and promised her a cup of tea when she came back. Martha closed her eyes and thought about getting some sleep. Then she saw Gordon Coulthard again, and her eyes snapped open.

To her surprise somebody was sitting at the bottom of her bed. She looked about, a bit startled, before blinking.

"Who are you?"

The woman sitting down was about to answer her when she started coughing. She held up a finger while her face turned scarlet, the fit getting worse. Martha wasn't sure if there was something she should do to help.

The mysterious coughing woman rummaged about in her handbag. She pulled out an inhaler and sucked on it hard. Holding her breath, Martha watched her count to ten before letting out a big, relieved breath.

She sat still for a moment as though expecting another bout of coughing. When it didn't arrive she spoke to Martha.

"Sorry about that," she croaked. "Bloody asthma, honestly. I've been told these new inhalers are meant to make life *so* much easier. But I'm still out of puff when I climb the stairs."

"Oh," said Martha. "Have you thought about taking a lift instead?"

"Well, you see, that's the thing. I'm claustrophobic. Can't stand being trapped in a metal box climbing up twenty, thirty floors. That's a nightmare for me. Do you have any idea how big a distance that is to fall if the cables snap? Think about it."

"I'd rather not," said Martha.

"Yeah, I know. There's lots like that. Speed you drive at down the motorway, the amount of people in a crowd at a gig, it's all terrifying. You're better just plodding through life never knowing these things."

"Yes, I think you're right," she said. "Now, I'm not being rude or anything but, would you mind telling me who you are?"

"Oh yes, bloody hell, sorry," said the woman, clapping her hand against her forehead. "Sorry, yeah, I get carried away with things, especially after I almost cough up a lung. Sorry. Here's my ID."

She rifled through her handbag again. This time she produced a small leather wallet. Flipping it open, the unmistakable shape of a police medallion appeared. Martha gulped.

"Detective Sergeant Pope," said the sickly woman. "I've got a couple of questions for you."

"Oh, right," said Martha, suddenly feeling very nervous. "I mean, yes, of course."

"Of course what?" asked Pope.

"What?"

"What you just said," said Pope.

"What?"

"You just said of course. Of course what?"

"Oh, nothing," said Martha. "Nothing at all. How can I help you Detective Sergeant? I take it this is about Gordon Coulthard."

"How did you know?" said Pope, leaning back in her chair. "Yes, it's about Gordon Coulthard. Unless of course you're talking about *another* Gordon Coulthard who was found dead this afternoon that I don't know about."

Martha was in such a shock she didn't know if Pope was being serious or not. Only when the policewoman started laughing did she feel silly.

"Right," she said. "Sorry, it's been a very long day and I'm not really with it."

"No, I'm sure," said Pope. "Every day is a long day in my work but hey, got to put food on the table somehow right."

"Yeah."

"Anyway, I'll cut to the chase Martha, I know you're in your sick bed so I won't keep you long. I've just got a couple of questions for you."

Martha couldn't feel her legs she was so nervous. She'd never been interrogated by the police before. Then again she'd never found a dead body before either.

"I'm sorry," she said. "I'm sorry, I just… it's been a bad day, like I said. I'm a bit nervous."

"That's okay," Pope smiled. "It's just routine that's all."

"Am I in trouble?" asked Martha.

"Well, that's what I'm here to establish, Martha."

"Am I under arrest?"

"No, you're not," said Pope. "Not yet anyway."

"Not yet?" Martha blurted.

A few of the other patients in the ward looked around. Pope cleared her throat. She leaned in a little closer to Martha.

"Look Martha," she said quietly. "I'm just doing my job here. You're not under arrest, and I hope you don't give me any reason to put you under arrest. Okay?"

Martha gulped again. Her mouth and throat were dry. She didn't think all of this stress could be good for her heart. And here she was, in hospital, because of her heart.

"Okay," she said, trying to calm herself. "Okay."

"Just a few questions, that's all."

"Right, just a couple of questions, okay. I can handle that."

Pope produced a small notepad from her coat pocket. She clicked her pen and turned to a fresh page.

"So you discovered the body?" she asked.

"Yes," said Martha. "Well, no, technically not."

"Technically?" the policewoman cocked her eyebrow. "You either found it or you didn't. What's this technical malarkey?"

"I mean, yes I found the body, along with my sisters. We got in there just after Estelle. But we all got there after Tracey. Do you know who Estelle is? I don't know her last name. Sorry."

"She's the mistress right," Pope pointed her pen at Martha. "Yeah I know who she is. Blonde, dumb and from a bad background. Not so much a tart with a heart as a tart with a flash car. Gotcha."

"Yeah, something like that."

"And your relationship with Mrs Coulthard. What's that exactly?"

"We're her employees," said Martha. "Well, I say employees, she hired us."

"Us?"

"Myself and my sisters," she said. "We're private investigators. I run Parkers Investigations. We help people who think their partners might be cheating on them."

"I get it," Pope smiled, writing the name down. "Parker is the family name, parking is the family business. Nice."

"We try to make a difference," said Martha sincerely. "Although sometimes it doesn't work out that way."

"And if I check with Companies House you'll be all up-to-date on your tax returns, VAT, all of that yeah?" asked Pope.

"Of course," said Martha.

The policewoman laughed. She kept scribbling away on her notepad.

"Just checking," she said. "So you were hired by Tracey Coulthard to spy on her husband, yeah?"

"Yes."

"And that's why you were at his penthouse?"

"Yes," said Martha. "We'd raced up the stairs and when my sisters and I got into the lounge together we heard Estelle scream. See we'd all come up after Tracey, that's Tracey Coulthard. Her and Estelle had been fighting in the street and Tracey had taken the lift. We all chased after her."

"So Mrs Coulthard was in the flat alone with Mr Coulthard then?"

"Yes, I guess so," said Martha, thinking as she spoke. "I mean it couldn't have been for very long."

"How long?"

"I don't know, I can't really think. A few minutes maybe?"

"Five minutes? Ten minutes? Can you remember Martha, it could be important," said Pope.

"Five minutes then," said Martha. "As long as it took me to try and run up twenty flights of stairs."

"Right. And what was Mrs Coulthard doing when you found her?"

"Nothing."

"Nothing?" asked Pope.

"She wasn't doing anything. She was just sitting there, in the corner while… while…"

A flash of the scene appeared in Martha's mind. She became stiff, rigid, like she'd been turned into a statue. She gripped the sheet around her tightly hoping it would help. But it didn't.

"Are you okay?" asked Pope suspiciously.

"Yes, sorry," said Martha. "It's just… it's just seeing Gordon Coulthard like that. Face down in the water, not moving, it was horrible."

"I'll bet," said Pope, finishing her notes. "Look, I'm sorry to distress you. We're just checking all the facts add up that's all. You've been very helpful Mrs Parker."

"Miss Parker," said Martha. "Parker is my maiden name. I never changed it."

"Right," said Pope, getting up and coughing to clear her throat. "Yeah, we're just following procedure."

"Procedure for what?" asked Martha. "Is this... is this a murder investigation?"

Pope smiled. Her mouth stretched out across her thin, pale face like a clown's makeup. She shrugged.

"I'm not at liberty to say," she said.

"But it is, right? You think Gordon Coulthard was murdered."

"I can't say Martha, sorry. Get well soon. I know what it's like being stuck in these places, not very nice. My asthma, gets me every change of season and I'm laid up for days while they shove tubes up my nose. Nasty. Take care. If there's anything else I'll be in touch."

She tapped the bars that ran alongside Martha's bed. Just as she was about to leave, and Martha could breathe again, she stopped. She rifled around in her handbag again and pulled out a card.

"If you think of anything else though," she said. "Anything at all. Just give me a call. Sorry for the state this is in, must have spilled some cough syrup on it."

She handed the card to Martha who took it. She was getting quite a collection of these things. She looked at the name: 'Detective Sergeant Aileen Pope, Maryhill Police Station' and a host of numbers. A big, bright yellow blob had covered the top quarter of the card and made it wrinkly.

"Anything that comes to mind just pick up the phone," said Pope. "I'm always on duty."

"Sounds horrible," said Martha. "I mean, sounds like hard work."

"They're one and the same thing, Martha. Take care of yourself and get better soon."

She waved a little before leaving the ward. Martha watched her go. When she was sure that the policewoman wasn't coming back, she lay back down in her bed.

She thought about trying to get to sleep. She thought about getting up and discharging herself. But most of all she thought about what was going on.

She needed to speak with Helen and Geri straight away. She needed her sisters.

Fourteen

MARTHA DIDN'T GET home until the following morning. By the time her twelve-hour observation period was over it was the middle of the night. The medics had thought it best just to keep her until a sensible hour before turfing her out.

In truth she had been quite excited about it all. Despite everything that had gone on, she had relished the chance to sleep in a single bed with no distractions or grievances.

Not that she'd been able to sleep. She'd spent the whole night tossing and turning. Either she was too hot or too cold, too uncomfortable or too restrained. She'd seen the clock above the nurse's station hit every hour before finally the lights had come on. Some bland tasting porridge later, her husband, Geoff, had picked her up and driven her home.

He'd had to go to work, making various apologies. A quick call from her daughter, Margot, to make sure she was still alive and Martha was alone in her house.

She'd taken to watching out the window, waiting for that familiar sound of an old Mini coming spluttering up the road. When it finally did she almost fell down the stairs running to answer the door.

"You should be in bed!" Helen shouted.

"Yeah get into bed, Martha. I'm not carting your old, spotty backside back to the hospital again. I've got a seminar this afternoon that I *really* should go to. And Christmas shopping to do."

"I'm glad to see you both too."

She hugged and kissed Helen, then did the same to Geri. She opened up the office and put the kettle on, chasing Toby the thieving tomcat away before Helen could get her hands on him.

"So, what did the doctors say?" asked Helen. "We'd just missed the visiting hours I think, and they wouldn't let us in. They said it was some sort of observation ward you were on? Strictly out of bounds to us mortals."

"Never mind all of that, come on, tell me," said Martha hurriedly. "What happened after I was escorted out of Coulthard's flat?"

"Would you listen to that?" said Helen, sucking her tongue "She's just had a heart scare and all she's worried about is some dead banker."

"I know," said Geri. "You think she'd get her priorities right, eh?"

"It's not like we've been worried sick or anything," Helen pressed. "It's not like we've been ringing the hospital, and your husband too I might add, asking what's wrong with you."

"I was so worried I didn't even get any studying done last night," said Geri.

Both Martha and Helen turned to their younger sister, incredulous. She was about to protest but just smiled, and busied herself with the kettle.

"Oh alright then," she said. "I went for a pint. Sue me. Anything was better than moping around the house feeling sorry for you. What good would that have done?"

Helen tutted loudly. Martha didn't care. She waved her hands.

"Come on, I'm fine. Thanks for your concern but I'm okay, really I am. So tell me," she said. "Tell me what happened when I was taken away."

Helen crossed her arms and let out a big sigh. Geri brought over the teas and sat down at her desk.

"What's wrong?" she asked. "You're not telling me something."

"We're not telling you *anything*," said Helen.

"Why not?"

"Because you're ill."

Martha wandered over to her desk. She found a letter opener and held it up at her sister.

"If you don't tell me Helen, I'm going to take this and cut off all your hair when you're asleep."

"I'd like to see you try," said Helen, grabbing her curls.

"Oh she's very trying," said Geri. "She's got that crazy, bored, middle-aged look in her eyes."

"Hey! Less of the middle-aged," said Martha. "Now come on, spill your guts. It's making me more stressed that you won't tell me."

Helen let out a flustered sigh. She looked at Geri who nodded in approval.

"The police arrived just after you left," she started. "An inspector came in. She was funny looking, coughing all over the place."

"Pope," said Martha.

"Yeah, Pope, that's it," Helen snapped her fingers. "How do you know?"

"Because the good detective paid me a visit in hospital, that's why. Inhaler and all."

"Now there's a woman who looks middle-aged," said Geri.

"Never mind what she looks like, I want to know what happened?"

"It was pretty straight forward I guess," said Helen. "I mean, I imagine it was pretty straight forward. I've never been questioned by the police before."

"What did they ask you?"

"Just the usual stuff, how we knew Gordon Coulthard, what we were doing there. Geri and I were taken into the bedroom and given the once over by a couple of, quite frankly far too attractive policemen. Cleared my hangover up like a shot."

"Once over?" asked Martha.

"Steady on Mart, it's not what you think," laughed Geri. "They frisked us to make sure we weren't carrying anything suspicious."

"That's what I said," Helen winked.

"So what about Estelle and Tracey?"

Helen hesitated, glancing over at Geri again. The youngest Parker sister shrugged.

"You might as well tell her," she said. "She's going to get it out of you anyway."

"Get *what* out of you?" Martha yelled. "Would you two just tell me what the hell happened?"

Helen took a big breath, scratched her mop of frizzy, untidy hair and blinked. When she was finished stalling for time she answered Martha.

"They arrested Tracey," she said. "Slapped on the cuffs and took her away in the back of one of the squad cars."

"Arrested?" Martha blurted. "On what charge?"

"Murder of course," said Helen.

Martha could feel the sensation in her legs vanishing. She couldn't be sure it wasn't a side effect of her recent illness or just sheer panic. In the end she sat down at her desk and stared numbly at the wall.

"Are you alright Martha?" asked Helen, reaching over to her.

"Of course she's not alright, look at her!" Geri snapped. "I told you we should have kept our mouths shut."

"What? You just told me to *tell* her what happened."

"Yes, I know, but I didn't mean it *literally*."

"Oh so you tell me to do something and not expect me to do it?" Helen yelled. "That doesn't even make sense."

"So if I told you to jump off a cliff you'd do it Helen? Would you? Would you do that?"

"Of course I wouldn't."

"Well this is the exact same thing."

"It *so* isn't Geri and you know it."

"Would you two shut up?"

Martha's voice sounded big and imposing in the close confines of the office. Immediately Helen and Geri were quiet. They stood like two scolded children, their hands behind their backs and their heads bowed.

Martha leaned on her desk, her brow furrowed. She had definitely suspected foul play. Even when she was getting questioned by Pope in the hospital. Suddenly the detective's pensiveness, her steadfast nature not to share anything with her made perfect sense.

This was a murder inquiry, lips had to be tight. Which made it even worse that Martha and her sisters were up to their necks in it all. Her eyes fell to the vault in the corner of the room. Like some hideous, supernatural pulse, she thought she could hear the money calling to her. Blood money, that's what the newspapers would call it. Blood money to bump off the husband.

She could see the headlines already. But more importantly she could hear the knock from the police coming from the front door. She could smell the polished mahogany of the courtroom. She could taste the rancid air of prison. She could even feel the shame of being convicted of murder—of a crime she hadn't even committed.

It was all too much. She shot up from her desk and hurried over to the safe.

"What are you doing Mart?" asked Geri.

Martha didn't answer her. She twisted the dial back and forth until the door opened. Inside was the brown envelope, the mound of cash sitting waiting for her. She grabbed it and waved it at the others.

"We can hand it back," she said. "We can just go around there and give May the housekeeper the money. It'll be like we were never involved."

"Wow!" Helen shouted. "Let's not be too hasty here! We earned that money Martha, we can't be expected to do our jobs for nothing you know."

"No, we can, we really can," said Martha. "We can when the client's husband winds up dead. That's work we don't want any part of. Come on, we can be around there and back in half an hour. Thirty minutes, that's all, and we're out of this."

"Mart, you sure you're feeling okay?" asked Geri, sidling up to her.

"What?"

"You just… I don't know. You don't seem to be acting like you've got all your marbles is all."

"What are you talking about, I'm fine," Martha continued, waving the money about. "I'm trying to protect us, I'm trying to get us out of this mess. Can't you see?"

"And what good is giving the money back going to do?" Helen sounded panicky. "I mean, they're not going to miss twenty-grand, especially if Tracey is behind bars. We sure would miss it though."

"Martha, maybe you should sit down," said Geri.

The two sisters were slowly backing Martha into the corner. She looked at them in turn, her head twitching like a scared animal. She was scared, terrified even, and she had nowhere to go.

"Just give me the cash Martha," Helen held out her hand. "Just give me the cash and nobody gets hurt."

"For god sake," Geri rolled her eyes. "It's twenty grand Helen, not a friggin' gun."

"I don't care, it's my next semester paid for Geri, so shut it."

"What's wrong with you two?" asked Martha. "Am I the only one who's bothered by any of this?"

"Well, yes, quite frankly," said Geri. "I don't think there is anything really to be worried about."

"Oh so being at a crime scene with a client of ours, who paid us this money, isn't something to worry about?"

"No, it isn't!" Geri fired back. "It's not like we killed the guy or anything."

"Tracey didn't either," Martha retorted.

"How do you know that?"

"Because…"

She trailed off. The question had phased her, knocked her off her guard. *How did she know that?* It was like she had been trying to ask herself the same thing since it happened, but hadn't been able to come up with the reason. Hearing it from Geri suddenly made things a whole lot clearer.

"She didn't kill him," she said again. "I just know it."

Seizing her chance, Helen snatched the envelope from Martha. She quickly returned to her desk and sat on the money, folding her arms.

"You're not getting at it again," she said. "Absolutely not. At this rate you'll be selling *us* rather than take payment for cases."

"What do you mean she didn't kill him?" asked Geri, ignoring her sister. "It's pretty clear that she did."

"I don't know," said Martha, wandering across the room slowly, like she was in a trace. "I can't tell you why I know, but I do. Tracey Coulthard didn't kill her husband."

She slumped into her chair. The casters creaked under her weight. She rolled back and forward, listening to the squeaks. Somehow she found the sound comforting, like it soothed her mind. She could concentrate doing this, it was a nice distraction.

"She didn't kill him," she said again. "She didn't kill him because she couldn't have killed him."

"But," said Geri. "She was up there before us. He was dead when we arrived. She didn't look all that sorry her husband was lying face down in the bath. She didn't even flinch when the cops took her away."

"And don't forget the motive," said Helen. "She had plenty of reason for drowning that slippery bugger. I mean, how angry would you be if you'd just found out your husband was engaged to another woman. And not just *any* woman, that Estelle or whatever her name is. Pretty brutal if you ask me."

"Estelle," murmured Martha. "Estelle."

The name rang around the inside of her head like a church bell. The mistress, the violent woman with a murky past. Surely her role in all this wasn't as clear-cut as Helen, Geri and the police were thinking. It couldn't be—Martha knew it. And her answers, at least in the short term, lay with Estelle.

"Okay," she said, clapping her thighs. "Okay I think I've got an idea."

She got up and looked about for the car keys. She spied them on Helen's desk and snatched them up.

"Where are you going?" asked Helen.

"We've got work to do," Martha shouted back, already in the porch. "Come on, hurry up. You can't just sit about all day, you've got to earn your wages in this company."

"But Martha," Helen shouted. "What the hell are *we* supposed to do? Here, we're not taking this money back are we? Because, you know, I think it would quite like to stay."

"You mean *you'd* like it to stay," said Geri, sardonically.

"Don't give me that, student girl," said Helen. "We're not all able to squeeze into tight fitting tops to get our drinks paid for us. So button it."

"Meow," Geri made cat claws out of her hands.

"And don't make cat noises at me either. I'm going to boot that Toby one's backside as soon as I see him for eating my biscuits!"

MARTHA HONKED THE horn of the Mini. Helen and Geri dashed outside, locking the office behind them. They climbed into the car as Martha threw it out of the driveway.

"Do you want to tell us just what the hell we're doing?" asked Geri.

"Yeah a little clue might be nice," said Helen.

"It's simple," said Martha, smiling at her two sisters. "We're going to solve the murder."

Helen and Geri exchanged looks. Then they both rolled their eyes in unison.

"Great," said Geri. "And there was me thinking we had nothing else better to do."

Fifteen

"ARE YOU SURE this is it?" asked Martha.

"Of course I'm not sure," said Geri, leaning between the two front seats. "Do you have any idea how many Estelles work in hair salons in this city? And how they *all* look the same?"

"Let me guess," said Helen. "Blonde, blue eyes, fake tan and lots of lip gloss."

"Bingo," smiled Geri. "But the question remains. How many do you think? In fact, don't answer that, I'll tell you."

She ran her finger up and down the screen of her phone. Counting out loud, she showed the screen to her sisters.

"Fifteen," she said. "Fifteen people called Estelle work at hairdressers or salons in this one city alone. Can you believe that?"

"Is that bad?" asked Helen.

"So why have you brought us to this one in particular then?" asked Martha. "If there are fifteen of them across Glasgow, why this one, here?"

She pointed out of the windscreen. A row of rather sad looking shops sat directly across from them. Most of the units were either empty or abandoned, their metal shutters painted in bright colours with graffiti tags from local gangs. All around the place was flat and empty.

Martha could remember there being high-rise flats here once. She used to see them on the bus to school. Now they were gone, reduced to rubble and nothing but a landscape that looked like something out of a post-apocalyptic movie remained. Emptiness and this forlorn row of shops.

At the end was a salon. The doors were open, an old neon sign buzzing above the huge window that said 'Paradise Hair and Beauty'. There were posters outside, advertising cut-price discounts on washing, blow-drying and styling. It looked like anything could be performed in the dismal little place. From facial treatment to manicures and pedicures, it was a one-stop shop for everything beauty. A pity that didn't extend to the outside of the actual building itself.

"This can't be right," said Martha. "I thought Estelle's salon was new. This place looks like it predates the war."

"Would you at least pretend to have some faith in me?" asked Geri. "Otherwise I'm getting out right now, walking back to my flat and pretending I don't have sisters who drive me mad."

"I wouldn't get out around here," said Helen, holding the money tight to her chest. "You might catch something. Or something will catch you."

"Geri, the salon," said Martha, growing impatient. "Why here, why this one?"

Geri repositioned herself. She held out her phone so her sisters could see. On the screen was a page advertising the shop across the street.

"Blimey," said Helen. "It doesn't look any better on the internet. I hope their marketing manager gets the sack."

"Exactly," said Geri.

"Exactly what?" asked Martha.

"Exactly, where's the marketing manager? Where's the style, the elegance, the decoration, even the bloody half-decent sign. Where are all these things ladies? Where? Nowhere, that's where. They don't exist here."

She looked at her sisters expectantly. Martha didn't mind admitting she didn't have a clue what Geri was talking about.

"Nope, you've lost me kiddo," she said.

"Me too," agreed Helen.

"Really? You don't see it?" asked Geri surprised. "Look at this."

She flicked through pages on her phone. Each time another salon appeared, each one shiny looking, glossy and professional. They all put the one across the street to shame.

"There are fifteen salons in the city with an Estelle either working at them, owning them or regularly checking in at them, right. Well they all look like they've had everything put into them, professional through and through. Except this one. Keeping up?"

"So far," said Martha.

"Just about," said Helen.

"So remind me again what Estelle, *our* Estelle's recently departed fiancée did for a living?"

"He was a banker."

"Yes, not just any old banker, a *very successful* banker. On his way to the top by all accounts. So what do successful, hotshot bankers have lots of?"

"Money," said Martha.

"Precisely," agreed Geri. "Money and plenty of it. Come on guys, throw me a bone here. The Christmas tree outside their house is bigger than all of our gaffs stacked on top of each other. He's driving flash cars, has a separate penthouse *and* got a real nice mansion in the suburbs. So what's his air-head fiancée doing working in a place like this?"

The sisters were silent. They all stared across the street at the dilapidated, run-down looking row of shops. Geri was right, something didn't add up. Martha's confidence was growing.

They'd barely scratched the surface and already nothing appeared as it seemed with these people.

"Now do you get me?" asked Geri.

"What's Estelle doing working here?"

"Smells like a front to me," said Geri. "It's too grimy. It's almost like we're supposed to ignore that it's here. Makes a pretty good outlet for laundering money."

Martha tapped the steering wheel. She hadn't thought of that. Now that she was outside the salon, it made perfect sense. There was nothing around here, the whole area felt like it had been abandoned. Across the river she could see the bright, sparkling glass towers of the inner city. Here it was old and worn down.

"What is it people say?" asked Helen. "Hiding in plain sight."

"Good point," said Geri. "So what's the move Mart?"

"I think we need to talk to Estelle," she said. "We need to know where she met Gordon, how they know each other."

"But if she's playing the grieving fiancée," said Helen. "She won't want to talk to us. Hell she might not even be here. Would *you* be?"

"We'll just have to see," said Martha, getting out of the car.

The three sisters strode across the street towards the salon. As they approached, the sound of raised voices came floating out of the door. Shouting and swearing—an argument in full flow. Then something shattered.

"Wow," said Geri. "Somebody's not happy."

"Maybe we should come back another time," said Helen, cowering behind the others. "I mean, if they're chucking stuff in there, I don't think I want to be a target. I had enough of that with Tracey Coulthard thank you very much."

"Come on," said Martha, undeterred. "Keep your wits about you in here. Don't touch anything or look at anybody the wrong way. Just… keep it together alright?"

She led them into the salon. The main room was empty. There were no other customers, just empty chairs and sinks looking back at the sisters. The shouting was coming from the back room. Martha strained to listen over the radio, and thought she recognised one of the voices.

She was about to say something when a woman appeared at the door. It was Estelle.

"You three?" she spluttered.

"Who?" asked another woman, older than Estelle with a haggard face suggesting she had had more than a hard paper round, a cigarette hanging from her blood red lips. "Who the hell are these three?"

Estelle ran before she could answer. She shoved the old woman out of the way and disappeared into the back room. Without a second thought Martha gave chase.

"Stay here," she barked back at the others. "Don't let her leave."

She pushed past the older woman. Estelle was quick, much quicker in flat shoes than she was in her stilettos. Like a bleached blonde blur she weaved through the back of the shop. She pulled chairs behind her trying to block the way.

Martha wasn't giving up. She leapt over the debris as Estelle shouldered a door and bolted outside.

"Bloody nora," wheezed Martha.

She followed. Estelle had a good ten yards on her, maybe more. But she wasn't giving up. At least outside there was nothing to bash her shins.

Estelle took off across the derelict land. She was running full pelt, occasionally looking back over her shoulder to see where

Martha was. The distance was getting bigger. Martha had to think. She was never going to catch her up in a flat race. The hairdresser was much too agile, younger and fitter than her.

They reached the other side of the empty ground. A chain-link fence surrounded it, a flimsy protection. Estelle began to climb, her manicured nails causing no impediment. Martha hammered her legs, seizing her opportunity to gain some ground.

Closer and closer she got, watching the young woman try frantically to climb the fence. She wasn't making enough progress, but Martha was. Bearing down on her prey, she was just about there when... something tripped her up.

She could feel herself falling. It was almost like she was out of her own body now, watching as she began tumbling forward towards the gravel in slow motion. She could feel the burns on her hands and knees already where the skin would be grazed. She only hoped she'd keep some of her teeth.

By some strange stroke of luck, she was close enough to the chain-link fence. It partially stopped her, but only partially. Her forty-years of life-experience, knowledge, wisdom and above all else, weight, thundered into the flimsy barrier.

There was a moment's pause while the fence thought about what had happened. Then, deciding it wasn't strong enough, it gave way.

Martha was bundled onto the pavement with a thud. She was just happy it wasn't as bad as it could have been. A trip at that speed was bound to be nasty.

More importantly Estelle had been felled. She landed awkwardly on the ground, twisting her ankle as she went. She let out an agonising scream and began rolling around.

"My ankle," she shouted. "I've broken my ankle. *You've* broken my ankle, you stupid cow."

"Me?" puffed Martha, getting up. "I didn't touch you."

"You did. You broke the fence, you kicked it down. I'm going to sue you."

"Now hold on a minute here, you're the one who ran—"

The hard, tinny honk of a police siren cut her off. A white squad car pulled up in front of the two women. Detective Sergeant Pope appeared, sucking on her inhaler.

"Well, well, well," she said. "Fancy running into you two here. Together. Isn't that a turn up for the books?"

"Arrest her," shouted Estelle. "Get the cuffs out. She's just assaulted me."

"I did not," Martha replied. "You shouldn't have run away."

"I was running away from *you*."

"That doesn't matter, you shouldn't have been doing it."

"You shouldn't be poking about in my business."

"I wasn't doing anything like that."

"Enough!"

Pope's voice echoed across the space. It was deceptively loud and imposing. Martha didn't think a woman so small and obviously ill was capable of such noise.

"What is it about you two?" asked the policewoman. "First, I hear about you fighting at a party, then you're both at a crime scene. Now I find you're rolling about the ground causing some property damage, *council* property damage I should point out."

She kicked the fence. Estelle was still on the ground, although her screaming and moaning had stopped. Martha stared at her feet, noticing a tear in her jeans.

"Now before I call in an ambulance for Lady Estelle here, is there anything you two want to tell me?" asked Pope.

Martha said nothing. Estelle did likewise.

"Fine," said the policewoman. "Looks like we'll have to have a cosy little chat down at my place then."

She stood to one side. A uniformed officer opened the back door of the squad car.

"Shall we?" she asked.

"Great," said Martha, tasting sweat on her top lip. "This is all I need."

"Join the club, Parker," said Pope. "But I'll warn you, there's a waiting list."

Sixteen

MARTHA HAD NEVER been in a police station before. But she'd seen plenty of them on television and in the movies. That was little consolation now though. The reality, as always, was much grimmer.

She sat in a draughty interview room. A cup of stale tasting tea sat on the table in front of her, perched beside a recording device. There was a mirror on one side of the room that she assumed was two-way. Occasionally, she looked over and wondered who was staring at her from behind it.

Then she'd get scared. She'd look away, stare at the other three walls, her feet, the table, the ceiling, anything. She didn't like this, she didn't like it at all.

The silence of the place was about the only comforting part. In here she reckoned the world could end and start again a few dozen times and she wouldn't notice. It might just be an ordinary interview room, but it may as well have been solitary confinement.

On more than one occasion she wondered if the police had forgotten all about her. She wondered if the door would ever open, if she'd be let go, back into the free world. After all she hadn't done anything wrong. She'd only wanted to speak to Estelle. That wasn't a crime—was it?

The door opened. A young woman in uniform appeared. She paused for a moment at the door, staring at Martha. Then she nodded at the cup of tea.

"Do you want a refill?" she asked.

"No, thank you," said Martha glumly. "I'd much rather know why I'm here to be honest with you."

"Yeah, I'm sure you would," said the young officer. "I just thought you might want some caffeine to tide you over."

"Any chance of speaking to Detective Pope?"

"I'm not really at liberty to say."

"Great," droned Martha. "So I'm just to sit here and look at the four walls is that it? I mean, I haven't done anything wrong."

The young woman bit her bottom lip. She poked her head out of the door and looked around. Then, sneaking back into the room, she whispered to Martha.

"Look, you didn't hear it from me right but Pope is on the war path," she said.

"The war path? How do you mean?" asked Martha.

"Sssshhhh," said the young policewoman. "Keep your voice down."

"Sorry," said Martha. "But what are you talking about 'war path'? I don't understand. Surely she's not allowed to keep me here for no reason?"

"No she's not," said the officer.

"Can I go home then?"

"No you can't."

"Well that doesn't make any sense."

"I know, but it's the truth," the officer collected the half-drunk tea. "Pope is working her team overtime to crack this case. She's got the bit between her teeth. And there's a lot of pressure from upstairs given who's involved. She has her reasons for keeping you here."

"I still don't follow."

"Don't you read Twitter? Or even a newspaper?" the officer said. "Gordon Coulthard, the journos got a sniff of it this morning, it's all they're reporting on. Now what was a routine murder inquiry is front page news, and Pope is at the centre of it. She's pulling in every lead she has."

"So that's why I'm sat here like a plum pudding, counting away the minutes of my life."

"I guess so," shrugged the young officer.

"Alright MacDonald, that'll do."

Pope appeared at the door, flipping pages of a file. She glided into the interview room and sat down across from Martha. MacDonald, the young policewoman, scurried out of the room. But before she went she winked at Martha.

She closed the door behind her leaving the two women alone. Martha sat politely quiet, watching the detective across from her. She was young, much younger than her clothes and haircut suggested. Martha wondered just how much her obvious asthma affected a woman like that.

She was committed to her job, no wedding or engagement rings on her finger. She didn't wear makeup and there was always the smell of coffee off her breath. This was a professional, thought Martha. She gulped.

"Okay," said Pope, finishing her reading. "Do you want to start or will I Martha?"

"I don't understand, start what?"

"You want to tell me why you and your dopey sisters were sniffing around Estelle Kennedy."

"They're not dopey," said Martha. "Don't talk about my family that way."

"That's not what I hear," Pope leaned back on her chair. "From my officers who rounded them up at the salon."

Martha could feel a lump forming in her throat. While she hadn't been happy with her treatment, she had accepted it. Now that she knew Helen and Geri were involved, she felt herself unravelling a little.

"What have you done to them?"

Pope's face tightened. She leaned forward, her hawk-like features narrowing on her across the table. She clasped her hands together and pointed her index fingers.

"Oh, is that a temper I detect there Martha?" she asked. "That was quick wasn't it? Do you often lose your temper? Do you have a short fuse? Do you have anger management issues? You know, have you ever thrown something at a wall, kicked something really hard? Have you?"

"Why are you asking me all of this?" Martha shouted. "I haven't done anything wrong. You haven't even arrested me for God's sake!"

"No I haven't," said Pope. "Is there any reason why I *should*?"

"Of course there isn't. Why are you being so bloody nasty to me?"

"I don't think I *am* being nasty Martha. That's just your opinion."

"Give me a break," Martha rolled her eyes.

"So, you want to tell me about Estelle?" Pope took up her file. "Because I've got witness accounts here from a party you two were at on Saturday night saying that Miss Kennedy was overheard shouting and bawling about a woman who matches your description. You want to tell me about that?"

"What? No. Yes. We had a bit of a run-in."

"What kind of a run-in?" Pope pounced.

"She started pulling my hair, she thought I was after Gordon."

"And were you?"

"Of course I wasn't. I didn't want to be at the party in the first place, it was just… work."

Martha could feel herself getting short of breath. Pope's interrogation seemed more aggressive than necessary. She wasn't sure she even needed to be here. After all she hadn't been charged with anything.

She had to remain calm and focussed. She forced herself to concentrate, to think and not to be sucked into the disorientation Pope was trying to create.

"Am I under arrest?" she asked again, going on the offensive.

"No," said the detective.

"Then why am I being held against my will?"

"You're not."

"Well it feels like I am. Can I go home now please?"

"Just another question or two then I'll let you go."

"But you said I'm not being detained," said Martha. "You said I'm not under arrest."

"You're not."

"Then I'm not answering anything until I have a lawyer here. Does that sound fair enough?"

Pope clamped her mouth shut. She sat back again, her incisive eyes taking a measure of Martha. Martha kept breathing. She had broken her opponent's stranglehold on the conversation. But it had been hard. She felt like she could sleep for a week and not get up.

"Look, I'll level with you Parker," said the detective. "I'm trying to solve a murder case here. I don't know how much you know about *real* police work but it's not as easy as you think. We've got Coulthard's wife banged up in the cells and it looks like a clear-cut case of revenge killing. But it's not as simple as that, okay? I'm just trying to get a hold of all the facts."

"I understand that," said Martha. "But you can't go about bullying innocent members of the public. What if I decide to make a complaint?"

"You can make all the complaints you want, madam, that's your prerogative," said Pope. "But you have to at least see it from my point of view that, when I go to speak with one of the people who discovered Gordon Coulthard's body and find her brawling with another person who was there, alarm bells go off in my head. I'm a police officer Martha, it's my job to hear those alarm bells."

She opened up her hands and shrugged a little. Martha kept watching her, wondering what she'd say or do next.

"So help me to help you," said the detective. "Help me clear everything up by telling me what you were doing with Estelle Kennedy."

"Nothing," said Martha. "Honestly, nothing."

"Nothing? You broke a fence and almost her ankle."

"She almost broke her *own* ankle, that wasn't my fault. I tripped and fell into the fence."

"Why were you there in the first place?"

Martha let out a sigh. She placed her trembling hands on the table and tried to keep breathing.

"I know this is going to sound crazy but… I don't think Tracey Coulthard murdered her husband."

If Pope was trying to hide her surprise, she was doing a really bad job of it. Her eyebrows had shot half way up her forehead and her eyes looked big in the gloom of the interview room. She nodded.

"And you're sure of this, are you Mrs Parker?"

"*Ms* Parker," said Martha. "Parker is my maiden name."

"You don't think Tracey killed her husband?" asked Pope. "And why, might I ask, do you think that? Is there something you know that I don't? Should I be getting my cuffs ready to pull you in as the real culprit?"

"What? No, of course not, I didn't kill him," said Martha. "And neither did my sisters by the way, I'd like to make that very clear. I just... I just have this feeling that's all, a hunch."

"A hunch?"

"Yes, a hunch, it's like a bowling ball sitting in the pit of my stomach. Do you know what I mean?"

"So you don't think Tracey Coulthard is guilty, a woman with known anger issues, with all the motive in the world and who's yet to protest her innocence is not the one who killed Gordon Coulthard? And you're telling me that it's some psychic bowling ball in your belly that's telling you this?"

"Yes," said Martha. "Well the bowling ball isn't *actually* there obviously. It's just a feeling I've got."

Pope let out a half-laugh, half-wheeze. She looked around the room as if trying to summon some support. When none was forthcoming she pointed at Martha.

"Are you being serious right now?" she asked. "You're telling me you've risked yourself becoming a suspect in this case, just because you think Tracey Coulthard is innocent?"

"Yes," said Martha. "Although I wasn't planning on becoming a suspect, if that's what you're saying I am. We... I just wanted to do a little investigating of my own."

"And that's why you were at Estelle's place?"

Martha nodded. Pope laughed again. She leaned forward on the desk, eyes burrowing into Martha.

"You're not lying are you?" she said. "You actually believe that Tracey Coulthard is innocent."

"Why would I lie?" asked Martha. "In fact, shouldn't you be taking a leaf out of my book?"

"What?" gasped the policewoman. "What do you mean?"

"I mean shouldn't you be taking a much more open-minded approach to this case. You said it yourself you're trying to establish the facts, but it sounds to me like you've got Tracey banged to rights and you're damning any other possibility. As my old mum always says, you'll meet yourself coming and going that way."

Pope shot up from the table, her chair squealing as it flew backwards. She was about to launch into a tirade when she burst into a fit of coughing. Her pale face began to darken, her cheeks and forehead turning a deep shade of scarlet. Martha wasn't sure if she should do something. She'd seen asthma attacks before with Margot.

Her fears were eased when the detective pulled out her trusty inhaler. She sucked on it twice before the coughing subsided. Catching her breath, Pope opened the door of the interrogation room.

"Out," she demanded. "Before I throw the book at you."

"You mean I can leave?"

"I wouldn't recommend going anywhere except straight to a good psychiatrist but yes, you can leave this station at least."

Martha quickly gathered herself up. She felt her knees crack as she hobbled over to the door. She was about to leave when Pope grabbed her arm.

"Just watch yourself, Parker," said the detective, pulling her in close. "I don't want you skipping town anytime soon. And do yourself a favour and leave the detective work to the professionals."

"I'll be careful Detective Pope," said Martha, pulling her arm free. "But you should pay heed to what I've been saying. This case, it's not as cut and dried as you're making it out to be. Tracey Coulthard is innocent, I know it. That means there's a murderer on the loose out there somewhere and you don't know who it is. Not the best thing to be happening when the media are all over the case now, is it?"

Pope didn't react. Martha could see the detective's temples twitching, the tendons in her cheek flexing. Eventually, she nodded down the corridor.

"On your way," she seethed, before turning back into the room.

Martha didn't need a second invitation. She hurried down the corridor and out into the reception area of the station. There Helen and Geri were waiting for her. They were, as usual, arguing.

"All I'm saying is these blokes and women that model for these information posters, they're going about saying they're models," Helen was lecturing. "But I bet if you met one of those guys in a pub somewhere and tried to talk to him he'd be really pretentious."

"To you maybe," Geri smarmed.

"But he's not like a *model* model, if you know what I mean. He's a model for a police poster about neighbourhood watch programs. It's hardly Paris Fashion Week is it?"

She stopped when she saw Martha standing at the desk. They both shot up and raced over to their sister.

"Bloody hell are you alright?" asked Geri. "You were in there for ages."

"I'm fine," said Martha. "I just want to go home. Are you two okay?"

"Yeah, can't complain," said Helen.

"They didn't hurt you did they?" asked Martha. "They didn't mistreat you, because if they did I'm happy to lodge a complaint."

"No, don't be daft," said Helen. "We were brought to the station and told to sit here and wait for you. Which we did."

"Dutifully," said Geri. "Although you owe me extra wages Martha. If I have to listen to another one of Helen's lectures about models for public information posters being pretentious, I reckon my head will explode."

Martha hugged her sisters. She fought back tears as they left the station. It had been another long day. They were becoming a recurring theme. But at least she had her two favourite people in the world to be with. That was making it all just a little bit easier to handle.

Seventeen

CHRISTMAS PRESENT WRAPPING was supposed to be therapeutic. The repetitiveness, the jolly colours, even seeing her handiwork piled up beneath a Christmas tree should have all helped to lift Martha's mood. Nothing, she feared, would be able to help her today.

She sat in the middle of her living room floor surrounded by the mess and debris of her wrapping. There was sticky tape in her hair, her fingers were sore from tying ribbons and if she ate another mince pie she'd burst. At least now it was over. Everything was wrapped, and ahead of schedule, too. Amazing, she thought, what looking for a distraction can do to my productivity.

At least there had been no *Fairytale of New York* playing in the background. That would have really pushed her over the edge.

She had hoped the wrapping would take her mind off of everything. But it was no use. She was still too distracted by the Coulthard case. And why wouldn't she be? Every time she closed her eyes she could *still* see Gordon's body.

That's why she'd been staring at Christmas wrapping paper for almost five hours straight. That's why she was hoping that when she went to bed she'd be dreaming about Santa Claus, reindeer and snowmen rather than that terrible scene she'd walked in on.

She wasn't convinced though. She looked at the clock on the mantelpiece. It was almost two in the morning. Even the TV had abandoned her, various adverts now showing everything from fitness equipment to slow cookers were now dancing across the screen.

Geoff had gone to bed hours ago. He'd be fast asleep now, snoring his head off so loud that even if she wanted to nod off she wouldn't be able to. Martha was in a quandary, stuck between a rock and a hard place. And it felt like there was nowhere to go.

She got up. Her legs were sore, from her thighs right the way down to the tips of her toes. She twisted her hips trying to relieve some of her discomfort. She blamed all of the running. Taking off after Estelle, a woman half her age, had been foolish at best. Now she was paying the price for doing little to no exercise in over twenty years.

She limped into the kitchen and switched on the lights. Tea would help, a cup of tea *always* helped. Martha had learned that from her mum. There was no problem on earth that couldn't be sorted with a nice cup of tea and a big talk. The thought made her smile. How many times had she sat with her mother in their old kitchen and talked about problems? Everything from school exams to boys and Morag's illness. Everything in between too. The two of them, just sitting, talking, laughing and loving together.

Martha would have given anything to have another one of those talks now. She spied her phone sitting on the kitchen table and thought about calling her mum. But she couldn't. It was too late at night for one thing, her mother would be sound asleep.

How could she even begin to explain to her mum what was going on? She was in enough trouble as it was poking her nose in where it wasn't needed. That's why she'd been hauled into a police station and given the third degree by Pope.

Her thoughts flooded back to the interview. Hard as she tried, she couldn't get that moment where the detective had mocked Helen and Geri out of her head. Something had twinged in Martha right then. She'd realised how much of a danger she'd put her sisters in. It was *her* fault they had been in that penthouse. It was *her* fault they were on this case. She had to do better for them. She was their older sister, she was meant to be the responsible one.

Martha suddenly felt a little emotional. Her nose had started to run and her vision fogged. She shook it off, loading up the dishwasher.

"Silly bugger," she said, laughing. "Standing here crying like a big kid. Pull yourself together woman."

She busied herself with the kettle. If she couldn't speak with her mum she was at least going to have a cup of tea. Then she'd go to bed. Everything might work itself out by morning. There was always a chance.

Martha reached up to get the teabags from a cupboard but stopped short. Her breath was taken from her in an instant as she saw a figure move past the kitchen window. She was about to scream for Geoff when the porch light went on.

"Geri!" she shouted, dropping the teabags.

She rushed to the front door. A cold wind blew in from the night as Geri came staggering towards her. The young woman collapsed into Martha's waiting arms.

"Geri! My god! Are you alright?"

"Hey Martha," she said. "Good to see you."

"What the hell happened to you?"

"Nothing... nothing at all."

Her face quickly twisted into a pained frown and she started to cry. Martha hugged her close into her chest and patted her hair.

"What's the matter Geri? What's wrong? Has somebody done something to you? Have you been attacked?"

"No," Geri sniffed. "No, nothing like that. I've just... I've... can I come in?"

"Of course."

Martha pulled her into the house. She closed the door and they made their way into the kitchen. Martha fetched Geri a spare dressing gown and wrapped her up in it tightly, rubbing heat back into her sister's bare arms.

She poured two mugs of tea and sat one down beside Geri. The young woman was shivering. She held the mug up close to her face, breathing in the warmth.

Martha noticed her makeup was smeared across her face. Her hair was messy and her shoes were spattered with mud, grass and dirt. *What had happened?*. She just hoped Geri was comfortable enough to tell her.

"So what brings you here at this time of night?" she said with a wry smile. "Let me guess, you've solved the case—Tracey Coulthard *is* guilty after all and I'm getting carted off to the psychiatric ward."

Geri laughed. She leaned on the table, her thin arms red with the cold. Martha had to bite her tongue to not chastise her sister for going out without a coat. She thought she'd give her the benefit of the doubt in the circumstances.

"No," said Geri. "I haven't solved the case. I've had other things on my mind Martha. I've got a life outside work you know."

"You call what we do work?" Martha smiled. "It's not according to Detective Sergeant Aileen Pope."

"Is she the one who looks like the pole up her backside has a pole stuck up its backside?"

"Not sure I appreciate the imagery there Geri but I know what you're getting at. Yes."

"Yeah I thought as much. She's the one who was sniffing around the salon after you were taken away."

"She's leading the investigation. Not that you can call it that. She pretty much told me today in no uncertain terms that they've got the killer in Tracey Coulthard and that's that."

"Why'd they haul you in then?" asked Geri, taking a sip.

"She wants to be thorough—her word not mine."

"I see."

Martha let Geri warm up and settle. She'd learned from her own mum and her own daughter how to handle others being upset. As much as she was curious to find out why her youngest sister had appeared at her door, half-dressed and frozen in the early hours, she knew she had to play it cool. Go charging in and Geri would clam up. She was better than that—she wanted to help not fight.

Tears began to roll down Geri's face. She sniffed, trying to hide her upset. But after a while she gave up and let the floodgates go. Martha reached over and hugged her tightly.

"Oh darling," she said, softly. "What the hell's the matter? What could possibly have happened to make you like this? You're supposed to be the *strong* one, remember?"

Geri grabbed her sister. She squeezed and squeezed, her grip like a vice. She kept sobbing, crying into Martha's shoulder so much that her top was sodden with tears and snot. She let Geri cry until there was nothing left.

"I'm sorry," said Geri, eventually. "This is awful."

"What are you sorry for?" asked Martha. "You don't have to apologise to me, I'm your sister. This is allowed you know."

"I know, I'm just… I'm just so bloody upset."

"I can see that. You want to tell me what this is all about?"

Geri rubbed her face and let out a frustrated groan. The sadness in her face was gone, replaced by anger. She looked to the ceiling and clenched her fists tightly. Martha thought her sister was going to erupt like a volcano.

"Bloody men," Geri said.

"Men?" asked Martha. "What about men?"

"I hate them Martha, I hate every single last one of them. Every bloody one. That's it, I'm becoming a feminist, screw it. Long hair, boobs down to my ankles, the works. In fact, I might just start borrowing Helen's clothes and be done with it."

"I don't think Helen is *that* kind of feminist Geri. I'm not sure that was ever really what feminists looked like outside of cartoons."

"I don't care, I'm doing it. I'll start up my own branch of feminism, I'll call it the 'I hate men because they're all scumbags' movement. We'll get a website, a Twitter, we'll hold demonstrations, blockade public men's rooms, go to the football and burn our bras and throw them on the pitch. It'll be great Martha, we'll show them, we'll show them all."

If Geri was indeed a volcano then this tirade was surely her lava. Martha thought it was best to let her vent. She obviously wanted to, the scarlet in her face beginning to subside. When Geri had finished she slumped into her stool by Martha's breakfast bar and sighed.

"You feel better now?" she asked.

"No, not really," quipped Geri. "But at least I've got it out of my system. Thank you."

"Always a pleasure Geri, you know that."

The sister exchanged smiles. A long, comfortable moment passed between them.

"So you want to tell me what's brought this on?" asked Martha. "Because you don't have to if you don't feel like it. I'm happy to go to bed and let it lie."

"No," said Geri, wiping her nose. "No it's alright. You deserve to know. I owe you that at least."

"You don't *owe* me anything Geri."

"No I do Martha, really I do," she reached out and took her hand. "I want to tell you. Besides, you've got patience enough to take me in at silly o'clock in the morning."

"You're family Geri, you're my sister, in case you've forgotten. I don't turn family away, ever."

Geri nodded. She smiled but started to cry again. Martha fetched her a box of tissues and she cleaned herself up.

"So, come on then, what's this all about?"

Geri took a gulp of tea. She rubbed her forehead and rolled her shoulders. She was calming down, Martha could see that. She was glad. Her sister was dear to her and sometimes she forgot just how young she was. At only twenty-one she wasn't as independent or capable as Martha, even though she liked to pretend she was. Sometimes she couldn't hide the fact she was still a young woman, a girl even.

"I've been seeing someone," Geri started. "For the past few months. We've been getting close, real close. I thought he really liked me."

"Do you really like him?"

"I thought so," Geri nodded. "But it's not the case."

"How so?"

"I got home tonight and he was coming round. Except he was already in the flat, his car was outside. I didn't think anything of it, I just thought he'd changed his plans and come round."

"What's his name?"

"It doesn't matter," Geri said, bitterly. "All I know is I get into the flat, expecting to see him, and he's there laughing and joking with my flatmate."

"Oh," said Martha. "What's wrong with that?"

Geri darted her an 'it's obvious' look. She let her mouth hang open, mimicking a corpse.

"Come on Martha, I know you've not been on a date in centuries but even you should know what I'm getting at."

"Depends on what you mean by laughing and joking," said Martha. "I don't know your flatmates, I've never even been *in* your flat Geri. Maybe this thing happens all the time."

"With no clothes on?"

"Ah," said Martha. "I see. So laughing and joking means something completely different to what it meant when I was your age."

"I could have gone into the gory details for you but I thought maybe you would spare me the excess embarrassment."

"Thanks."

"So yeah, that's been my evening."

"And you left?"

"Not after I had probably the biggest hissy fit in the history of the world. Proper spoiled brat stuff Martha, smashed plates, slammed doors and everything. You would have been proud."

"I don't think so somehow," smiled Martha.

"Anyway, the pair of them tried to palm me off with excuses, the usual crap you know. It wasn't my fault, they'd fallen in love, all the rest of it. I felt like I was in a Disney movie, that I was supposed to look over the whole thing and we'd carry on like I'd never clocked it."

"Sometimes these things are for the best though Geri. I mean, look at what we do for work, we're catching these people out all the time. Wouldn't you rather know than be left in the dark?"

"Yeah I get that, that's why I'm so upset Martha," said Geri. "You'd think somebody who's seen as many cheating wives and husbands as I have would have noticed something iffy by now."

She let out another frustrated groan. Shaking her head she looked off into the distance.

Martha felt for her. The smart, witty and intelligent young woman she was growing up to be was still, after all, a child. She had so much to learn and so much still to experience. Geri Parker liked to walk and talk with the best of them, to pretend she was the great street-wise girl of the twenty-first century, but at heart she was just like her sisters. Emotional, trusting and honest—even if that meant she got hurt.

Martha rubbed her shoulders. She held her sister tightly and made sure she heard what she was about to say.

"This isn't your fault Geri. Don't think it is," she said. "You're just starting out on the great road of life and, unfortunately, this isn't the last time your heart's going to be broken."

"I'm not broken-hearted," said Geri. "I just feel like a total and complete idiot that's all. There was me thinking that I might, just might, have something special with this guy. And then he goes and does this. I mean, if I can't tell that then what can I tell eh? Maybe I'm not cut out for this line of work."

"Hey, don't say that," Martha said sternly. "I won't have you or Helen bad mouthing yourselves. Life's hard, nobody's denying that. And there are plenty of people out there who are quick to jump on the bandwagon against you. Let them be the critics, you can ignore them. You don't need *yourself* piling more onto the load. You stand tall and walk proud and be who *you* want to be, not what anybody else wants you to. Do you hear me?"

"Yeah I hear you," said Geri. "Thanks Martha."

"Don't be daft, you don't ever need to thank me and you don't ever have to apologise to me either."

"Can I get that in writing?" she smiled.

"Maybe later."

Martha raised her mug. She gestured to her sister to do the same. She held the tea up high and they clinked their cups together.

"What are we drinking to?" asked Geri.

"Us," said Martha proudly. "You and me and maybe your sister too. The three of us, family, being together and sticking by each other no matter what. If we do that then there's nothing we can't do."

"Even solve this Gordon Coulthard murder case?" asked Geri.

"Well, we'll see," said Martha. "I haven't quite gotten around to thinking that one through yet. But who knows, maybe. I don't see why not."

"Well we'll need to start thinking a bit harder then, won't we?" said Geri. "I mean, Tracey will be in court soon enough to answer charges, submit a plea and all the rest of it. It won't take them long to slap something on her. Once that's done it makes the whole thing nigh on impossible to fix. And that's even *if* there's anything to fix in the first place."

"I know," said Martha. "I know. We just need a breakthrough, something that would buy us a little bit of time."

"Maybe there's nothing to find Martha," Geri sounded sceptical. "I mean, maybe Pope and the police are right. Maybe in the time it took us to get up the stairs she bonked him over the head, dumped him in the bath and left him to drown."

"Maybe…"

Martha sat up. She looked at Geri sitting on the stool beside her. The younger woman felt very self-conscious suddenly, wrapping her dressing gown about her.

"What?" she asked. "Why are you looking at me like I've got two heads. Do I have a zit or something?"

"What you just said there," said Martha. "What did you say?"

"About Tracey drowning Gordon?"

"No, before that."

"That she might have actually done it—because she had plenty of reason."

"No, no about his head."

"Who's head?"

"Gordon's head. You said something about in the time it took us to reach the penthouse Gordon could have been hit on the head."

"Yeah."

"What made you say that?"

"Because he had a lump on the back of his head," said Geri. "Didn't you hear Tracey?"

"Oh yeah. Of course."

Geri licked her lips. Martha leaned forward. She could feel the tiredness retreating from her. There was a renewed sense of urgency now. The buzz of the chase was coming back.

"When Helen took Tracey out of the bathroom she spoke to us, remember?"

"Yes," said Martha eagerly. "She told us she didn't kill him."

"That's right. She also said she didn't give him the lump on the back of his head. Don't you remember?"

"Are you sure?"

"Positive."

"You didn't mishear her or anything?"

"No, definitely not. That's what she said to us. Lump, back of his head and that she didn't put it there."

"Fascinating."

"What is?" asked Geri.

"I don't know about you but I'm starting to think maybe we've been looking at Tracey all wrong in this," started Martha. "I mean, we've been just assuming she's been so overcome with anger and rage that she's been *resigned* to accept responsibility. But maybe she's been telling the truth all along. I've always thought she didn't do it. What if I'm right?"

"So what do we do? Examine the body?"

"We can't do that," said Martha. "It'll be locked up in the morgue."

"Says who?" asked Geri.

"Says police procedure."

"We're not police Martha, as much as you'd like to think we are. We don't have to play by their rules."

"Geri," said Martha, drawing out her sister's name for effect. "Whatever you're thinking I want you to unthink it right now."

"Oh come on, don't be such a sourpuss, we'll be in and out before anybody notices."

"You're not serious are you? We can't break into a morgue!"

"It's for the greater good Martha, come on, you drive, I've had three pints and about a dozen boxes of chocolates. I'm in no fit state to be behind the wheel. You can thank my now ex-boyfriend and his *new* boyfriend for that."

"New *boyfriend* did you say?" asked Martha.

Geri got up and took off her dressing gown. She wandered over to a cupboard near the Aga.

"What?" she said, pulling out a wax jacket and throwing it about her shoulders. "You didn't think he was messing around with another woman, did you?"

"I… no, nothing," said Martha.

"Come on Mart, it's the twenty-first century. Get a grip of yourself."

"You're right, sorry," she said. "Now put some decent shoes on, there's a pair of walking boots in there too. If we're breaking into a morgue I want you to be at least wearing something sensible on your feet."

"I think that's probably the most sense you've made all week Martha."

"Ironic then," she said aloud. "Just as we're about do the least sensible thing possible."

"Live a little," said Geri, heading for the door. "You might enjoy yourself."

"That's what I'm afraid of."

Eighteen

"DID YOU REALLY have to wake me?" moaned Helen, yawning loudly. "I mean, fine, great, I like that you guys always think about me and stuff, but you woke me for this? Really? Couldn't you two have managed on your own?"

"We didn't want to leave you out," said Geri. "Because if we did we would never hear the end of it."

"That's true," Helen said, battling sleep as she drove erratically down the motorway. "I can't really deny that. You know me too well, sis."

"Thanks," smiled Geri.

Martha sat in the front passenger seat of the Mini. They were hurtling along through the night. The city shone in the distance, bright colours dancing off the new buildings and making the whole place seem alive. As they crossed the River Clyde the skyline reflected on the dark water. It was beautiful, hypnotic even.

Martha only wished they were seeing it under better circumstances. For the millionth time since they'd left her house she asked herself whether she'd taken leave of her senses. Were they really about to break into a morgue and find Gordon Coulthard's body? It was breaking so many rules she wasn't even sure she could count that many.

Yet somehow she kept coming back to the same answer. It was the right thing. Doing the *right thing* seemed to be a recurring feature of this case. Ever since she'd first met Tracey Coulthard, it had felt like she was questioning every decision she made. The consequences, the execution, everything had been up for debate. And now that it had all taken such a sinister turn, Martha found she was doing it more and more.

"Remind me why we're doing this again?" asked Helen.

Martha refrained from answering her with a glib remark. She wasn't sure if she'd feel any better if she voiced their plan aloud. Somehow, it felt quite conspiratorial, like they were plotting an assassination or something. She kept her voice low, just in case.

"We have to take a look at the lump on the back of Gordon Coulthard's head," she said. "I hadn't noticed it, but Geri says Tracey was adamant she hadn't put it there."

"Right," said Helen. "So why do we have to break into a morgue in the middle of the night? Shouldn't we just tell the cops?"

"Where's your sense of adventure, Helen?" asked Geri from the back. "Where's the fun in just handing it over to Pope the Dope?"

"Eh, it wouldn't be against the law for one thing," she replied. "You can't go about breaking and entering, that's a criminal offence you know."

"So's sending an innocent woman to prison for a crime she didn't commit," Geri snapped. "How would you feel about *that* on your conscience?"

Helen didn't answer. Martha didn't say anything either. Geri was right, the stakes were as high as they could possibly be.

"So what are we looking for then?" asked Helen. "I mean, it's just a lump, so what? The morticians and forensics guys will have seen it surely. What will we find that they won't already know?"

"That's why we needed you here," said Martha.

"Me? What do I know, I'm not a pathologist, Martha. Although I did think about taking it once, you know, a sort of morbid fascination."

"You're morbid enough as a relation Helen, don't make it worse," quipped Geri.

"It's that fascination we're counting on, Helen," said Martha. "That and your overall knowledge about, well, everything medical."

"Well… when you put it that way," she said modestly. "But I mean, what am I looking for?"

"Anything," said Geri. "You tell us if you see anything out of the ordinary."

"Out of the ordinary, what do you mean?"

"Use your imagination, let your creative and academic juices flow."

"I don't know about juices flowing, that sounds a bit… well… we won't bother with what that sounds like."

"Whatever, just go in there and do your thing Helen," said Geri. "We're counting on you."

"We're always counting on you," said Martha. "And we believe in you too."

"Wow, thanks guys," Helen tapped the steering wheel. "That means a lot."

"But first, just try to get us there in one piece," said Geri.

THE MORGUE WAS on the outskirts of the city centre. Sitting across the street from Glasgow Green, the city's famous park, it was a short, squat little building that had stood for over a hundred years.

The sisters were all quietly glad there was only one mortuary in the city. The last thing they wanted to do was go searching in different places for a corpse at all hours of the night.

Helen parked the Mini around the corner. The streets were quiet at this time, no traffic, no people. Tall, red sandstone tenements were dark and mysterious all about them. Even in the hard glow of the streetlights Martha thought they looked beautiful and otherworldly.

The three sisters hurried around the corner and spied the morgue. All the lights were off and the doors looked firmly closed and locked. Martha had never broken into a place before. She didn't know where to begin.

"Is it too obvious to just knock on the door?" she asked.

"Yeah that would be too obvious Martha," said Geri.

"It would also make us the worst cat burglars in history," chirped Helen.

"I'm not so sure that's such a bad thing."

"What's that big place around there?" Geri asked.

She pointed to the far side of the morgue. There was a huge building that joined on to the mortuary. Tall and dark columns guarding its entrance.

"That's the old High Court," whispered Helen. "It's been closed down for years since they opened up the new one down the street."

"Are they linked?" asked Geri.

"I don't know," said Martha. "Not surprisingly I've never been in it."

"Then let's go take a look."

Geri ran out into the street. Martha tried to grab her, thinking this time she'd be able to catch a hold of her sister before she did something rash. But once again she was too late.

"I hate it when she does that," Martha said, racing after Geri.

They chased her down the road. Running past the morgue, they spied Geri hopping a stone wall and into the grounds of the old High Court. Martha and Geri followed behind her.

An old, slime-covered staircase dropped down beneath the street level. It was dark and wet, Martha holding on to Helen for balance and her sister doing the same. Geri was at the bottom.

"You two took your time," she said. "I've found a door."

"Where does it go?" asked Helen, steadying herself.

"How the hell should I know. This is the first time I've ever been here."

She tried the door but it wouldn't move. She barged her shoulder into it but nothing—just a hard-sounding thud.

"Stand back," said Martha, pulling a pin from her hair. "Let an old professional have a go."

She kneeled down and focussed. Slipping her hairpin into the lock she began trying to unpick the mechanism.

"You see, you youngsters, you forget the simple things," she said. "Forget your hi-tech fancy solutions. All you need is a bit of old-fashioned know-how and a little gumption."

There was a click. Martha gave the door a little push and it nudged open. She looked back at her sisters.

"See," she said. "Nice and simple."

"Yes, yes, alright Miss Marple," said Geri stepping past her. "Now let's get in before you start telling us what it was like when the world was still in black and white."

"Steady on Geri, I'm not that old," she laughed.

The three sisters crept into the old courthouse. It was dark inside, the air smelling stale and musky. They lit their way with the torches on their phones, following the corridor as it wound its way into the bowels of the building.

"Do either of you have any idea where we're going?" whispered Helen. "Or are we all following each other?"

"The morgue was ahead of us when we came in here right?" said Martha. "That means if it's connected to the court, then there should be a door around about here somewhere."

"Will this do?" said Geri.

She flashed her light above them. An old mahogany sign with the word 'morgue' in faded brass letters appeared overhead.

"Bingo," said Martha.

They tried the door. It opened easily. Inside, a corridor stretched beyond them. Lights flickered into life overhead, lining the hallway. The sisters walked in carefully, making sure nobody was following them or that they made too much noise.

Martha's heart was thumping. She didn't like this at all, it was so alien to her. She tried to keep reminding herself that she was doing it for a good cause. If she didn't push on, then Tracey Coulthard would go down as a murderer. And she wasn't, she wasn't. Martha knew, she didn't know how, she just *knew*.

"Where do we start?" asked Helen. "This place is like a maze."

"There must be a main room, or a vault," said Martha.

"A vault? This is a morgue Martha, not a bank. They're human beings in here."

"Eh, guys," said Geri. "Whatever you want to call it, I think it's in here."

She was standing at a door, her head poking in. The others joined her and they all stepped into the room.

More lights flickered on automatically. It was cold—a bitter draught coming from somewhere around their ankles. There was a table in the centre of the room, although it looked more like a slab. There was a sink and what looked like a workbench, a computer sitting in standby mode close to the windows.

All along the far wall were little doors. Martha and the others didn't need an explanation, they knew what they were.

"Fridges," said Geri. "Bloody hell, it's like being in the supermarket, you know, the frozen aisle."

"Geri," said Helen. "Show some respect, would you? There are people in there."

"They *were* people."

"It doesn't matter, they're *still* people."

"Yeah I know, I know. I just... I just wasn't expecting it to be, you know, so clinical."

"You okay?" asked Martha.

Geri was pale. There were big, dark bags under her eyes and she looked like she was about to throw up.

"I'll be fine," she said. "Maybe this wasn't such a good idea of mine."

Helen walked over to the wall of fridges. She pulled a pair of rubber gloves from a box by the doors and began scanning the little labels that were above the hatches. Up and down she went looking for Gordon Coulthard's name. When she found it, she snapped her fingers.

"Here we go," she said. "Mr Coulthard's room."

She opened the door to reveal Coulthard's body. Pulling out the tray, Martha and Geri remained at a safe distance from the cadaver. His feet poked out from beneath a clinically white sheet that covered everything else. His skin was waxy white. Martha felt Geri shuddering beside her.

"Why don't you fire up that computer," she said to her sister. "Keep your mind on the job, try and pull up his file. We might get better luck in there."

Geri did what she was told. Martha made sure she stood between her and the body as Helen rounded her patient. Pulling back the sheet, Gordon's face came into view.

He looked just the same as the last time Martha had seen him. He was a little paler, but he still retained the selfish arrogance of a man drunk on his own wealth and power.

Helen carefully began her examination with gloved hands. She tilted Coulthard's head upwards and began feeling around beneath his hair. Martha watched her sister closely, not wanting to look at the body in great detail or for very long.

"Well?" she asked. "Is it there?"

"Oh yeah it's there alright," said Helen. "And it's a doozey, a real big one. God knows what caused it, but it's big."

"Big enough to have killed him?"

"Big enough that I'm surprised he's still got a head, to be perfectly honest with you. It feels like there's an ostrich egg beneath his scalp!"

"So what could have caused it?"

"I don't know. It's tough to say," said Helen. "I mean, if Tracey had hit him just right with something big and hard, then maybe. But what he was hit with, and what damage was done inside, I don't know."

"How about a fractured skull?" said Geri.

Martha turned to her youngest sister. She was leaning over the computer looking at Coulthard's file.

"You found that quickly," said Martha.

"Please Martha, give me some credit now and again. Passwords are easy," she smiled cheekily. "They're even *easier* when the computer is left logged on."

"I hope you don't know any of *my* passwords," said Helen, laying Coulthard's head back down on the tray.

"Way too easy. But you've got nothing worth stealing, so I don't bother."

"What does his file say?" asked Martha, interrupting another potential round of bickering.

"Let's have a look," Geri clicked on a few windows. "It looks like they're saying he drowned. Which makes sense when he was found face down in the bath."

"What about the bash on his head?" asked Martha. "Is there anything more about that?"

"You're really obsessed with this now aren't you?" asked Geri. "Let's see? More about the pathology, heavy drinker, smoker, damage to his liver blah, blah, blah," Geri scrolled down the file. "Oh, here we are, this is interesting."

"What is it?" Martha leaned in closer.

"There is a hairline fracture in his occipital bone, whatever that is."

"Occipital?" asked Helen. "That's the big bit at the back of your head."

"Okay. But it says here that he had a *severe* coup-contrecoup injury causing a bleed in his brain."

"A contrecoup? What's that?" asked Martha.

"Beats me," said Geri.

"Coup-Contrecoup?" asked Helen. "That's when you get two different injuries to different parts of the brain."

"What do you mean?" asked Martha.

"They happen in road accidents, like if you get impacted from the front, your brain swishes around in its fluid, imagine like an egg in a lunchbox when you shake it. You get damage to the bit directly under where you hit, kinda like a bruise. But the brain also gets damage to the back of it, because it keeps moving backwards when your skull has already stopped, like I said, an egg in a lunchbox. Or side to side injuries can do the same.

Basically it's if you're hit with enough sudden start-stop force you'll cause damage to different parts of the brain at the same time."

"Bloody hell," said Geri. "Poor guy."

"You mean if he hadn't ended up in the bath he would have died anyway?" asked Martha.

Helen shrugged. She looked down at Gordon and pulled the sheet back over his face.

"I don't know, it sounds pretty awful," she said. "But I'm no pathologist, but if it's a coup-contrecoup, that's something altogether more powerful. And awful I might add."

"Like what?" asked Geri.

"It means he was hit hard. Very hard."

"Too hard for a small slip of a thing like Tracey Coulthard?" Martha mused.

"I'd say so," said Helen.

Martha stood in the middle of the morgue, her brow furrowed, staring at Coulthard's body beneath the sheet. Her head was full of questions, her mind racing.

It felt that this case became more complicated and confusing by each turn. The more she knew, the less she felt she understood. It was infuriating and fascinating in equal measure. She was conflicted, but she didn't mind admitting she was sort of enjoying it.

Martha let out a long breath, unsure of how their trip had helped. If anything, it had just raised more questions. The sudden urge to forget it all and let the police do their job came over her again. It was only when the sound of footsteps came from the corridor outside did she snap back to her senses.

"What's that?" whispered Helen, her big eyes staring at her sisters.

"It's trouble," said Martha. "Quick. Hide."

Nineteen

"THIS ISN'T GOING to work," said Geri, her hands on her hips. "Have you ever seen a tiny little car and around twelve clowns trying to climb in at the circus. That's what this is like. And we're the clowns."

"Would you shut up and get in," hissed Martha.

Helen was already in the small cupboard, her arms folded around behind her head as she jammed herself into the back of the cubbyhole. Martha stood at the door, hopping up and down anxiously.

"I'm *not* getting in with you two. This is stupid," said Geri.

"No it's not. It's our only option," pleaded Martha.

"We could run."

"Where can we go? We can't, there's nowhere to go."

"Out the window, anywhere."

"There is no bloody window," said Martha, exasperated. "Please Geri, just get in."

The footsteps were getting louder now. Voices joined them, and Martha had broken out in a cold sweat. She stared at the door of the examination room. Shadows danced beneath the gap. There were people out there and they were coming. If Geri didn't get in the cupboard now then they'd be caught. And if they were caught Martha didn't know what would happen.

"Geri, please," she said. "Please, as your sister, I'm begging you to get in this cupboard with me and Helen. Otherwise we're going to get caught and probably arrested. And we're no good to Tracey Coulthard if we're behind bars with her."

There was a creak behind them. The door of the examination room slowly opened. Voices drifted in as Geri leapt forward and into the cupboard. Martha was right behind her as the three Parker sisters squeezed themselves into the impossibly tiny space.

Martha felt something twinge in her shoulder, as she pulled the cupboard door behind her. She didn't care, they had to remain out of sight. Geri and Helen were making muffled moans of agony. Martha hushed them down as she tried to keep the door shut.

The door wouldn't close fully. There was still a thin gap, enough to hear the voices from outside. Martha concentrated, she thought she recognised one of them.

"My foot," whispered Geri. "You're standing on my foot."

"Well stop squirming," moaned Helen.

"Be quiet," hissed Martha. "Listen, is that… is that?"

"Detective Pope this really is out of the ordinary," said a man's voice.

"Pope," gasped Martha.

Geri and Helen stopped moving immediately. They were frozen, like two statues hidden away in the back of a cupboard of some dusty museum.

"I don't care if it's out of the ordinary Doctor Mason, I'm conducting a murder inquiry here," said Pope.

Martha felt the blood inside of her freeze. If she thought things would be bad if they were caught before, they would be a hundred times worse now that Pope was here.

If the door she was holding onto for dear life were to slip open, that would be it. Arrested on the spot, thrown in jail and her reputation lost forever.

"It's the middle of the night and you've got me opening up the mortuary," said Doctor Mason. "Couldn't this have waited a couple of hours? I mean, they're not going anywhere, are they?"

"I'm afraid crime doesn't stick to your nine to five schedule, doctor."

"Quite."

"Where's the body?" she asked.

"Where it was the last time you saw it."

Martha heard the two of them walking to the far side of the room. Her grip was slipping on the door. She had to adjust but she couldn't risk being seen. She bit her bottom lip, staring at her hand and willing it to keep steady.

There was a clank from outside. Doctor Mason grunted as he opened the door of the vaults. Martha stifled a squeal; she couldn't hold the door any longer. She quickly let go of the door and tried to catch it again but it slipped.

The door opened up completely. Martha stood there for a moment, her eyes wide, the whole of the examination room opened up in front of her. The sisters were completely exposed, ready to be caught red-handed.

To Martha's relief, Pope and Mason had their backs turned. The doctor was pulling a tray out from the vaults while the detective watched him. Martha stood frozen to the spot for a split second, although it felt more like a century. Then her mind and limbs kicked back into action.

She quickly reached for the cupboard door and pulled it closed again. The sisters all waited, nervously, none of them breathing. They waited, then waited some more, each of them expecting the door to open and Pope to discover them. The longer they waited the more anxious they became. Until finally they heard the policewoman start talking to Doctor Mason.

"What's the verdict then?" she asked. "What have you found?"

"You mean you haven't read my report?" asked the doctor.

"Mason, I'm a busy woman, that's why I'm still awake at this time of night. Or is it up at this time in the morning, I can never tell. Either way, cut the crap and tell me what we're looking at here. The report said drowning. But it also said something about an irregularity. A contusion? Blunt force? I'm trying to run an investigation here. I need clarity. Now."

The doctor gave a long, tired sigh. Martha heard him walking around the table, his shoes squeaking on the floor tiles.

"It seems our friend Mr Coulthard here took a rather nasty knock to the head," said Mason.

"And that's what you've found?" sneered Pope. "That's your irregularity? You've had the body for days, man—I could have told you that ten minutes after I arrived in his flat."

"When I say a knock on the head I'm not talking about a little bash. This man has suffered a severe coup-contracoup injury."

"A contra-what?"

"Coup-Contracoup, it's the damage seen to the brain when a direct impact causes a head to hit a solid object at speed. Injury to opposite sides of the brain because the brain has been bouncing around inside his head."

"Ah, the old egg in a lunchbox?" asked Pope.

"See," whispered Helen from the back. "I told you."

Martha shushed her. She held onto the lip of the door with both hands now. But she was shaking. Half in fear of being caught, but half, she realised, in excitement.

"Exactly," continued Mason. "Couldn't have put it better myself actually."

"I try," said Pope. "And it didn't take five years of medical school to come up with that. So a bump on the head then. A bad one. Resulting in his being unconscious when he went into the water and thus drowning?"

"I'd say," said the doctor. "Though it's reasonable to say that the blow was severe enough that, if he hadn't been found face down in water, there's a good chance that he would have died anyway."

"Right," said Pope. "That's very interesting. Was this contra-wotsit caused by a blunt object then? A hammer? A bat?"

"Yes. But you're the detective," said Mason. "What did you find at the scene?"

"You mean, apart from the soon to be ex-wife, the lover, and a trio of frankly delusion sibling detectives? Nothing."

Martha felt Geri bristling and gave her a warning nudge.

He clanked around again. Martha assumed they were putting the body away. There was a hard thump as the vault door was closed and they walked across the room towards the cupboard.

"So no weapon of any sort?"

"Could it have been done with a stiletto? Or a court-shoe?"

Martha heard Mason laugh. She was the only one of any of them who wore court shoes. Surely she was not still a suspect?

"Give me your medical opinion doctor," said Pope. "What am I looking at here? Could the wife have hit him hard enough?"

"I couldn't possibly say," said Mason.

"For god sake Mason, give me a break," said Pope.

She sounded angry. She was wheezing now between breaths. Martha wondered if she'd have an asthma attack. That meant they could be stuck in the cupboard for a while as they waited for help. She didn't know how much longer her aching fingers would hold out for.

"Just give it to me straight, would you? What's your gut instinct?"

Doctor Mason let out another long sigh. Martha knew how he felt. She'd been put through the same rigmarole with Pope. It wasn't pleasant and could be really tiring. Especially at this time of night.

But she wanted to know too. Every part of her was dying to jump out and throttle the doctor—force him to spit it out. Thankfully she was much too sensible for that.

"If I had to make a guess," said Mason. "The damage was caused by something severe. He could have been involved in a car accident or something, I don't know if that helps you but that's the levels of severity we're dealing with here."

"A car accident?" asked Pope. "Very interesting."

"Or an equivalent force. Does that help?"

"No, not really," she said. "But it's still interesting. And you're saying that it would have killed him anyway, even if he hadn't drowned."

"Almost certainly. The damage to his brain, the bleeding throughout and the swelling of his brain tissue would have been irrevocable. Whatever happened to Mr Coulthard, whatever his head was put through, car accident, high speed collision, whatever it was, was the real fatal blow. The bath water was just a lucky coincidence."

"Right," said Pope. "That's put a bigger spanner in the works than those the three witches lurking about this case."

Martha almost swallowed her tongue in shock. Somehow she kept herself composed enough to keep the door closed.

"I don't follow," said Mason.

"It's nothing," said Pope. "The wife hired three amateur private eyes to spy on Coulthard. Now they think they're Sherlock Holmes, Poirot and Inspector Gadget, all rolled into one. They're making life a hundred times harder for me because they were at the scene and there's no way I can properly rule them out. The oldest of them is a complete dingbat, determined to prove that Tracey Coulthard is innocent. And now you're saying she just might be."

Geri had to stifle her laughter. Helen did the same somewhere in the back. Martha wasn't sure if she should be shocked, angered or unsurprised. In the short time she'd known Detective Sergeant Pope, the policewoman hadn't pulled any punches. And she certainly wasn't now.

"Right, fine," said Pope. "I'll let you get back to bed."

"Thank you," said Mason. "Although there's no real point now, is there? By the time I get back to the house, it'll be just in time for my alarm to go off."

"Where do you live?" asked Mason.

"Am I being asked in a professional or personal capacity detective?"

"Forget it then," droned Pope.

Their footsteps walked past the cupboard door. Martha closed her eyes tightly as they passed. When they were gone she lingered for an extra moment. Then, slowly, she eased the cupboard door open and stepped out. Geri and Helen were behind her, unfolding themselves from the storage cupboard like accordions.

"Bloody hell," said Helen. "Now I know how sardines feel. That was awful."

"I think one or both of you has broken either one or both of my feet," said Geri, cracking her neck.

Martha didn't say anything. She stood and stared at the vaults, her head pounding.

"I reckon we should give them five minutes," said Geri. "Let them get out of here and then we do the same. This place is giving me the creeps."

"I agree," said Helen. "Maybe I can get back to sleep."

"Hey, you moan when we don't involve you and then you moan when we do. We can't win."

"I'm just messing with you that's all," smiled Helen. "There's nothing I love better than spending an evening skulking around a morgue with my sisters. Who *wouldn't* want that? I'm so lucky."

Geri sucked her tongue. Then they both looked at Martha. Immediately their moods changed, obviously sensing their sister wasn't happy.

"A car accident," she said. "That's what could have caused the damage to Coulthard's brain. That's what that doctor said wasn't it?"

"Yeah," said Geri.

"I told you that."

"But his car was fine," said Martha. "It was parked outside his flat, remember we saw it, just before Tracey arrived. There wasn't a scratch on it."

"Yes," said Geri. "So what are you getting at?"

"If he wasn't in a car crash," started Martha. "Then what the hell did that to him?"

A chill ran through all three of the sisters. They each came to the same conclusion at the same time. Only Martha was brave enough to say it.

"Or more importantly," she whispered. "*Who* did that to him?"

Twenty

THE PARKER SISTERS sped through the city, chasing the early morning sunrise. The pungent smell of the morgue wafted from their clothes, filling the car. Even with the windows down and the air conditioning on they couldn't seem to escape it.

Martha didn't mind it so much. The moaning and fidgeting from the others were the only reminder it was even there. She was too busy running over every little detail of this case in her mind.

"I'm going to smell of antiseptic for a week," snorted Helen.

"And who's going to notice?" scoffed Geri. "It's not like you're going out anywhere."

"And how would you know about my social life?" Helen darted back. "For all you know I've got a date with a tall, dark, handsome fireman tomorrow night."

"And do you?" asked Geri, twisting in her seat.

"Do I what?"

"Do you have a date with a tall, dark, handsome fireman tomorrow night?"

"What?"

"Exactly," Geri smiled. "I thought not. And take it from me sis, you don't *want* a date with a guy like that. Believe me, they'll only go and break your heart. Or worse still go running off with one of your best pals."

"Would you two keep it down," snapped Martha. "I can't hear myself think. Just give it a rest."

Helen and Geri were quiet immediately. From the corner of her eye she could see they looked hurt. She knew that look, it had been a staple of their upbringing. Any time their parents have given them a talking to, each of the sisters pulled the exact same face. Drawn, forlorn and totally ashamed.

"Don't look at me like that," she said.

"We're not looking at you," said Geri.

"Yeah, we're looking at everywhere *but* at you. In case you bite our heads off again," said Helen.

"Don't be like that," said Martha. "Look I'm sorry. I didn't mean to snap, I'm just... I'm just tired."

"No wonder," said Geri. "It feels like we've been awake for days. Weeks even."

Martha smiled a little. She could feel her limbs crying out for sleep, her mind aching for a rest. The past few days had been a strange whirlwind of surprise, danger and mystery. She just wanted to lie down in a quiet room and not have to think about it anymore.

She knew that was impossible of course. They were too deep into this now, too far gone to simply walk away. And with the new information from the morgue and Pope, it felt like they were getting closer to proving Tracey's innocence with every passing moment.

"We're missing something here, something important," she said sighing. "This doesn't just happen, people don't just get violent bumps on the head. They aren't just murdered for no reason. What are we missing? What is it we're not seeing?"

"I don't want to sound rude or anything Martha," started Helen. "But if we knew what we weren't seeing then we wouldn't not be seeing it would we?"

"That's just confusing Helen," said Geri. "And the last thing we need now is *more* confusion."

Martha shook her head again. More bickering, she was getting sick of it all. She wanted answers, proof, clear cut evidence that what she thought, what she believed of Tracey Coulthard, was true. The others didn't seem bothered, did they even care that an innocent woman might rot away in jail.

Martha still wasn't sure why she actually *did* care. But that hardly mattered. She cared enough that this whole thing was chewing her up from the inside outwards. And she wanted it to stop.

"Well what do we know?" asked Geri, interrupting her thoughts.

Martha felt sluggish. She felt old, like the whole case had aged her by about twenty years. She saw her eyes in the rear-view mirror and almost didn't recognise them. When had those big bags and dark rings arrived? She remembered what they used to be like—bright and cheerful, with an eternal optimism. Not now. Now they looked like Gordon Coulthard's – dead.

"Facts. We need to do a fact checking exercise," Geri said. "We get taught it all the time in psychology. You make a list of all the parts and variables of the problem and go through them, one by one, until you can assimilate the problem. This is just the same, only it's a bit more sinister. Am I right?"

The others didn't argue with her. She held her hand up and began counting off with her index finger.

"Okay," she said. "We've got—"

She was cut off by the screeching of tyres. The car lurched around a corner. Geri thumped into her chair while Helen rolled around in the back. The car straightened and they both caught their breath.

"What the hell?" screeched Geri.

"And you have a go at my driving, Martha!" Helen protested.

"If we're going to do this," Martha said. "Then I need coffee, and eggs, bacon, sausages, black pudding, potato scones, mushrooms, tomatoes, lots of toast and a big, sugar coated doughnut to finish it all off."

"Oh bloody hell," said Geri, smiling as they pulled up at the side of the road. "It must be serious."

"And where are we going to get that kind of feast from?" asked Helen, righting herself. "I mean it's only three, four, five in the morning? It's five in the morning already. Where the bloody hell did the night go? I haven't had any sleep."

Martha smiled and pointed out the window. A tiny little café stood lit up on the dark street. There was a Christmas tree in the window, its lights slowly blinking on and off in a gentle, soothing rhythm. Above it was an equally bright OPEN sign that seemed to draw the sisters in.

They got out of the car, shuffled into the little café and placed their huge orders. They were sat down, pouring tea and coffee, buttering toast and tucking in to their early morning banquet within fifteen minutes. And with a fuller stomach, Martha began to feel a little better.

"You were saying," she said to Geri, gulping from a chipped mug of warm, black coffee. "Problems."

"Oh yeah, I forgot, sorry. All this fried food, it's gone to my head I think."

"Spit it out," said Helen, picking her teeth. "Problems, what are they?"

She leaned in to the others and kept her voice down. The young girl behind the till looked tired, yawning every few seconds, as she stood looking numbly at the door. In the background there were Christmas carols playing, but still no *Fairytale of New York* to Martha's delight.

"Right. Problems. We've got an arrogant, selfish, cheating, dishonest and very much dead banker on our hands, that's problem number one," started Geri. "Number two is his wife and fiancée, although they technically count as two things they're still the same problem. He was cheating on his wife, he told his fiancée he was leaving his wife, and that makes them both potential murderers."

"God this sounds horrible when you say it out loud," said Helen.

"Problem three," Geri ignored her. "As our little midnight raid on the morgue has shown us, with a little inadvertent help from Constable Pope, the damage that happened to Gordon Coulthard's brain was so bad that he would probably have died anyway, but there was no indication that either the wife or the fiancée hit him. Problem four, well, that's the sticking point isn't it?"

"What is it?" asked Martha, sucked in by her sister.

"Problem four is that if Gordon Coulthard was hit hard enough to cause that much damage, were either Tracey Coulthard or Estelle even capable of physically inflicting that damage? And if not, then who did that to our Gordon? Those, my sisters, are our problems."

She sat back in her chair. Martha and Helen did the same. While those same questions had been spinning around inside Martha's head for the past hour, hearing them aloud seemed to help her a little.

"You know something," she said. "This was a good idea."

"It was?" asked Geri, surprised.

"It *was*?" asked Helen, even more surprised, since she was obviously not feeling it.

"Yes, it was," said Martha. "It was helpful because it means I'm not going crazy with this case. If you think all of these things are problems too, then I'm not insane."

"Always glad to help," Geri said with a laugh.

"Helping is all very good," Helen butted in. "And I'm glad you two are feeling cosy and proud of yourselves. But it doesn't take us any further forward. All that we've established is that Tracey Coulthard *probably* didn't kill her husband—which she has already told us—and that there's a killer on the loose somewhere out there. Hardly cut and dried is it?."

"No, it's not," said Geri, sounding a little defensive. "But it's a start, isn't it? It's a leaping off point where we can go *somewhere*."

"Where though Geri? Where?" asked Helen. "We're still no closer to catching whoever did this. And by the sounds of it, Pope is in no hurry to let Tracey go."

"She always has to spoil things, doesn't she?" Geri shoved her chin into her hand and stared into space.

Martha rubbed her temples. Her sore head was coming back again, she'd probably have to take some painkillers. She didn't like to do that, she never had done. Ever since she was a little girl she'd always had an over-sensitive gag reflex. She hated tablets, no matter what shape or size they were.

She'd suffered as a result. Every headache, every cold and flu sickness, even her pregnancy had been long suffering and painful. Now she was still suffering, even into her middle-age.

"You okay?" asked Helen.

"No," she said. "I'm not. For all of the reasons above, for you two bickering and for this bloody sore head of mine. I feel like I'm ready to burst."

"You shouldn't have had those eggs then," Geri quipped.

Martha didn't react. Instead she shook her head and slowly got up from the table, starting towards the door.

"Martha?" asked Geri. "Oh come on, don't be so sensitive, I was only messing around with you."

"Yeah come on Mart, don't be daft," said Helen. "We love you really, don't huff with us. It's been a rotten night, we're only trying to cheer you up."

"I know," sighed Martha. "But I'm just not feeling great, okay. I was just in hospital, you know? I don't think I should be overdoing it as much. I think…"

She trailed off. Geri and Helen stared at her standing by the door of the café. A worrying moment passed as all three sisters remained silent. The cheery chimes of *Jingle Bells* echoed in the distance but none of them could hear it. Geri and Helen watched breathlessly on as Martha slowly reached into her pocket.

She pulled out her phone. The screen was flashing brightly, a single name highlighted above the vibrations. From where they were perched, Geri and Helen could see who it was.

"No way," whispered Geri.

"Surely not," said Helen.

Martha swallowed a stale gulp. The coffee was already drying in the back of her throat and she could hear her breakfast churning away in the pit of her stomach. She licked her lips and held the phone to her ear.

"Hello?" she said, more of a question than a statement.

"Martha Parker?" came the brittle, croaky voice from the other end.

"Tracey?" she said. "Are you alright?"

"What do you care?" answered Mrs Coulthard.

"I'm sorry. What can I do for you?"

"What can you *do* for me?" Tracey laughed, her voice like a chugging steam train on the other end of the line. "Oh Parker, if only you *knew* what it was you could do for me. But I don't think you've got those kinds of talents."

Martha swallowed. Her head was pounding now, a cold sweat making her shiver. Tracey Coulthard sounded like a ghost. She was ethereal, spirited, like she didn't exist and was beaming directly into Martha's head from another world.

"Are you okay, Tracey?" Martha asked again. "I mean, where are you?" She suddenly had a thought that Tracey may have elected her as her one call from prison. She quickly dismissed it as silly.

"I'm at the police station," said Tracey, her voice now little more than a whisper. "I need you to come and collect me."

"Collect you?"

Helen and Geri looked at each other. They could only hear Martha's side of the conversation. But it was enough to get them out of their seats.

"I don't understand," said Martha. "I thought... I thought the police were holding you for the... for the murder of your husband."

"You're going to come and collect me," said Tracey. "Right now and you're going to take me home to my house. Then, you're going to leave me alone, *everyone* is going to leave me alone. And that will be that. Do you understand?"

Martha swallowed again. Her tongue was totally dry now, the back of her throat like an arid piece of desert. She nodded.

"Now," said Tracey. "Collect me now."

"Okay," said Martha. "What police station are you at?"

"You'll work it out," said Mrs Coulthard. "You're good at working out things. You're a clever one Parker, very, very clever. You'll work it all out."

The line went dead. Martha stood for a second, listening to the insistent beeps telling her the connection had been cut. She'd never been so glad to hear them.

"So?" asked Geri.

"What did she say?" asked Helen. "What's going on?"

"You know what I'm going to say," said Martha, opening the door. "It's the same answer I've had since we took on this bloody case. Three simple words."

"You don't know?" asked Helen.

Martha didn't answer her sister. Instead she started out the door and headed towards the car. At least she was adding more to her resume during this case. As if undercover agent, forensic pathologist and cat burglar weren't enough, she was now a taxi driver.

Twenty-One

"I'M GETTING A bit sick of jumping through hoops for this woman," said Geri. "I mean, one call and we're off chasing our tails again."

"Geri don't," said Martha. "I'm not in the mood."

"I'm being serious," the youngest sister continued. "It's like if she says jump we say how high. Yes Tracey, no Tracey, can we flush the toilet for you Tracey, it's getting right on my nerves."

"I said don't!"

"She has a point Martha," Helen chimed in. "I mean, I know we've been paid a lot of money and all the rest of it but we've more than done our bit for her. Why are we still running around after her? Surely she can afford a taxi home from the nick?"

"Because…"

Martha couldn't finish that sentence. It wasn't that she didn't want to. She just couldn't. Something was stopping her from forming the words, putting them into a sentence and speaking them to her sisters. It was like there was a barrier between her brain and her mouth. And she couldn't get around it.

"We're just going to pick her up," she finally said. "And that's that. We owe her that at least."

"That's just it, Mart. We don't *owe* her anything," said Geri.

"Do I need to remind you what this woman's just been put through?" said Martha quickly. "Her husband's just been killed. She's been accused of killing him, when we're pretty sure she didn't. And before any of that, she learned that the slimy bugger wasn't just seeing another woman behind her back, but that he was actually engaged to her. And you think we should just ignore her? Come on Geri, you too Helen, our mum raised us better than that. Where's your solidarity?"

None of the others argued with her. Martha felt a little bad. She hadn't intended on ramping up the emotional blackmail quite so much. But she didn't have time to lament. She was speeding through the city towards a police station to collect Tracey Coulthard. She had to be at the top of her game, she had to stay sharp.

"So where is she?" asked Helen.

"She didn't say," said Martha. "But I have a feeling she's in the centre of town."

"Why?"

"She told me to work it out," said Martha. "She said I was clever enough to work it out. And aside from trying to polish my ego, I reckon somebody as important to a high-profile case as this will be in the centre of the city, where there's plenty of protection."

They pulled around the corner. Martha slammed on the brakes to stop the car from hitting a parked van.

"What the hell?" she shouted.

The road ahead was completely blocked off. Vans with large satellite dishes barred the way. There were people running around, some in hi-visibility vests, others with TV cameras mounted on their shoulders. Other photographers dashed between the vans and parked cars, all racing towards the one point.

"No way," said Helen. "It's a media circus."

"Circus is right," said Geri. "Look at the number of people here. Are they all here to see Tracey?"

"What do you think?" asked Martha. "Don't you remember what Pope said? It's all over the news. Papers, TV, the murder of a high-profile banker is a big draw in Scotland."

"Yeah, I know, but still," said Geri. "This is total overkill. They've blocked off the street."

Police officers were trying to redirect traffic without much success. Waving away cars and arguing with media representatives who were manoeuvring their vans for a better sightline of the police station further up the street. A cop began walking towards the car. Martha felt her hands begin to shake so she grabbed the steering wheel a little tighter.

"You can't come through here!" he said, rapping his knuckles on the window. "Go back the way you came, this street is closed off."

"Yes, hello," said Martha, rolling down the window. "We're trying to get to the station, we're picking somebody up."

"No way," said the cop. "This street is closed off, turn around and be on your way."

"No, wait, you don't understand."

"Just get moving. Now."

"Hey, you can't talk to her like that," Helen snapped from the passenger seat. "We're tax-paying citizens, we have a right to speak."

"I've told you to move on," the policeman was getting angry.

"I don't care what you've told us," Helen fired back. "We're trying to get through here to pick up a very important person."

"Helen," said Martha. "Take it easy."

"Look! I'm not telling you again darling, just get moving."

"Darling? Darling! Did you seriously just call me darling?" blurted Helen. "I'll show you darling."

"Helen," Martha warned.

"Officer, I'm sorry," said Geri, leaning out the window. "My sister, she didn't get much sleep last night, she's a little on edge."

"On edge?" Helen coughed. "I'm not the one being a misogynistic plonker."

"She's tired and emotional," Geri fluttered her eyelashes. "We're here to collect somebody from the station. In fact, we've been called by the very same person I reckon all these reporters are here to see. So if you let us through, we'll happily take her off your hands and you can get the street open again. How does that sound?"

Geri did her best to sound friendly and alluring. Martha didn't normally approve of her sister's flirting, especially when she was there to see it. But it had to be better than Helen's haranguing. She hoped it worked this time for all of their sakes.

The policeman took a moment to consider the offer. He straightened himself and folded his arms.

"And how do I know you're not with the press yourselves?" he asked. "Never trust a journalist, eh?"

"Oh come on," said Geri smiling. "I would have thought a big, strapping, brave policeman like yourself would be able to tell that us three are far too attractive to be journalists. Am I right?"

That cracked it. The officer's face went from stern and suspicious to relaxed and almost friendly. He laughed and tipped the brim of his hat upwards.

"Has anybody ever told you that you're a charmer, sweetheart?" he said.

"Sweetheart?" Helen mumbled. "This guy just doesn't get it."

"Shut up, Helen," Martha hissed. "Call ahead, if you like. Ask Detective Pope. Tell her the Parker Sisters are here to collect their client."

"Okay, okay" said the policeman, flinching at the very mention of Pope's name. "But if I find out you three are lying to me, I'm going to have you booked before your feet touch the ground, understand?"

"Oh come on," said Geri. "You don't have to play hard ball to get my number. All you have to do is ask, officer."

"Yeah, yeah," he said, reaching for his walkie-talkie. "I've heard it all before, love."

He spoke into the device and warned his colleagues that Martha, Helen and Geri were coming through. They raced through the barriers and past the journalists, TV news crews and other officers.

The central police station was a grand old building, all towers and red sandstone. It loomed large over the rest of the street, imposing on the other buildings around it. This was a grand cathedral to the law, built when Glasgow enjoyed great wealth from trading with the rest of the world. Martha afforded herself a little longer look than she probably should have. She always loved beautiful buildings and stunning architecture.

She pulled up a little away from the main entrance. A large group of journalists and photographers had gathered at the bottom of the steps that led to the door. Martha and the others recognised them from television. It appeared all the networks' big guns were turning out to catch a glimpse of Tracey Coulthard.

"Somebody must have tipped them off," said Martha, getting out the car.

"I wonder who that could have been?" asked Helen sceptically.

"You don't think it was Tracey do you?"

"I don't know anything is ever certain with that woman," she said. "She's full of surprises. But put it this way, if she'd phoned us to come pick her up and then put a call into every newsroom in the country, I wouldn't be surprised."

Something about what Helen had said didn't sit right with Martha. Was it that there was a real possibility it could have happened? Or was it that she didn't want to believe her sister? Either way they were in the middle of a media storm. They had to be careful.

"Okay, gather round," said Martha.

"Are we huddling?" asked Geri.

"I think we are," said Helen. "A Parker huddle, we've not had one of those for years."

"No, I'm excited," said Geri laughing.

"Would you two be serious for a second, please," said Martha.

They stayed close to the car. Martha didn't want to get any closer to the journalists, not before she'd briefed her troops.

"This is a big story, okay," she started. "The journalists are going to be all over anything and everything Tracey Coulthard touches, looks at, breathes on even. And that includes us. So I want us to be professional, quick and efficient. We're just going in there, collecting Tracey, driving her back to her mansion and that's it. Simple. Got that?"

"Crystal clear," said Helen.

"You're not going to get any complaints from me, sis," said Geri.

"Really?" asked Martha. "No protests? No smart-alecky remarks? Nothing?"

"We're not stupid Martha," said Geri, pulling out her phone. "We know what's going on here."

"Yeah, do you think I want to be plastered all over the news at six?" asked Helen. "I've got my academic reputation to uphold you know."

She turned her nose upwards at the others. Martha didn't say anything, she was still in a little shock that, for a change, her sisters were doing what she'd asked.

"Fine, good," she said. "If that's settled then we can go ahead. Yes?"

"Lead on," said Helen.

"Eh, guys," said Geri, her head still in her phone. "You know how you said you didn't want to be all over the news?"

Martha and Helen gathered in a little closer. Geri showed them her phone.

"Is that?" asked Martha. "Is that…"

A newsreader was standing on the street, speaking into the camera. The screen was being broadcast live and when Martha got her bearings she realised they were across the road from the journalist.

"We're on TV guys, like right now. I say TV, the internet, but that's as good as TV now isn't it. Watch."

Geri began waving. Martha watched her, not beside her, but on the screen on the phone.

"That's us there, do you see us?" asked the youngest sister. "Just over that woman's left shoulder. Coo-eee, say hello to all your friends and family watching all around the world."

"Oh god," said Helen. "I think I'm going to be sick!"

"For god sake don't do *that*," Martha said, bundling her sisters down the street. "That's the last thing we need, you throwing up all over the place in front of a live audience. Get moving, hurry up!"

The sisters marched down the road towards the large gathering of journalists that had congregated at the bottom of the steps. Jostling and pushing their way through the group, Martha led Helen and Geri all the way to the front door. There was some shouting and angry calls from the journalists and photographers, each unhappy that the sisters had just barged their way to the front of the huddle.

Martha didn't care. This wasn't her scene at all, she didn't like being the focus of attention—especially not from the press. The plan, stick to the plan, she kept telling herself. In, out and away, it was so simple it was bound to work. It *had* to work, there was no other option.

She was about to push her way through the revolving doors when a voice shouted out from behind her. Her teeth clamped together and she cursed under her breath.

"Oi! You! You're Martha Parker aren't you?"

It was a journalist. He was broad shouldered with a pot belly, his tie loosely fastened about his bullish neck. Martha panicked, she didn't know what to do or what to say. In the end, she couldn't lie.

"Yes," she said.

"Weren't you one of the people at the scene of the crime?" asked the reporter.

Another wave of panic. It was getting worse now, the other members of the media were warming up. Like a pack of lions circling their prey, they thrust their voice recorders into the air and turned on the lights and flashes of their cameras.

"I was, yes," said Martha, still shaky.

"Eh Martha, I don't think..." Helen was interrupted.

"What can you tell us about Gordon Coulthard Mrs Parker?" asked the reporter.

"Did Tracey Coulthard kill her husband Mrs Parker?" came a third voice.

"Do you know who *did* kill him Mrs Parker?" asked another.

"What's your relationship with Tracey Coulthard?" and another.

"What are you doing here Mrs Parker?"

"Have you been arrested Mrs Parker?"

"Were you paid to kill Gordon Coulthard Mrs Parker?"

"Stop!"

Martha was shaking. She held her hands up as a flurry of camera flashes engulfed her. She wasn't used to being bombarded like this.

"My name isn't *Mrs* Parker," she declared. "It's *Ms* Parker, Parker is my maiden name."

The congregated journalists all scribbled the information on their notepads. They all looked back up at Martha and the others in unison, like a swarm of hornets.

"And I'm not answering any of your questions," said Martha sternly. "You'll be hearing from my solicitor if I get harassed like this again."

There was a momentary pause. Then they all began shouting at once. A wave of questions from the sea of faces washed over Martha. Thankfully something grabbed her from behind.

She was pulled backwards through the revolving door. When she emerged on the other side, a little dazed and blinded by the camera flashes, she saw Helen and Geri scowling at her.

"Thank you," she said. "That was madness."

"And answering their questions is bloody madness too," Helen quipped. "What do you think you were doing out there? You don't need to speak to them, they're just the press, they'll make it all up anyway, twist your words. Come on Martha, get your head together."

"Yeah, after you told us to be on our best behaviour too," said Geri with a wry smirk.

"Yes, you're right," said Martha, rubbing her forehead. "I'm sorry."

"Apology accepted," said Helen. "See, just like that. Take note dearest sister, it's alright to forgive each other from time to time."

Martha clapped her sister on the shoulder. She walked past her, Geri following close behind, as they made their way to the front desk.

Inside the police station was in upheaval. Uniformed officers were dashing about throughout the lobby. Voices echoed down the wide staircases, bouncing off the marble walls and floor like tennis balls on a court. The ambiance of the place was somewhere between panic and anger. The whole station felt like it was on lockdown.

At the front desk a rather haggard looking woman in a uniform was furiously lifting, answering and then slamming down phones. When she saw Martha, Helen and Geri arrive, she threw up her hands.

"Oh no," she said. "No way. Nope, I'm too busy."

"Too busy for what?" asked Geri.

"I'm not putting through another complaint from you Women's Institute lot, absolutely not. We've got every reporter in the country camped outside, the street blocked off with television trucks and my superintendent ready to pop a blood vessel or twelve so no, I'm sorry ladies, we won't be able to deal with your overgrown hedgerows requests today."

"No, sorry, you don't understand," said Martha. "We're here to collect someone."

"Collect?" sneered the policewoman. "You lot, you three, are *collecting* somebody? Are you sure?"

Martha, Helen and Geri looked at each other. None of them could be sure this woman wasn't having a joke at their expense. The look on the officer's face however was stern enough to tell them she wasn't.

"We're picking up somebody," said Helen. "In fact it might even make your life easier."

"Oh yeah?" the policewoman leaned forward. "And can you three possibly make *my* life easier? Go on, I'm all ears, I could do with a laugh."

"Because they're here to pick up Tracey Coulthard. And about bloody time, too." Pope's rusty voice boomed in the marble lobby.

Martha looked up to see the detective standing at the top of the stairs, surveying her kingdom with an angry pride. The policewoman at the desk immediately stood up.

"Tracey Coulthard?" she repeated. "These three? Are you sure?"

"I know sergeant," said Pope, stepping down. "Hard to believe isn't it? But it's true. She made a phone call to them just after five this morning. It seems that these three are Tracey's knights in shining armour. And they're going to take her off our hands. Isn't that right, Parker?"

Pope's eyes burned into Martha's with a white-hot intensity. Martha held her ground though, she wasn't about to be bullied by the detective any longer. As much as she was worried about Tracey and more than a little unsettled by her, she still thought more of her than Pope.

"Where is she?" she asked. "We're here to take her home."

"Yes," said Pope. "I'm sure you are. How does the old saying go again? Thick as thieves, is it?"

"We wouldn't know," said Geri. "Since none of us are thieves, detective."

Pope curled the corner of her thin lips into a smile. She wheezed a little before eying each of the Parker sisters in turn.

"Fine," she said. "You want her, you can have her. But mark my words. Whatever you lot are covering up for her, I'm going to get to the bottom of it. Understand me?"

Nobody said anything. Eventually Pope took the hint and turned away. Martha breathed a little easier now that the detective wasn't shoved right up in her face.

The sisters followed Pope at a safe distance. They were going to get Tracey Coulthard and take her home. In, out and away—it was simple. So why did Martha feel so uncomfortable?

Twenty-Two

POPE LED THE three Parker sisters through the police station and down towards the cells. She was uptight, tense, her shoulders stiff. Martha could tell she was under a lot of stress. The muscles in the back of her neck looked taut. They could have supported a flyover they were so tense.

Martha couldn't really begin to imagine what it was like to be in Pope's position. She'd spent the past few days worrying about Tracey Coulthard and how there was a killer on the loose. But that was the first time it had ever happened to her. Ordinarily her cases were much more sedate, tranquil even.

For Pope though, this was all part of the day job. Murderers, thieves, general villains, they were all cause for concern for the law. And the law in these parts appeared to be Pope.

Martha wondered how she felt now. She wondered what was going through that pale, oily haired head of hers. Maybe she had been too hard on the detective. Maybe she should have tried to be a little more sympathetic, to try and help, not hinder the official investigations.

Pope swiped her identity card on a panel next to a door. It swung open and the detective stood to one side.

"She's in there," she said. "Get her and get lost. And don't skip the country, we might still need you – *all.*"

Martha's thoughts of sympathy were immediately diminished. She decided it was Pope's manner and demeanour that made it so hard to like her. Stern and bitter, all of the time, it wasn't very personable.

"Thank you," she said, passing the cop. "Where is she?"

"Where she's always been," said Pope. "Wallowing in her cell crying and shouting. Do me a favour Parker, have a word with her when you can. The spoiled little rich kid routine works fine when you're twelve years old, not when you're a fully grown woman. It's birds like her who give us a bad name."

Martha couldn't argue with that. She nodded politely and stepped beyond the security door with Helen and Geri. A policeman stood on guard next to the open door of a cell. When the sisters approached he retreated.

"All yours," he said, passing them.

"Thanks," said Geri.

The sisters stopped at the open cell door. Tracey Coulthard sat on her own on the edge of her bed. Her head was tipped forward, long hair covering her face. Her sinewy little arms looked white in the cold light of the place. Martha thought, very briefly, that she might even be a ghost. It was only when she spoke that those fears were extinguished.

"You're here," she said.

"Yes, we're here to pick you up," said Martha, stepping into the cell. "Are you ready to go?"

"Ready. To go?" Tracey looked up. "I shouldn't have been here in the first place Parker. I told you, didn't I. I *told* you I didn't kill him."

"Yes, yes, you told me," Martha said nervously. "Now please, Tracey, let's get you out of here. You don't want to say anything that might… that might make things complicated."

"Complicated," she laughed. "Complicated she says. How much more complicated do you think this can get?"

"Oh Tracey," Martha said, looking at the ceiling. "That's a question I've been asking myself on an hourly basis. Believe me."

"Yes, well, I'm sure you have," spat Tracey. "You've had plenty of time to do it, moving around, walking about as a *free* woman. All the while I've been stuck in here. Do you have any idea what it's been like for me? Do you know what it *feel*s like to be treated like a common criminal? Do you? Do you!"

"Oh shut up, you mad fruit bat," Geri snapped.

Martha wasn't sure who was the most shocked at the outburst – herself or Tracey. The young woman stood up and pushed the hair from her face. She revealed a gaunt, grey complexion, eyes ringed with red.

"Excuse me?" she said, marching towards Geri. "Who do you think you are talking to me like that?"

"Oh give over would you!" Geri fired back. "You've treated us like dirt since the moment we first met. Get off your high horse love, we're trying to help."

"I've been locked up!" Tracey screamed. "They're saying I killed, *murdered*, my husband!"

"Yeah, yeah, we know. Not that you'd ever let us forget about it."

"I'm the victim here!"

"Victim of your own snotty attitude maybe, that's about it."

"How dare you!"

"Look, both of you need to calm down," said Martha, stepping in between them. "Remember where you are. There's an army of policemen and women upstairs and they've got *more* than enough between their teeth to try and lock us all away for a very, very long time. So please, *please*, I'm begging you all to just knock it off until we get out of here!"

Silence ensued. The four women stood looking at each other. Martha was breathing hard. She could feel her own anger welling up but she knew she had to stay focussed, for all of their sakes. Tracey's bony little shoulders were bobbing up and down as she fumed with the world and everybody in it. Across from her Geri looked bored, thoroughly fed up with everything.

Then there was Helen. The middle Parker sister looked terrified beyond all belief. The fright on her face was like she'd just woken up from a bad nightmare. Martha had to get them all out of there. And she had to do it now.

"Okay," she said. "I think we should all get some fresh air and maybe a cup of tea or something. Calm us all down and we can clear our heads. So Tracey, please, if you're ready, our car is waiting outside."

Tracey paused for a moment, milking the attention for every second she could. When she was satisfied, she stormed past the sisters and out the door.

"Guess that's us then," said Geri. "We wouldn't want to keep Cleopatra waiting would we?"

"Geri, please," said Martha. "Just humour her. We don't have long left. Just upstairs, out to the car and then back to her house. Then we're done, okay?"

"We're done?" asked Helen. "You mean we're not going to, you know, catch the killer."

"We're *done*," said Martha.

She pushed past the others and chased after Tracey. The fierce Mrs Coulthard had reached the end of the row of cells and was approaching Pope. Martha got there just in time to stop the fireworks from erupting.

"Like I said to your friends Mrs Coulthard, don't go hopping on a plane any time soon," said the detective. "This case is far from closed and we still don't fully know what happened to your husband."

"I'm not going anywhere," said Tracey. "And you'll be hearing from my lawyers about this. Wrongful arrest is a very serious crime Pope. My father was a Lord Advocate, but then again you already knew that didn't you."

Martha had to stifle a little cheer. Pope's face was turning more sour by the second. She quite liked seeing the detective put in her place with such authority. For the briefest of moments, Martha felt that she was on the same side as Tracey.

"Is that all?" asked Mrs Coulthard.

"On your way," said Pope.

"Hold on, wait a minute," Helen interrupted them. "We can't go out there, out the front I mean. We'll get torn limb from limb by the journalists and TV crews."

"She's right," said Geri. "Is there a back door to this place? What am I saying? Of course there's a back door."

Pope's bitterness subsided. Instead she looked smug again as she sucked on her inhaler.

"Yeah, there's a back door," she wheezed, coughing a little. "But I'm not letting you use it. You'll just have to fend for yourselves."

Tracey didn't seem to take any notice. She strutted past Pope and started up the stairs. Martha and the others went with her.

"Don't forget to sign out at the *front* desk now will you," Pope called after them. "Can't wait to read what you thought of the place."

Martha's breath was getting short. She thought she could feel the strange strain in her chest again. She ignored it, chasing Tracey up the stairs and out onto the main landing of the police station's lobby.

"Tracey," she called. "Tracey, hold on. Maybe there's another way. Helen's right, we can't go out there, it's mobbed with reporters."

Tracey stopped at the desk. The stressed-out policewoman handed her a form to sign, which she did in a rage. She was given a parcel with her belongings which she left for Martha to collect. Then she made a direct line for the revolving doors on the other side of the lobby.

"Are you even listening to me?" Martha asked. "I'm telling you that the journalists out there will have a field day if you march out right now. Helen's right, they'll tear you limb from limb."

Tracey stopped quickly. She spun around and glared at Helen with her red-raw eyes.

"Do you think I'm stupid?" she spat. "Really? Do you think I'm an idiot? Do you think I'm just some bloody airhead that doesn't know what's going on around me? Do you think I'm that Estelle girl? Do you? Answer me."

"I don't think any of those things Tracey," said Martha. "I think, no, I know, that the moment you step outside that door it's going to be game over. Trial by media. Your world will never be the same again."

Tracey stepped back towards Martha. She was shorter but no less imposing. Keeping her voice low, her sharp little face contorted into a fierce scowl, she made sure Martha heard every word.

"My world is already gone," she said. "It was gone the moment I saw my husband face down in that bath. In fact, it was gone when he proposed to that piece of trash. Perhaps it was already gone the day I said 'I do'. So don't dare lecture me on what I can and can't do Parker. You have no idea what I'm capable of. And you never will."

"Fine," said Martha, feeling her bottom lip tremble. "You do what you like, Tracey. Like you always do. But there's a reason you called me to come and pick you up from here. And I'll bet that reason is you don't have anybody else who's willing to put up with you anymore. So you can keep treating me like something that's stuck to your Louie Buttons or whatever they're called, but I warn you, my sisters and I won't put up with it. We're just about the only friends you've got in this world and I'm warning you that if you step out that door you'll be hounded."

"Don't you think I know that, Parker?" Tracey asked, her face still a picture of anger. "Don't you think I know what's being said about me. What everybody thinks. Who do you think tipped off the press that I was being released?"

"What?" asked Martha.

"It was me, Parker, me. I let them know," she took a step back and held out her arms. "Because I'm nothing but meat to them now, I'm a rolling story, everything I do will be reported until the day I die."

"So why would you bring them here then?" Martha was pleading for answers now. "Why would you openly, willingly even, subject yourself to that?"

Tracey began to cry. The tears rolled down her cheeks but she was still frowning, still looking at Martha like she was the worst person in the world.

"It's the only power I have left," she said, sobbing. "It's the only thing I can control now. I've lost it all. If I can just tell them my story, my way, that's something isn't it? Isn't it?"

Martha didn't answer. She wanted to grab the woman in her arms and hug her tight. But she also wanted to strangle her. How could one person create such a discord, such a total conflict of emotion so easily?

"I'm going to talk to them," said Tracey. "I won't be long. I don't want to have to do any more than is necessary."

Tracey wiped the tears from her eyes. She sniffed and pulled back her hair. She looked so different now, almost like a proper human being. Her skin was still ashen white and she was visibly exhausted. But the ghostliness was gone and she had some life about her.

She took a few deep breaths. Then, pushing her shoulders back, she stepped through the revolving doors of the police station and into the sea of camera flashes.

Martha stood and watched her through the glass, a roar of voices going up as the press unleashed their torrent of questions. She lost sight of Tracey amongst the brightness, but she couldn't help wonder just how broken and damaged the woman had to be to face that wall of question and suspicion willingly.

"She's either really clever or she's mad as a box of frogs," said Helen, sidling up beside Martha.

"I'm going for the last one," said Geri, standing on the other side.

Martha didn't answer them. She wasn't sure what the right answer was.

Twenty-Three

THE CAR PULLED up outside the Coulthard's mansion. Thirty minutes had passed since Tracey had addressed the media but already her words were plastered all over the internet. Geri had been keeping tabs on what had happened the whole journey back to the suburbs.

Martha didn't even try to understand what was going on, she just knew that news like this spread like wildfire in the digital age. With social media and instant accessibility, there was no keeping a secret anymore. Not that Tracey wanted to keep a secret. She seemed to know exactly what she was doing. While Martha didn't agree with the way she was conducting herself, she certainly couldn't find fault in her courage. It took a lot of guts to get up there and tell her story to a pack of rabid journalists. And Tracy had done it with aplomb. And they had listened.

Now they all had to deal with the consequences. The house looked empty. The huge windows were dark and stared down at the street like empty eye-sockets. Even the vast Christmas tree standing outside the door seemed glum and uninterested. This was a house where the life and love had already departed— if indeed it had ever had any of the latter.

"Come in," said Tracey, getting out.

She opened the gates and marched up the driveway. Martha and the others watched her go.

"Should we… you know…" said Helen. "Just drive off."

"We can't do that," said Geri, looking up from her phone. "She knows where we work."

"She doesn't know where we stay though."

"It's the same place," said Martha. "For me, anyway."

"Oh yeah, sorry."

"No, we'll go in."

They got out of the car. Like three frightened children they slowly made their own way up the driveway towards the front door. Tracey had left it open, vanishing inside the huge house. It was cold. The weak winter sun providing no heat. Inside wasn't much better, the house was steeped in darkness—a cavernous pit of draughts and shadow.

"Talk about creepy," said Helen, shivering. "I've seen mortuaries with more life."

Martha puckered her lips. Helen realised what she had said and scratched the back of her curly head.

"Sorry."

"I'm hungry," Tracey called from upstairs. "Make us something to eat will you, Parker."

"Uh. What would you like?" asked Martha, a little confused.

"Anything."

"We're not her servants," said Helen quietly. "I say we get back in the car and get the hell out of Dodge. Let her fend for herself for a change. Where's her batty housekeeper, anyway?"

"She doesn't live-in. And we can't leave Tracey. You know we can't," said Martha. "She's not... she's not stable. I don't think she should be left on her own."

"Why the hell not?"

"Because." Martha's voice echoed about the lobby. She caught herself and shook her head. "Because we can't, I can't have that on my conscience. Look, if you two want to go then fine, take the car. I'll finish things up here and get a cab and meet you later. But I'm not leaving her. She's just out of custody, she's all over the news. That kind of pressure can't be good for somebody so… volatile."

"Parker!" Tracey shouted again. "Make me something to eat, will you?"

"She's volatile alright," said Helen.

"Fine. We're not going anywhere," said Geri. "But I think you guys should take a look at what those journalists are saying about Mrs Coulthard's little impromptu press conference."

She angled her phone between Martha and Geri. The news feed was filled with pictures of Tracey standing outside the police station. There were a dozen different headlines each detailing what the freshly widowed Mrs Coulthard had said. Maintaining her innocence, stressing she hadn't been charged and vowing to clear her name. It had been a strangely simple message as it turned out, Martha was impressed.

"Banker millionaire widow, Tracey Coulthard, pleads her innocence in dramatic display of emotion?" asked Martha, reading the last one out. "That's a bit over the top, isn't it?"

"News sells," said Geri. "Especially if it sounds dramatic. They've even started digging into us a little."

"What? How?" asked Helen. "What are they saying? Let me see."

"It's nothing," said Geri calmly. "They've just done a little profile of the agency. Actually, it might be quite good for business. Murder, suspected killer wives, you can't buy that sort of publicity."

Martha wasn't sure she agreed. She ignored it for the time being and walked towards the kitchen. At least she knew what to do there. Cooking was easy, it was mind-numbing, she didn't have to think about it too hard.

A quick rummage through the cupboards and pantry and she had the basics of a spaghetti Bolognese on the go. She wasn't particularly hungry herself, but she knew that if Tracey ate it she would be at least be full for a while.

The lady of the house didn't appear until it was ready. And when she did finally grace the others with her presence, she did it in her usual overly-dramatic style.

Dressed in a very thin, black silk gown, she glided into the kitchen. Her hair was back down over her face and the folds of her robe were dangerously plunging. She stalked around the kitchen, Martha, Helen and Geri staring at her with every step. Settling at the head of the table, she remained silent, waiting to be served.

"Yes, hello to you too, your highness," said Geri.

Tracey didn't respond. She sat perfectly still and stared straight ahead, her eyes unmoving behind her long strands of hair.

"I assume you're still hungry," said Martha, dishing out the food. "You know, I used to make this for these two when they were younger. We'd have it during the summer holidays, do you remember, ladies?"

"Yes, I do," said Helen. "When you were back home from uni."

"Didn't we used to have it like three days in a row?" laughed Geri.

"I used to make loads of it. It always tasted better on the second day, anyway. Remanded, that's what mum used to call it. Remanded Bolognese."

"By the third day, it must have had fur on it," said Helen. "I'm still surprised none of us got Botulism from that."

"Don't be daft, it was only mince and pasta," said Martha, serving her sisters. "And anyway, from what I remember, you always used to wolf it down."

"I was a teenager, Martha, I was getting a free meal. I'd have eaten your arm if it had been on the plate."

Martha laughed warmly. She dished out a small portion for herself and sat down at the table. There was, at last, a little warmth in the house.

"Where's May?" asked Geri.

Tracey shrugged her shoulders. Martha was surprised that the housekeeper wasn't about. She'd seemed like a permanent fixture in the Coulthard's house.

"She does what she likes," said Tracey. "She has her own life to lead. I can't tell her what to do."

"No, you just do that to us," said Helen.

"And you're getting well paid for that, no?" said Tracey spitefully.

"Hey, we were paid to do a job, and we've done it, thank you very much. You should be a little more grateful that we're still hanging around."

"Oh yes, grateful. Sorry, I forgot," said Tracey, pushing the hair from her face. "I'm grateful that my husband is dead. I'm grateful that I found out he had proposed to another woman. I'm grateful for the fact I've spent the past few days being detained and questioned by police on suspicion of his murder. And I'm grateful, of course, that you three are still gracious enough to keep me entertained with your parochial childhood memories. Yes, I'm grateful Miss Parker, I am the very picture of gratitude."

Helen had gone a little red. She concentrated on her plate of Bolognese rather than meet the daggers from Tracey. Martha cleared her throat to try and catch Tracey's attention.

"We know you've been through the wringer Tracey, Helen knows that, so do I," she said. "But we've been doing our best to help."

"Have you indeed?" sneered Tracey. "And what have you done to help me, Parker? Have you employed and notified my lawyers? Have you started a petition to order my release? Have you made arrangements for my husband's funeral? Please, tell me ladies, what exactly *have* you done to help me?"

Martha clenched her fists beneath the table. She was angry—angry that Tracey wouldn't show, couldn't show even the smallest bit of appreciation. She was so angry that her toes curled in her trainers.

"That's not what you hired us to do, remember?"

"You're just like everybody else," Tracey snapped. "You let me down, everybody does eventually. It's a common thread throughout my life. I'm not surprised you've done it too."

And just like that Martha's animosity was gone. She looked at the fragile little woman at the head of the table. Gone was all of her hate and spitefulness. Suddenly she was another daughter for Martha to look after. A lonely woman caught up in a world she hadn't asked for and didn't want anything to do with. She was alone, and frightened, and determined not to let herself be swallowed up by her circumstances.

Could Martha really blame her for being so bitter? What would she do if she were put in that position? Her fists unclenched, as did her toes. She did her best to stave off a sudden rush of tears too.

"If you feel that we've let you down, I'm sorry," said Martha. "But do you know something? We're still here. We're *still* here. And as far as I can see, we're the only ones."

Tracey's cheek twitched. She remained otherwise perfectly statue-like, but a relaxation washed across her face. Martha thought that maybe, just maybe, she had struck a nerve with her employer. She hoped so, she really did.

"I'm tired," said Tracey, getting up from the table. "I've not slept in what feels like months. I'm going to bed."

She glided across the kitchen again.

"Won't you please eat something?" asked Martha. "You said you were hungry, you could have just a couple of mouthfuls, you know, to keep your strength up."

"Alright, mum," whispered Geri.

"No," said Tracey. "I've gone right off the thought of food. I'm going to bed."

She moved towards the door. Martha, Helen and Geri followed her, leaving their plates behind.

"Tracey," Martha called after her. "Would you like us to stay? We don't mind keeping you company, you know, until you can get things in order."

Tracey stared at the three of them like they were from outer space. She let out a snort that was something vaguely like a laugh.

"No, thank you," she said. "I told you, Parker. I'm going to sleep. Goodnight."

"Yes, of course," said Martha. "But just one more thing, before you go."

Tracey sighed loudly. She let her head fall back, revealing her slender neck and pointed chin. She clenched her teeth tightly together, stretching the tendons in her gaunt cheeks.

"What is it?" she asked. "I'm *very* tired. I don't have the patience for your tiresome questions."

Martha cleared her throat. She could feel her stomach knotting already. What she was about to ask was dangerous and she feared a severe backlash. But she knew she had to ask it, otherwise this whole venture would be a waste of time.

"Yes, I know," she said. "But it's important Tracey. I need you to think very hard about what I'm about to ask you. Don't just jump straight in, take some time if you need to."

She paused, preparing herself as much as she was fighting back the little voice in her head that told her this was a bad idea. When Tracey looked at her with those cold, venomous eyes, she took the plunge.

"Your husband, Gordon, he was murdered Tracey, you know that don't you?" she said.

"Seriously?" Tracey asked. "That's your question? Are you stupid?"

"I know, I know," said Martha, patting the air to placate Tracey. "What I'm saying is, Gordon was murdered, you *know* that. But what we don't know is *who* did it. Even the police don't know that. That's why you weren't charged. That's why you're here now."

"Your statement of the obvious astounds me, Parker," Tracey sneered. "It's a small wonder there are so many unsolved crimes in the world with the likes of you here to investigate."

Martha's patience was wearing thin again. She fought the urge to snap and kept going.

"What we need to know, do you have any ideas, any ideas at all, who might have wanted to do this to your husband?"

"How can you ask me that?" said Tracey. "Do *you* have any idea what I've just been through?

"Yes, I do Tracey, but I need to ask."

"Do you think I'd keep something like that a secret?"

"No, I don't, but we're desperate here. I know you're angry with Gordon, but that doesn't mean we can just let his killer off scot free," desperation had crept into Martha's voice. "So I'm asking you—I'm *begging* you—please think. Just think. Who would do something like this to Gordon?"

To everyone's surprise, Tracey didn't immediately strike back with a torrent of derision. She sneered a little, but Martha could see that she was mulling things over. As fragile and worrisome as this woman was, she was also incredibly intelligent. Even if she did have a low estimation of the sisters, she wasn't stupid enough not to realise they were on her side.

"There's nobody," she said at last. "Nobody he knew would do something this bad to him. He had plenty of enemies in the bank. Who wouldn't though? He was a very powerful man. He was tipped for greatness, all the way to the top. That paints a target on your back. But I doubt any of them would have the balls to kill him. Not like that."

"Why not?" asked Martha.

"You obviously don't know bankers, Parker," she said, slowly. "In my experience they're all talk and no trousers. And believe me, they talk a good game but when it comes to action they don't have the guts to follow it through. I was married to one, remember. I know what they're like."

"So it could have been a stranger then?" asked Helen. "You think somebody had broken into the flat before we all arrived?"

"It's a possibility," said Tracey. "Although I highly doubt Gordon would have tried to fight them. He was a coward, fiercely so. If there was a chance he'd be in a fight, he would throw money at the situation, sometimes literally. No, my late husband was not the physical type, even though he played rugby."

"Rugby?" asked Martha. "Gordon played rugby. As in he *still* played rugby?"

"Every Saturday morning," said Tracey. "There's a study down the hall he lavishly called his trophy room. More like his ego polishing pit. You can have a look if you like, it's just cups and medals gathering dust from a lifetime of pretending he was good at sport."

"But he still played?" asked Helen. "He was still actively playing in matches."

"I said so, didn't I? Every Saturday." Tracey hissed. "I don't know if he actually played. He might have been with *her* then, who knows. But occasionally he'd come home with a split lip or a black eye. Bloody stupid, an imbecile—he'd spend the rest of the weekend worrying what they'd say about it in the bank on Monday."

Martha rubbed her chin. Her mind was forming those familiar spider diagrams again. Her tiredness was being chased away by the thrill of the case again. This was progress, she thought, they were finally making headway.

"May we see those trophies and prizes?" she asked. "Would that be okay?"

"I couldn't care less," said Tracey. "Like I said, they were meaningless to me, trinkets of a life he lived away from me. Why would I care about that?"

"You were his wife," said Geri bitterly. "You must have had *something* you both enjoyed?"

A wry smile crept onto Tracey's lips. She stepped out of the door and walked slowly towards the bowels of the house.

"Money," she said, over her shoulder as she departed. And then she was gone.

Twenty-Four

TRACEY HADN'T BEEN lying; Gordon really did like to collect all his old trophies. Martha, Helen and Geri stood in the middle of the room and tried to take it all in.

"Wow, this guy sure did think highly of himself," whistled Helen. "I mean, I've heard of a God complex, but this is taking it to a whole new level."

Martha couldn't disagree. The room was dimly lit, filled with large flat screen TVs, couches and a pool table. There were huge cabinets lining the walls, filled with medals, awards and trophies.

There were pictures too, mostly of Gordon and what looked like friends and family. There was a graduation photo, images of him alongside others on days out, after matches, covered in mud but always smiling. It was a side to the man that Martha would never have thought existed.

To her, he was all flash suits, fast cars and living a perpetual, adolescent lifestyle. He was a man who had cheated on his wife in the most dramatic fashion, and didn't seem to care. He'd throw money in the way of any problems he had because he could and the world just had to react.

But that wasn't the man shown in this room. In here, his private quarters, he was a human being. Martha felt a little numb at that thought. It made it harder to accept that he was dead. Worse still, he had been murdered.

"Talk about a man cave," said Geri, skimming a ball around the pool table. "I mean, this whole place reeks of overcompensating, does it not?"

"What's a man cave?" asked Helen.

"What's a man cave? Are you serious?"

Martha didn't know either. But she was happy for Helen to take the flack for being out of touch on this occasion.

"Whatever it is, this place doesn't look much like a cave to me," said Helen. "In fact I'm pretty sure this room is bigger than my whole flat. And that TV over there is probably *taller* than the building."

She waved at the massive screen that dominated the far wall. Geri was laughing. She put her hands on her hips and cocked her head towards the TV.

"Yup, definitely over compensating."

"We've got work to do," said Martha. "Come on, stop messing around. Have a look around, check out those pictures."

"What are we looking for?" asked Helen.

"Anything, everything. Something that might give us a clue about who Gordon Coulthard was," said Martha. "If we can find out what he was like, the company he kept—other than Estelle—then we might be able to work out just what the hell happened to him."

The sisters split up. They each took a third of the huge room and began raking through the drawers. Martha picked up and looked at every trophy that was stacked on the high shelves. Helen poured through the certificates, the awards papers, searching the drawers and looking for clues.

Geri started taking the pictures out of their frames and checking their backs. She leafed through photo albums and made sure she'd checked every image there was.

Soon the room was a total mess. Pictures, papers, everything was strewn about the floor, the couches and the pool table. Martha wouldn't have minded, but they still hadn't found anything.

"Bugger," she said, rolling her shoulders. "Did you get anything?"

"Nope," said Helen. "He was a high achiever, that's about it. But I swear if I see another swimming certificate or badge of honour I might go loopy."

"Geri?"

"He liked to take pictures of himself," she said, cracking her knuckles. "Well, with other people too, but I don't see anything out of the ordinary. There's Christmas pictures, birthday photos, winning big matches, holidays to the sunshine, everything really. It's kind of sad, when you think about it."

"What is?" asked Martha.

"It's just like, here's this guy's life, strewn about the place. That's it, nothing else can ever be added to it. Makes you think, you know?"

Martha didn't want to think about that. She was having a hard enough time without falling foul to sentiment as well.

"What about you?" asked Helen.

"The same," she answered. "He kept everything, down to the medals from when he was a schoolboy. There was even a cup he won when he was in primary school. Quite something."

"But not anything useful," Helen sat cross-legged on the pool table.

She steepled her fingers and rocked gently back and forth. Martha knew that look, it was one of total concentration. She pushed herself off the nearest cabinet and walked over to her sister.

"What?" she asked.

"What what?" replied Helen, her eyes closed to slits.

"You're thinking."

"No I'm not."

"Yes, you are," said Geri, joining the others. "You always sit cross-legged when you're thinking. It's your trademark."

"I don't have any trademarks," said Helen, continuing to rock. "I'm not a bloomin' cartoon character you know."

"What are you thinking?" asked Martha. "Come on, you wouldn't be doing this if you didn't think you were on to something."

"Maybe," said Helen.

"Come on Helen, please," said Martha. "We could really, *really* do with a break on this case."

She wasn't exaggerating. The mess around the place, the pictures of Gordon, Tracey's distress, the press presence… Martha's emotional burden was bordering on the impossible to bear.

"Okay," said Helen, clapping her hands together. "Take a look around you and tell me what you see."

"A bloody tip," said Geri.

"And what else?"

Martha was out of ideas. Geri looked tired and uninterested. Helen took to her stage.

"We've got a man here who quite obviously loved to be adored," said Helen. "Look at this place. It's a shrine to his achievements, going all the way back to when he was a little boy. Doesn't that tell you something about him? About her upstairs? About what he was doing with that Estelle girl?"

"What?" asked Martha.

"He's lonely, he's always been lonely," said Helen. "And his achievements, though plentiful, have always been hard fought and, thus, cherished. He quite obviously just wanted to be appreciated."

"By who?"

"By anybody. Look."

She bent down and rummaged through a pile of photos. She found one of Gordon and what looked like his parents.

"Mum and Dad," she said, reading the back.

She pulled another one out. This time he was among a group of twelve young people all in graduation robes.

"Pals and peers," said Helen.

Then she grabbed another one. She held it up to the light so Martha and Geri could see it properly. It was Gordon, hoisted up on the shoulders of a group of rugby teammates. They were celebrating, shouting, cheering, hailing Coulthard as the hero. Martha had never seen a look of such glee, such contentment on a person's face as she did on Gordon's in that picture.

"His rugby team," said Helen. "After a big match, they're the champions, and Gordon is at the centre of it all."

"So what does that all mean?" asked Geri. "The guy liked to be loved, so what, who doesn't. Are you saying all these people are suspects because he was a bit too much? They had to shut him up from his constant attention seeking?"

"No," said Helen, tutting. "Don't you ever pay attention, Geri? Honestly, I hope your retention is better at university than it is at work."

"What are you saying Helen?" asked Martha, before the sniping could get going in earnest.

Helen laid the picture of the rugby team down on the pool table. She stood up properly and pointed down at Gordon.

"I'm saying that he was a man who liked to do the most he could to be part of the crowd, to fit in," she started. "And if that's the case, you're going to do things you don't necessarily want to do, just to belong, to get along. So what happens when you get into a position of power, of wealth, of both? You stop doing those things, you stop playing up to the crowd and you start to get your revenge. Make sense?"

"Well, I suppose so," said Martha. "And you think Gordon Coulthard decided that when he was rich and powerful he was going to turn on all these people?"

"I'm not saying he did, not to all of them," said Helen. "It would only take a few, a choice few, those who had really pissed him off. Revenge can be a strong motivator. If you're a guy who's had to say 'yes sir, no sir', for long enough, surely when you get to a position of wealth and status, you'll want to make the most of it."

"But what's that got to do with these photos?" asked Geri. "He had a God complex, so what? That's a pretty self-centered lifestyle but is it enough to be killed for?"

"No, of course it isn't," said Helen loudly. "But it's enough to paint a target on your back. A pretty big one, just like Tracey said."

Martha let out a long breath. She stared down at the rugby photo on the pool table. She looked at the faces all around Gordon. They were smiling too, battered, bruised but happy. Then she spotted something.

"Do you remember what I said about Coulthard's brain injury?" asked Helen. "I said his head injury would have killed him whether he'd drowned or not. Do you remember what I said caused that kind of injury?"

"Yeah, Pope said it," Geri clicked her fingers. "A car crash, something with a shed load of force right?"

"Yes, an awful lot of force like a car crash. Now, if I remember correctly, I remember reading about some study in the states that said there's an increased risk for these types of injuries in high contact sports. American football is a big one but I don't see why rugby wouldn't be just as bad."

"Hell it could be worse," said Geri. "They don't wear any helmets."

Martha could hear her sisters but she wasn't acknowledging them. She was bent over the pool table, staring down at the photo. When Helen and Geri realised their sister wasn't paying attention they turned to her.

"Eh, Martha?" asked Geri. "Are we boring you or something?"

"What? No, of course you're not," she said, lifting up the picture. "It's just, I've noticed something here, something very, very interesting that might just—*just*—be a clue."

"Oh yeah?" asked Helen. "And what's that?"

Martha pointed to one of the men beside Gordon. He was sweaty and covered in mud, with a large black eye. His face was almost obscured with all the filth, but he was just about recognisable.

"Is that...?" Geri began.

"Mal," Helen blurted.

"That's right," said Martha. "Mal, Gordon's friend, his work colleague and your dancing partner from what I recall."

"Eh?"

Martha didn't have time to explain. The sound of the doorbell echoed in through the open door. The three sisters looked at each other, equally confused as to who it could be.

They hurried from the room, Martha tucking the picture into her pocket, and headed down the hallway. When they reached the front door they could see two large, dark figures standing on the other side of the frosted glass. Martha went to open the door but Helen stopped her.

"What are you doing?" she asked.

"We don't know who it is?" said her sister. "They could be anyone."

"Don't be ridiculous. We're not going to know until we open it are we?"

"Helen's right," whispered Geri. "I mean, don't you remember what you said to Tracey? There's a killer on the loose out there. Who's to say they won't want to finish her off. Or us too?"

Martha was about to protest. Then a shudder of frightening realisation made her tense.

"Who is it?" she called out loudly.

The dark blobs moved a little. They knocked on the door again.

"It's the police," came a gruff voice. "Open up."

"Police? What do you want?" Geri yelled.

"Open this door right now. Or we'll kick it in."

"We better do what he says," said Helen.

Martha cautiously unlocked the door. She pulled it open to reveal two tall, uniformed officers standing on the porch. They weren't happy, scowling at Martha from beneath their snow tipped caps.

"Who are you?" asked one of the cops.

"Never mind who we are. What are you two doing here?" asked Geri.

"We're here to guard the owner of this house," said the other policeman. "Tracey Coulthard. Is she home?"

"She's upstairs," said Helen. "Sleeping, we think."

"You think?"

"Yes, we think, officer, that's what I said."

"Protect her?" asked Martha. "Or make sure she doesn't go anywhere?"

She looked over their shoulders. There was a squad car parked at the end of the driveway, its blue lights still flashing. If Martha hadn't known any better she would have thought it was blocking the way out as well as in.

"She's a person of interest," said one of the policemen. "We've been assigned to give her twenty-four-hour protection and observation. So you can be on your way, if you like."

"Now hold on just a minute," said Geri, shuffling to the front.

Martha grabbed her by the arm.

"Great," Martha said, all too cheerily. "Thanks officers."

She shoved her bemused sister out of the front door and pulled Helen along with them. The three of them quickly trundled down the driveway, past the squad car. They climbed into Martha's motor and caught their breaths.

"Cops man," grumbled Geri. "They just come in and push us little guys about the place. You shouldn't have given in to them, Mart."

"I don't care about the cops," said Martha, starting the car. "In fact, I'm glad they're here. It means Tracey won't get up to anything untoward while we're gone."

"Where are we going this time?" droned Helen. "And if it's any answer other than bed then I'm going to be hugely disappointed."

"We're going to talk to a friend," said Martha. "And we're going to get some answers."

The snow started to fall a little heavier as she pulled the car out into the street. The clouds above were gathering over the city, bringing with them the early sunset and the night afterwards.

Martha knew it was going to be a long one. She could feel it already, her bones were aching, her heart was thumping, she was preparing to go back into battle. She had to be at her very best. There was going to be one shot at this, just one chance. If she didn't get it right, there would be consequences. And that terrified Martha Parker beyond anything she had ever known.

Twenty-Five

"HOW CAN YOU find somebody's home address on the internet?" Martha asked Geri, trying to keep her eyes on the road. "Isn't that private information?"

"Oh please Martha, listen to yourself would you?" said Geri sarcastically. "You're starting to sound like mum."

"I'm sounding like mum because it's a *serious* question."

"Have you never heard of a phone book Martha?" Helen chimed in from the back.

"Of course I have."

"Well it's the exact same as that."

"It's not really though, is it?"

"Why not?" said Geri. "You would have just looked up somebody's name in the big directory book and there you go, number, address, postcode, the works."

"But you had to opt in to that, it was a choice," said Martha. "At least with that there was a chance any old Tom, Dick or Harry wouldn't stumble across where you lived, what you did and what you had for your breakfast last Tuesday."

"Oh please, don't talk about food," moaned Helen. "That Bolognese you made is sitting right in the middle of my chest. I feel like I've got a brick crushing my windpipe."

Martha sped along the road. She didn't know where she was going. She was relying on Geri guiding them to their final destination. Feeling and sounding like a technophobe wasn't really her, she knew just how valuable and vital the modern world was to her work. There were still some things, however, that didn't sit quite right with her.

"Here we go," said Geri. "Malcolm Edwards, 76 Derrylee Road."

"Sounds nice," said Helen. "Wait, Dairylea? Isn't that a cheese?"

"Are you sure that's him?" said Martha, ignoring her sister.

"Hey, haven't we been through all this before," Geri sounded angry. "You know, when you question if I'm right about something, we argue and then you refuse to grovel when it turns out, as always, I'm right on the money!"

"It *is* him, right?" said Helen. "Like, you couldn't have made a mistake or anything."

"No. It's him. I'm friends with him."

Martha slammed the brakes on the car. It squealed to a halt, the smell of burnt rubber wafting in through the heating grills.

"You're *what?*" she asked.

"I'm friends with him, yeah"

"You're *friends* with Mal Edwards, Gordon Coulthard's mate and you haven't told us. What were you *thinking?*"

"Bloody hell, Martha," said Geri, steadying herself. "Relax would you?"

"Relax?"

Horns and honking rang out from behind them. Drivers flashed their lights at the car that had stopped for no reason in the middle of the road. Martha ignored them all. She had eyes only for her sister.

"What do you mean you're friends with him? Didn't you think to share that with us? Geri, do you have any idea what this means? You could be implicated, you could be compromised, you could be... it could be... complicated."

"Would you please relax," said Geri. "I'm serious, you and that dodgy ticker of yours, I'm not taking you back to the hospital when you keel over again."

"Do you want to explain yourself?" the oldest sister said venomously.

"I'm friends with him, yeah," said Geri. "But only on social media."

Martha had to think quickly. Sure she was getting older and she hadn't had much sleep. But she had to think what all of that meant.

"Social media? As in the internet?"

"Yes caveman, on the internet," Geri said with a smile.

"But… but you're still *friends* with him, though. Doesn't that mean, you know, you *know* him?"

"Oh come *on* Martha, you've got to be kidding me," Geri reclined in her seat. "Is she being serious, Helen? Are we really having this conversation, in the middle of the road, while gridlock forms behind us?"

"Answer me, Geri," Martha yelled.

Geri flinched. She sat up, blinking, a look of mild fright on her face. She wasn't used to Martha being so angry with her.

"Calm down, Martha," said Helen, touching her sister's shoulder. "Just take it easy would you? Geri's not friends with Mal in the traditional sense."

"What are you talking about? She just said she was."

"No, that's not how it works, not anymore," Helen explained. "You can be 'friends' on social media but that doesn't mean you know the person, or have even met them. It's just a phrase, terminology."

"You're not *friends* with him then?" she said. "You don't know him, socially?"

"No, of course I don't," said Geri. "But I added him as a friend on social media to get some more info, a bit of insider knowledge. I wasn't expecting him to accept me but he did, the dirty bugger, just after the party. Look, I can see his photos, where he goes, what he likes, everything."

She flashed the screen at Martha and scrolled up and down. Mal was there, along with pictures, bands and films she'd never heard of. The panic was starting to settle, replaced with relief.

"You had me going there for a moment," she said. "I thought you'd been keeping something *big* from me. And after the past few days I've had, Geri, I don't think I could have taken that kind of shock."

"That'll be why you almost blew my head off with the hairdryer treatment then," said Geri.

Martha kicked the car back into gear and pulled off. They were followed by a hail of horns, honks and hand gestures, but at least they were moving again.

"So you're friends with him on social media," said Martha, as if reiterating it would make it more real. "Nothing more."

"Nothing more, Martha, honestly, nothing more. Although I can't say the same for Helen."

"What?" said Helen in the back.

"Her antics are in the past now," said Martha. "We're looking at the here and now Geri. Tell me where we're going."

"Well, I've cross-referenced all his details and I think I've got his address. It's down by the river, in those plush new flats that overlook the old dock yards."

"I told you it sounded nice," said Helen.

"Great, another plush flat," said Martha. "Last time we were in one of those, we found a dead body."

"Hey, our luck has to change at some point, right?" Geri said chirpily.

Martha skipped lanes, heading through the inner city towards the river.

The areas along the Clyde were unrecognisable from their former shipbuilding glory. Where once the river had been lined with cranes and the skeletons of great freighters and boats in the process of being put together, now it was bare. The yards were almost all gone and in their place tall, glossy-looking flats and residential blocks. Balconies looked out across the river and the city, flash cars were parked in the garages and underground bays.

Martha grew up hearing about the death of that industry and everything that had gone along with it. She remembered being taken to see the cranes and being a little frightened of them. Images of those huge iron animals marching across the landscape had stuck with her all these years.

The land had been flattened, old tenements and streets completely wiped out. The ground had been empty and desolate for years, forgotten by almost everybody. That was until some bright spark saw an opportunity to make the area great again. The flats had sprung up and whole new blocks, streets and lanes had been created. People were flocking back to the Clyde again, to live, not work. And the region was thriving.

It had become very trendy for the city's wealthy young professionals. People like Gordon Coulthard and Malcolm Edwards and their partners. They were the new breed of Clyde-siders—a million miles away from the dirt, sweat and toil of their predecessors.

The tops of the buildings loomed large on the horizon. Swish flats with stylish facades appeared like a set of veneered teeth against the weak light. Martha gripped the steering wheel a little tighter, mentally preparing to go into battle.

"Can I ask you two something?" Helen piped up. "Do we *really* think that Mal had something to do with Gordon's murder?"

It was a question Martha wasn't sure she'd even wanted to ask, let alone answer.

"We're not accusing him of anything, yet," Martha said curtly. "We're just going to ask him some questions. We're trying to find out more about Gordon Coulthard, remember. What kind of man he was, who might want to cause him harm? One thing I've noticed about this case, there's been precious little in the way of people actually knowing who Gordon really was."

"Especially his wife," Geri said.

"Yes, well, Mal's his oldest friend, as far as we know. If he doesn't know him properly, no one will."

"So we're just asking him then," said Helen. "I mean, we're not going in there all guns blazing, trying to make a citizen's arrest or anything"

Geri twisted in her seat. She threw a suspicious look at her sister.

"If I didn't know better, I'd say you were nervous Helen," she said.

"What? Nervous? Me? Don't be ridiculous," Helen fumbled with her hands. "Why would I be nervous? We're going to interview a perp. I've done that dozens of times before."

"Yeah but you've never been up dancing on a table with one of them before," she giggled.

"I don't know what you're talking about."

"I think you do," said Geri. "I think you remember a lot more from that party than you're letting on."

"There's going to be none of that," said Martha sternly. "No flirting, no handing out numbers and certainly no dates coming out of this meeting. We're going in there, as *professionals*, and we're going to conduct an interview. That's all."

Geri turned back around and faced the windscreen. She clicked her phone off and smiled wryly.

"Spoil sport," she said.

"I'm not a spoil sport Geri, I'm a realist. We're here to do a serious job."

"Yes I know, you're still a spoil sport though," she said. "And besides, you never know, maybe using my technique of interviewing would be better than yours."

"And what does that remark mean?" asked Martha.

"Oh I don't know. I just thought, maybe, if Helen turned on the charm, gave a couple of pouts here and there and batted her eyelashes, we might get a bit more out of Mr Edwards without him even knowing it."

"Eh, you two do realise I'm sitting right here don't you," said Helen from the back. "We tried that before and look what happened. I ended up with a hangover that felt like the whole of existence was crushing my head."

"True, this is very true," said Geri. "But there won't be a drink in sight this time. And you'll have us two to back you up."

"No," said Martha. "Out of the question, it's too dangerous."

"Nonsense," said Geri, hopping up and down. "It's perfect. Helen does a bit of flirting, Mal pours his heart out and we get what we want. Piece of cake. It'll be over before you know it."

"No, I'm not allowing it Geri, that's final," said Martha.

"Come on Martha, just think about it would you?"

"Wait. Don't I get a say in this?" asked Helen.

"Be quiet Helen, I'm trying to convince our sister that this is a good idea."

"No, I'm not risking it, Geri," Martha said. "We've got one shot at this. Mal Edwards could be the key to unlocking who Gordon Coulthard's killer is. If we scare him off or make a right pig's ear of this then we'll be in big trouble."

"Eh, excuse me?" said Helen. "When you two are finished debating what *I'm* supposed to be doing, do you want to let me know so I can tell you what *I* think?"

Martha tightened her lips. Geri folded her arms in a huff.

"Great, thank you," said Helen. "Now the way I see it, Martha's right."

Geri went to protest but Helen stopped her. She held up her hand and quietened down her younger sister.

"Yes, we've got one chance at this and yes, we don't want to make a right royal mess of it," she started. "And I'm the first to admit that my flirting could more closely resemble a rain dance or something out of a zombie movie."

Both Martha and Geri laughed. A little of the tension eased away as they edged closer to the stylish flats by the river.

"But—and I hate to say this—I also think Geri has a point. A very good point actually," Helen continued. "We've been playing this straight the whole time. Maybe it's time we tried something new, something a bit different. I know you're worried Martha and I know you've only got my best interests at heart. I love you for that, but I really think if we want to make progress and nail this case, we're going to have to think and act a little outside the box."

The address Geri had found appeared on a wall as they sped by. Martha threw the car off the main road and into the gated complex of the block of flats. The looming, white tower block stood tall, reaching up towards the darkening sky.

She stopped the car and peered upwards towards the top through the windscreen. She swallowed, a bad taste forming in the back of her throat.

"I don't like this," she said. "I don't like this one bit."

"No, I know you don't," said Geri. "But Helen's right. What we've been doing so far is getting us nowhere. We've got to start making progress if we want to get old crazy Tracey off the hook. You know those cops weren't just there to protect her. They're keeping her under a dubious and probably illegal house arrest."

"Pope's work no doubt," said Helen.

Martha shook her head. She clenched her hand and thumped her knuckles gently off the steering wheel.

"I don't like this," she said, again. "I'm meant to protect you two. I'm meant to keep you out of harm's way. Now look at us. We're about to head into this man's flat and try to trick him into telling us who killed his best friend. That's not what a good big sister does."

"Oh Martha," said Helen, smiling. "That's *exactly* what a good big sister does."

"Yeah," said Geri. "How many other people can say their sister trusts them enough to let them do something like this? I mean, in a roundabout way, you're actually probably an exemplary big sister."

Martha sniffed. She rubbed the end of her nose on the tatty sleeve of her cardigan. She looked at Helen and Geri and stifled her tears.

"You two don't half come away with some nonsense," she laughed sadly. "I don't know why I listen to you."

"That's why you're such a great sister," said Helen warmly. "Now come on. We'd better get up there, before I change my mind and realise just how terrible an idea this is."

Martha was hardly filled with confidence by Helen's words, but she knew she had to trust her. She had to trust Geri too. They were right, of course, she knew that much. If they were going to solve this case before the police found a way to finally pin it on Tracey Coulthard, then they'd have to take more risks. And now was as good a time as any to start.

Twenty-Six

"IT'S AT TIMES like these I wish I carried extra strong breath mints," said Helen. "I think my breath smells like that horrible little café we were in earlier."

"Give me a smell," said Geri.

Helen leaned forward and blew some air into her sister's face. The youngest of the Parker brood stood for a moment considering her answer.

"Well?" asked Helen.

"Put it this way," said Geri, stepping back. "It's probably just as well that you're not going to try and kiss him."

"There will certainly be *no* kissing, is that clear?" said Martha.

She realised she was sounding more and more like an old headmistress. It wasn't an image she particularly wanted, but she felt she had no other choice. If she wasn't comfortable with what was happening, she was at least going to make sure it was as sensible as possible.

"Alright, I think I'm ready," said Helen.

She sucked in some deep breaths of air and shook her arms and hands. Like a runner gearing up for an Olympic level race, she hopped a little up and down on her heels.

Martha and Geri watched their sister. They were equally confused as they were mesmerised by Helen's warm up.

"Are you ready?" asked Martha.

"You don't look ready," said Geri.

"I'm ready," said Helen, clasping her hands together and closing her eyes. "May all beings everywhere be happy and free, and may the thoughts, words, and actions of my own life contribute in some way to that happiness and to that freedom for all."

"Wow," said Geri. "That's pretty deep Helen."

"It's a Yoga mantra, Geri. You should try it sometime."

"Yes, very peaceful, now press the button," said Martha.

The sisters stood at the entrance of the block of flats. The door was firmly locked and there was an intercom beside it. A group of thirty buttons, each with a name beside them, was lined up beneath the buzzer. They found Mal Edwards at the top, in the penthouse, naturally.

Helen moved to push the button. Her finger hovered over it for a moment before she pulled away quickly.

"I can't," she said. "I can't, I can't go through with this. Somebody else do it, go back to the original plan. I don't think I can do it."

She began pacing around the porch. Martha looked around to make sure nobody could see the scene she was making. Geri stepped forward and grabbed Helen by the shoulders.

"Helen. Helen, listen to me, look at me," she said. "You *have* to do this, okay? Just hold it together and be… yourself. Got that?"

"I can't Geri, I can't, the pressure is too much," Helen pleaded. "I mean, what if I say something out of turn, or I throw up on him or I just come out and accuse him of killing Gordon Coulthard. What if he just laughs at me? He's used to so much more. I don't think I could live with myself, or that kind of rejection. I mean, my self-esteem is at rock bottom as it is, you know? You do it, you're the natural flirt. You're great at it."

"I can't," said Geri.

"Why not?" asked Helen, desperate for a way out. "You do it all the time!"

"Yeah but I wasn't the one who got under his skin at the party," she said. "That was you, all you, only you. The dancing, the kissing, the leg up around his hips, that was you baby!"

"Leg up around his hips?" asked Helen.

"We can't make her," said Martha, stepping between them. "If she doesn't want to do it, then we can't force her to Geri."

"Sure we can, we're her sisters."

"No, we can't," said Martha. "I'm serious. We'll just have to think of another way."

Just then the door opened behind them. A young couple came strolling out, laughing at some inconsequential joke, their hands in the back pockets of each other's jeans. When they saw the Parker sisters standing on the porch, they stopped laughing and frowned.

"Can I help you?" asked the young man, his accent thick South African.

"We're, uh, the cleaners," said Geri, leaping forward to catch the door. "Left the key at home, didn't we girls? No need to worry, door's open now, thanks a million, see you later."

She dragged Martha and Helen into the building. The three sisters left the young couple looking perplexed outside. Martha thought she should apologise, but there was no time. Geri had already summoned the lift and Helen sounded like she was one good gasp away from keeling over.

Geri pulled her sisters into the elevator. She mashed the top floor button and waited for the doors to close. When she knew they were alone, she unleashed her fierce side.

"Now pull it together Helen. I'm serious," she snapped. "We need you to be on form here. We *need* you, Helen."

"Oh God," Helen said. "I'm not up for this Geri. Martha, tell her, tell her I'm not up for this. You know I'm rubbish at all this flirting malarkey. I'll blow it."

Martha found herself in a very difficult position. On the one hand she didn't want to force Helen into something she clearly didn't want to do. Her younger sister was having an attack of confidence and she'd aged a hundred years. But, on the other hand, time was against them. They were racing up the floors of the building towards Mal's penthouse. When they were at the top they were going to have to kick themselves into action. And she needed Helen to be on top form. If they were going to crack this case, she needed her sister to deliver.

Martha didn't like Helen talking about herself in such a negative way either. She didn't like her sister saying she couldn't do something. There was no room for negativity, Martha didn't believe in it in any part of her life. As hard as that was to put into practice sometimes, she stuck by it vehemently.

That gave her an idea. It was a long shot. But it might just work.

"Oh Helen," she said. "Don't talk about yourself that way. You can do *anything* you put your mind to. You're a beautiful, intelligent, witty and charming person. Don't ever think you're not."

She reached out and took her hand. Her sister was becoming a little bleary eyed. Martha snatched Geri's hand too and they stood united in the ascending lift.

"You too, Geri," said Martha. "I'm so very proud of both of you, of the young women that you've become. It's been an honour—a privilege even—to watch you both grow up. And I'm so, so glad I've still got you both by my side."

The lift came to a stop. There was a bing and the door opened to reveal a small lobby. Martha squeezed her sisters' hands tightly.

"This is our stop," she said. "Now let's go out there, do this, and go home. This case has hung over us for far too long already. We get in there, get what we want and we end this. Okay?"

"Okay," said Geri. "Sounds good to me."

"What about you Helen?" asked Martha. "I believe in you. Geri believes in you. We've got your back, we'll be with you every step of the way. Just keep the phone on and we'll listen in. We'll be in the car if you need us."

Helen squeezed back. She bowed her head a little and nodded.

"Blimey," she said with a big sigh. "This is *not* how I saw this day going, and that's for sure. But hey, what the hell, I suppose you've got to live a little sometimes, eh?"

"That's the spirit," said Geri. "What's the point in living if you can't feel alive."

Helen looked at her sister. She furrowed her brow.

"Was that Carl Marx?" she asked. "No, Plato? Gertrude Stein? Shakespeare?"

"You're way off," said Geri, smugly. "It's from a James Bond film. There you go, take *that* higher education."

The three sisters laughed. Helen took another deep breath and wiped her eyes.

"You ready?" asked Martha.

"Yes," she said. "I'm ready."

"Okay. Let's go."

Martha led Helen and Geri out of the lift and onto the landing. Geri checked her phone for the address. She pointed at the door directly ahead of them and nodded.

"Right," said Martha. "Remember, according to him, you're here on a social call. But you're trying to find out as much as we can about Gordon, Mal's relationship with him and who might have had something against him."

"And what about *him*?" asked Geri.

"Whatever happens, happens," said Martha. "Whatever happens… happens."

Martha rang Helen's phone. Helen answered it, smiled and tucked it into her pocket, the line still alive. When they reached the door, Helen shuffled her feet a little and composed herself. She gave a quick look back over her shoulder as Martha and Geri retreated back towards the lift. She smiled sadly at them as the doors closed on them and they were whisked back downstairs.

Twenty-Seven

MAL EDWARDS STOOD shirtless and dripping at the door. His hairy chest glistened, water running down his taut, muscular curves. He dried his hair casually with a soft towel that matched the colour of the one wrapped dangerously low around his waist.

"Hi," he said, flashing an expensive smile.

Helen did her best not to stare. It was pretty difficult though. The only thing distracting her from the mesmerising figure standing in front of her was the burning flush of her cheeks.

"Hello… I mean, hi," she said, trying to pull herself together. "It's me."

The words fell flat. She instantly cursed herself. Already she could feel Geri's scolding voice forming in the depths of her brain.

"Hi," said Mal, his smile beginning to wane. "Sorry… Do I know you?"

It was the death knell. Helen's fragile psyche wasn't built for this type of rejection. But she reminded herself just what she was doing and why she was there. She had to perform, she had to do well. This meant a lot to her and her sisters. Their reputation might be riding on this going well.

"Hi, yeah, sorry," she cleared her throat in as sexy a manner as was possible. "I'm sure you don't remember me, why would you? Helen Parker. I'm Helen Parker. I, we, met at a party a couple of days ago. You know, in that swanky place in town. I think it was something to do with your bank."

Mal's face was blank. He was about to shake his head, then something clicked. He snapped his fingers and leaned a perfectly formed, muscular shoulder on the doorway.

"Helen, right. Gotcha," he said, the winning smile returning. "Yeah I remember you now. How could I forget? What a dancer!"

"Yes, yes, that's me," she cocked her hip a little. "Helen the dancer, that's what they call me."

She wanted to crawl into the ground and die. But she kept going. Persistence was a Parker trait, no matter how humiliating it was.

"So you tracked me down, eh?" said Mal, his smile turning a little more devilish. "As you can see I don't have my dancing shoes on me at the moment."

He wriggled his toes.

"No, no you don't," said Helen, using the excuse to look at his feet as a chance to scan the rest of him. "Not that it bothers me... I mean... some dancers... Well, I mean... they dance in bare feet all the time. It's part of their culture you see, to be as close to the earth as possible and..."

She caught herself. The babbling was too much. Thankfully Mal was taking it in good humour. He draped his hand towel around his neck and looked at her.

"So, to what do I owe the pleasure of such a beautiful woman turning up on my doorstep? A guy doesn't get that lucky surely."

"Lucky, yes, good one," Helen snorted loudly. "Good one. I was... I was wondering if I could come in actually, Mr Edwards. Just wanted to speak to you about your friend, Gordon."

Mal's happy-go-lucky joy seemed to wilt. He pushed himself off the frame of the door, suddenly seeming to tower above her.

"Still a bit raw I'm afraid."

"I know, I know it is. That's why I thought I'd call. I figured you might need someone to talk to. It must be awful."

Mal gave her a slightly suspicious look. Then he seemed to accept her excuse and his face softened. He stood to one side and ushered her in.

"Come on in," he said, warmly. "Living room is down at the end of the hall. If you give me a minute, I'll just go get some clothes on."

"Oh, don't worry about that," said Helen. "You don't need to go to any effort… I mean…"

He disappeared into another room. Helen made her way deeper into the apartment and found the living room. It was, as Helen had expected, spectacular. Everything looked new, like it was straight out of the shop. Greys, blacks and whites were the order of the day. The obligatory plasma TV and glass dining and coffee table ticked all the boxes of a wealthy professional's penthouse apartment. Even the views out through the balcony windows were like something from a postcard or poster at an airport.

"Hey," came Geri's voice from the phone.

Helen panicked. She fumbled for the device and whispered into it.

"Be quiet, he'll hear you," she said.

"Just relax would you? You're coming on to him like a drunken trollop on a Saturday night."

"I am not!" Helen protested, a little too loudly. "And besides, how would *you* know what a drunken trollop does on a Saturday night anyway?"

"Just rein it in a little, that's all I'm saying. I thought you were going to start drooling on the carpet at one point."

"Can you blame me? You should see him. I just caught him coming out of the shower. He's like a Hellenistic Greek sculpture for goodness sake."

"That's the geekiest reference I think I've ever heard," said Geri. "And that's really saying something for you Helen."

"Quiet," said Martha. "He'll hear you."

A door closed somewhere beyond the living room. Helen quickly hid her phone again and tried to look relaxed. It was about as impossible a task as any human being had ever been asked to do.

Mal strode in confidently, still drying his hair. He'd covered his muscular frame in a grey sweatshirt and tracksuit bottoms, his feet clapping against the hardwood flooring in a pair of designer flip flops.

"Can I get you something to drink? Tea, coffee? Something stronger?" he asked, heading to the open plan kitchen.

"No, I think I'm alright," she said, her throat achingly dry. "So, Mal, how have you been?"

She waltzed over to the banker in as elegant, alluring a way as her odd, gangly frame would allow. Trying to mimic Tracey Coulthard but coming across somewhere between an ostrich and a bag of golf clubs.

"How am I?" he laughed, drinking from a bottle of water. "I've been better Helen, to be honest. A lot better actually. But then I suppose my best friend *has* just died."

"Ah, yes," she said, shaking her head. "Really, really horrible. So tragic. So young."

"Hmm. Dreadful."

She was losing him, she had gone in on too serious a note. Helen tried to quickly think of something to say that wasn't talking about his loss, but her mind froze.

The silence grew between them. She looked about for something, anything. Then she spotted it. Like a great, shining beacon of hope in the darkness, the main spire of Glasgow University called to her from across the skyline.

"You have a wonderful view here Mal," she said, hurrying over to the panoramic windows. "You can see pretty much the whole city from up here."

"It's a penthouse suite," he said. "That's kind of the point of it."

"It's just wonderful," she said, this time not lying. "You know I've grown up looking at the uni building. I used to ask my grandmother what went on there and she said that's where all the clever people went. I never thought I'd get to go."

"You're a student then," he said, retreating to the couch.

"Post graduate teaching associate is my official name," she said, starting to feel a little more relaxed on topics she knew something about. "At least that's what my mum tells her friends."

"So what are you really doing here?" he asked, wrong-footing her immediately.

"I… uh…" God, why was this so hard?

He waited. Helen couldn't think of anything else to turn to as a safe conversation haven. *Just get on with it.* Reminding herself she was here to do a job, she took a deep breath and launched in.

"I wanted to talk to you about Gordon," she said.

"Why the big interest in him?" he asked, tilting his head to the side. "I wouldn't have thought he'd have any draw among the dusty old books and postgraduate programs. No offence."

She turned away from the window, tearing her eyes from the glorious view.

"He wasn't academic then?" she asked.

"Gordon? Academic! Don't be daft," Mal smiled. "He'd be lucky if he even knew how to use a *calculator*, let alone understand mathematical theory."

"But... but he was a banker," she said. "And a pretty successful one, at that."

Mal raised his eyebrows and took a long, drawn gulp from his bottle. Helen could feel her heart racing. She was making progress. She could feel a small crack opening up in his cool veneer.

She eased herself over to the couch where Mal had reclined. Sitting down on the edge, she kept her focus on him.

"I mean, he had to have some kind of talent for it, to get where he did so young?" she asked him, needling that crack.

"Huh," he laughed. "You know, he was like a brother to me. For the good *and* the bad of that statement. We were at school together, all the way through uni. I was always there to make sure he didn't blow things, do something stupid. And like I said, academics weren't his strong suite. He needed my help with even the most basic things. We studied economics, and it's not the easiest of subjects. But he always managed to get there in the end. I don't know how he did it to be perfectly honest with you."

"And you both joined the bank at the same time?" she asked him.

"Yeah," that brought another smile from Mal. "The pair of us started there on the same day. It was crazy, it was just like being back in school. Except this time we were dealing with multi-million-pound shares and accounts, futures, trading, everything. It's a glamorous life Helen, and it has its rewards, as you can see."

He waved his hands around the opulence of the penthouse.

"But it's not all so much fun when you're working in it I'll bet," she said, prodding him, nudging him, completely flying on her wits.

"Is it that obvious?" he said.

"Well, you read about it, don't you?" she said, relaxing even more. "About how high profile, high stress environments can take their toll on the psychology of an individual. There are dozens and dozens of studies on it."

"I'll need to take your word for that," he reached over and took her hand, squeezing it.

Helen felt a tingle run up her arm and down her spine. Mal retreated again, rubbing his face and flattening his wet hair.

"You know, when you're younger, you think you're indestructible," he said. "I've been working in the banking sector for ten years. I'm barely in my thirties but already I'm considered one of the old men. You think football is bad? This is even worse, believe me. The only way you can survive in this game is to keep your head on a swivel and hope that you get the call upstairs before it's too late."

"Call upstairs?" she asked. "What does that mean?"

"Promotion," he said.

Mal got up, a sudden energy about him. He began pacing around the living room.

"Gordon was a great guy, I loved him to bits," he continued. "But he was a bloody pain in the arse too. His brown-nosing was on a whole other level. And I mean a whole *other* level. What he lacked in knowledge, he more than made up for in the patter stakes. I always remember at uni, folk would say he could charm the birds from the trees. But believe me Helen, it wasn't just the flying kind of birds he was charming. You know Tracey right? Well she was just the best of the bunch. There were quite a few to pick from, trust me."

Helen tried to keep her face neutral. Having women referred to as 'birds' was one of her pet hates, but she had to put that aside and let him press on.

"Gordon always knew the right things to say, the right things to do. He knew where to be, when to be there and what was going on. I always used to joke with him that if he spent as long on his actual job as he did working out what players were in the game, then he might actually get by on some merit."

"Like you, you mean?" Helen offered.

That stopped Mal from his pacing. He stared down at her, a seriousness creeping over his good looks.

"Yeah," he said. "Yeah I suppose you're right. A bit like me. Not that I was ever given the same chances as Gordon. Maybe I didn't do *enough* brown-nosing. Or maybe the bosses just loved to have him around. He was good company, great company. A totally self-obsessed arsehole, but a charming one at that."

He finished his water and placed it carefully on the coffee table between them. Helen felt a chill go through her again. Only this time it wasn't pleasant. Something about the mood in the room had changed, just like that.

"Why are you so interested in all this anyway?" Mal asked, straightening back up. "Who are you really? Not another journalist hoping for a scoop? You'll get nothing out of me on that."

It caught Helen a little by surprise. Of course, they hadn't told Gordon or Mal what they did for a living. She was ready to retreat, a panic making her hand drop to her pocket where she hoped her phone was still listening in.

"I'll be honest with you, Mal," he said, strengthening her resolve. "My sisters and I are trying to find out what happened to your friend." She kept her voice calm, watching his body language. "We don't think Tracey, his wife, had anything to do with it all. And we don't want to see somebody innocent go to prison."

"Isn't that the job of the police?" he asked. "Isn't Tracey the main suspect? I mean I heard about what she did to Estelle. I mean, the woman's not exactly what you'd call stable, but Estelle didn't deserve that."

"I suppose that's not up to us to decide though, is it?" said Helen, feeling more and more uncomfortable by the second. "Tracey was hurt when she found out about Gordon's engagement. Understandably. But that doesn't mean she killed him."

Mal cocked his head to the side again, that hard, suspicious look returning. He cracked his knuckles, his shoulders set square. Gone was the attractive, welcoming man that had invited her in. Instead he looked like a club bouncer with an incredible sharp mind, who was more than capable of doing damage.

"Like I said," he snarled. "What's it got to do with you? Why don't you leave it to the police?"

"I… uh…" she stammered again. *Just tell him. You're trying to get justice for his best friend. Just tell him.* "I'm a private investigator. My sisters and I run a company. Tracey hired us too…"

"She's trying to pin Gordon's death on me, is she?" He stood up, furious. Helen stood too. It was time to make her exit.

"I'd best be going," she said, making to walk past him. "We're only trying to help."

She didn't get past him though. In a flash, he grabbed Helen's wrist and cranked it up behind her back. She screamed.

Mal covered her mouth and forced her against the living room door with a hard thump. Martha and Geri were shouting now, their voices echoing from the phone in Helen's pocket. Incensed, Mal reached in and pulled it out.

"What's this about, eh?" he snarled. "Trying to get a confession from me or something? That's entrapment, and it's against the law."

He smashed the phone against the wall, cracking the screen and causing it to spark. It dropped to the floor in pieces. Helen saw it lying there and felt her heart sink—it had felt like a lifeline, knowing her sisters were listening and could come to her aid. Surely they'd come running now.

The tears welled as Mal continued to shout at her, barking questions like a rabid dog. She was trapped, with nowhere to go. She wished her sisters were there to help.

Twenty-Eight

"OH GOD, WHAT have we done? What have we done?" Geri asked over and over.

Martha couldn't hear her. She was a million miles away. She stood counting the numbers on the lift display as it zoomed up the huge block of flats, barrelling towards the penthouse floor. In a strange way she almost didn't want it to reach its destination, for fear of what she might find. Helen's phone had gone dead suddenly. But her sister's scream and Mal's shouting before the line cut out would haunt her for a long time.

"I should be protecting you both," she said quietly to Geri. "It's my job, I'm your sister. I should be protecting you, not sending you into the lion's den with only a stupid bloody phone for protection."

"It's not your fault Martha, it's not!" Geri protested. "I shouldn't have goaded Helen into doing something like this. She's not cut out for undercover work."

"This wasn't undercover work. This was suicide. We should have just let the police deal with it, this is too much for us to cope with. And if anything's happened to Helen…"

"You're *not* to blame."

"No, I am. I should be protecting you both. Nothing is worth risking your safety. Nothing at all."

The lift pinged as it reached the top floor. The doors opened with a swoosh to reveal an empty corridor.

"Helen," Martha called desperately, hurrying towards Mal's flat. "Helen are you ok?"

The door was ajar. A terrible sense of dread washed over Martha. They dashed inside, calling out for Helen, searching every room until they finally came to the living room.

"There's nobody here," Geri said, clapping her hand against her forehead. "Oh God, where is she Martha? What's that pig done with her? Where could they have gone?"

Martha remained silent. She spotted the broken phone lying by the door. Kneeling down, she sifted through the debris. She didn't need a lab to tell her it was Helen's. And while the tension and fear were multiplying all the time inside her, making her chest tighten, she knew she had to stay calm.

"Think, Geri," she called over to her youngest sister. "Just think for a moment. We can worry and panic and blame each other all we want when we have Helen back. But right now I need you use that brilliant brain of yours to try and work out what's happened here."

The mini pep-talk seemed to work on Geri. She started breathing with a lot more control. She blinked, as if resetting herself.

"He can't have gone far with her," she said. "That was only what two, three minutes ago we heard them on the phone, and we were in the lift…"

"That means they must still be in the building," said Martha.

"Or if not in the building then somewhere nearby."

A loud screech from outside startled them both. They raced over to the huge windows of the living room. Far below on the darkened street, a bright green supercar drove dangerously fast through the narrow entrance to the flats. The tyres squealed again as it roared around a corner and headed in the direction of the city centre.

"That's him," said Geri. "That's Mal's car. I recognise it from his pictures online. He's got her, come on."

"No," Martha said.

"No? What do you mean no? He's got Helen!"

"We can't go after him, we have to be smarter than that," she said.

"But he's got Helen, Martha."

"I know he does," she said, her voice catching in her throat. "And he's also got a supercar with a head start. We'd never catch him up, not now. We have to think a few steps ahead. Where would he be going with her? He's got to have a safe place, somewhere he can hide out if he's cornered, like he is right now. Think Geri, think, please."

"But Helen..."

"I know," she said, her heart breaking. "I know. But she's tough. And this might be our only chance at saving her."

Calm and collected now, Martha headed for the door. She produced her phone and with it the small card with Pope's number on it. To her surprise, she wasn't shaking when she typed it in. Instead she felt totally in control.

"Pope," came the bitter tones of the detective. "Who is this?"

"Parker, Martha Parker," she said.

"Parker, I don't have time for your woolly jumper antics just now, I need to—"

"Mal Edwards," Martha cut her off.

"What?"

"Mal. Edwards," said Martha, deliberately pronouncing every syllable of the banker's name. "He attacked my sister Helen in his flat. Now he's kidnapped her. He's driven off in the direction of the city centre. I'll send you a picture of his car. Please try and find him."

"This better not be a joke Parker."

"I'm not joking."

She hung up and tossed the card over to Geri who was following closely behind.

"Here's Pope's number," she said. "Send her a photo of Mal's motor, she's expecting it."

"Gotcha," said the youngest Parker sister. "What's our next move?"

Martha didn't have a clue. She stopped to catch her breath. This wasn't easy. This was hell.

"Right, Pope has it," said Geri, coming up beside her. "She says that they're putting out a city-wide alert to try and stop him. And she says we're not to move from this place, she's sending a squad car around to pick us up. Hopefully the flash git is caught before he does anything stupid."

"God, I hope so," Martha said, her voice catching.

Geri reached out to her sister and put her arms around her. The pair of them embraced for a long moment. Both on the verge of crying. Martha was first to pull away.

"God, I hope she's okay," she said. "She must be terrified."

"Helen? She'll be fine," Geri sniffed. "It's Mal Edwards I feel sorrier for. You know our sister Mart, she can't go above twenty miles an hour before she gets car sick."

Martha laughed. Snotty and sad, she wiped her face on the sleeve of her old, tatty cardigan. She looked about the hallway.

"She's some woman," she said. "How could I have sent her up here on her own? I knew it, I bloody knew something would happen to her."

"I told you, you can't blame yourself. We were just as guilty, if not more so. You heard her, she said she wanted to do this. And I goaded her into it. We're all in this together, you hear me Mart? We're all in this *together*."

Martha nodded. She appreciated what Geri was saying. But it didn't make it any easier to bear. She should have known better, she *did* know better. But that didn't help Helen now, did it?

Martha felt like she could still hear the sound of Mal's grunting on the phone. He had been like an animal, like something wild that had just been triggered. She could still hear Helen's screams too. It made her shiver.

"God, just look at this place would you?" said Geri, slumping down on the floor. "Do you think they all get the same decorators in? They must do. No two people could be so equally lacking in creativity when it comes to their lovepads."

"I wouldn't know," said Martha. "Unlike you, I don't get to visit too many lovepads. Are they all like this?"

"Only the ones with money," smiled Geri. "You must be going to the wrong parties."

"We've *all* been going to the wrong parties, Geri."

That drew a laugh from the youngest Parker. She started to pick at the carpet, lifting bits of the thread out and twisting it around her finger.

"Do you remember my thirteenth birthday party?" she asked.

"Of course," said Martha, sniffing loudly. "It was in the back garden of mum's house. We got you a bouncy castle."

"I know. What was *that* about?"

"You'd always loved bouncy castles. I guess we just thought you still loved them. Shame that you had to go and burst it with a knitting needle."

"I maintain my complete and total innocence," said Geri. "You and I both know it was that pimple-faced weirdo who lived next door."

"Michael," smiled Martha. "And his mum and dad, Gert and Harry. They were a lovely couple."

"Their son was a dingus."

"He had really bad acne."

"That's not an excuse."

"No, but he did fancy you. You could have been a bit nicer to him, I suppose. Still, all in the past now. You don't have to worry about him fancying you now."

"Who's *worried?*"

Geri pretended to flick the long, luscious locks she didn't have. She leaned back against the wall, staring up at the bright, hot spotlights.

"Families eh? Who would have them, Martha?"

"Who indeed?"

Martha leaned on the long, rectangular table that ran along the wall of the hallway. She needed the support, otherwise she would fall down. She spied a dish filled with one and two pence coins, a spare set of keys for the flat and other bits and bobs. Odd, she thought, that even the mega rich still kept hold of mundane change.

Beside it was a stack of unopened envelopes. Martha started pawing through them, reading Mal's name over and over again along with the address of the flat. A brown one was at the bottom. That usually spelled trouble, she thought. She flipped it over and saw the familiar logo of HMRC at the top right.

"Oh dear," she said to Geri. "Looks like somebody…"

She trailed off. Geri, obviously sensing something was wrong, looked up at her sister.

"Looks like somebody what?" she asked.

Martha didn't speak. Instead she turned back around to face Geri, the envelope in her quivering hand.

"Martha?" asked the youngest Parker, getting to her feet. "What is it?"

She took the envelope from Martha. Scanning it, Geri saw nothing out of the ordinary. Only when she was about to protest did she spot who it was addressed to.

"Paradise Hair and Beauty," she said. "But that's... that's..."

"Estelle's salon."

The words were like a starter's pistol. Martha and Geri bolted from Mal Edwards' apartment as quickly as they could. There was no time to wait for their police escort.

Twenty-Nine

THE CHRISTMAS LIGHTS zoomed past Martha and Geri as they raced through the city. It was getting late but the pavements were still full of shoppers. The distant sound of carollers came and went as they passed them. Martha hadn't even started her Christmas shopping. It was literally the furthest thing from her mind. The whole festive season seemed to pale in comparison to everything else that had been happening to her and the others.

They whizzed past a pair of police cars, blues and twos adding a dose of reality to the holly, jolly scene of Glasgow at Christmas time. The police were heading in the opposite direction, running around searching for a supercar that only Martha and Geri knew was hiding.

"I can't believe it," said Geri. "I just can't believe it. What does it mean, Mart? Mal Edwards and the salon. What does it *mean?*"

Martha tried to concentrate on the road as they sped towards the salon. Names, faces, facts, figures, hearsay, conjecture, everything they had learned was whizzing around in her mind. It was so distracting that she was amazed she hadn't hit any cars yet, or worse, any pedestrians. The tiredness and aching in her joints was dragging her down, too. She felt like her hands and feet were made of lead. And it wouldn't be long before her eyelids felt the same.

The car barrelled over the River Clyde and into the inner city. The tall, shining, shimmering buildings of the city centre vanished almost immediately. The landscape grew flat and desolate the closer they got to their destination.

"We're almost there," said Geri. "You got any ideas what we're planning on doing when we get there?"

"No," said Martha. "I had been quietly hoping that you would have come up with something before we reached it. Any ideas?"

"Hey, you're the leader, remember."

Martha choked back a wave of tears.

"I'm not any kind of leader," she managed to get out, before her voice cracked again.

"Yes Mart, you are. You always have been. You're always there for us, both of us, for everyone in your life. You're a wonderful woman. And an even better sister. I love you. I know that Helen loves you too. No matter what."

To hear her speak so kindly filled Martha with pride. She loved both of her sisters dearly. They were her life. And she would do anything and everything for them. But this was not the time to be emotional. Not yet. Helen's safety was her first priority, her only priority. When she had her back, then she could finally let her emotions in.

"There it is," she said.

The street was dark, save for the headlights from their car. The horrid gloom of the winter's night hung over the place like a hard, dangerous blanket. The street lights were too far apart and darkness thrived in between them. And in that shadow, a bright, neon green Italian supercar stood out. A thing of strange, elegant beauty among barbaric emptiness.

A jolt of energy passed through her. She'd been right. Mal Edwards could have gone anywhere in his fancy motor. But he'd chosen the wrong place, the wrong time and the wrong private detectives.

"Turn the lights off," said Geri.

"What?"

"Turn your headlights off. They'll see us coming."

She leaned over and clicked them off. Martha slowed to a trundle as they passed the supercar.

"There's nobody inside," she said, whispering.

"They must be in the salon. Look."

Geri pointed a little way up the street. The ramshackle row of shops stood out in the darkness. Their long, rectangular shape blotted out the streetlights and houses in the distance.

She pulled the car onto the pavement and switched off the engine.

"Anything coming to you yet?" she asked.

"Sorry Mart, I'm all out," said Geri. "Looks like we might just have to wing this one."

"Bloody hell. I don't like the sound of that."

She stared silently for a moment just looking at the horrid little salon steeped in darkness. How had it come to this? She should have been at home, wrapping Christmas presents with her husband and kids, singing carols, calling her mum and feeding the cat. Instead she was in a bad area of the city, about to charge in headfirst to save her sister from a potentially very dangerous man. Life had never been this exciting before. It had never been so dangerous either.

She reached over and grabbed Geri's hand. Geri squeezed back and they both looked at each other.

"For Helen?" asked Martha.

"For Helen," said Geri, firmly.

They got out of the car and closed the doors as quietly as they could. A dog barked somewhere down the street and Martha almost jumped out of her skin.

"Hold on, wait a sec," whispered Geri.

She opened up the boot and rummaged around. Then she appeared with something in her hand.

"What's that?"

"A little insurance policy," she said, waving the wheel wrench.

"I didn't even know I had one of those."

"Shame there's no crowbar, but this will do," said Geri.

They hurried along the pavement towards the salon. There was nobody about, and the shop looked empty. It wasn't though. Martha was sure of that.

The sisters eased their way up to the main door. The shutters were down over the huge window. Martha peered through the glass of the door. It was dark inside save for a tiny sliver of light beneath a door at the far side. As she stared she thought she heard raised voices coming from the back.

"There's definitely somebody in there," she whispered.

"Right," said Geri "Stand back."

She shoved Martha out the way and pulled the wrench back. Before she could smash the glass, her sister stopped her.

"Hold on," Martha said, her breath smoking. "There must be another way in. That door round the back. But how do we get there?"

"Oh, c'mon. Helen could be hurt in there, we need action Mart."

"I know, I know. But we can't just smash our way in. We've got surprise on our side, Geri. Remember what I told you. Think."

She let go of Geri's arm and stepped away from the door. Looking at the shop front, there was nothing that stood out. It was plain and boring, as good as a blank block of concrete. Then she spotted something at the end of the building.

"A drainpipe," she said. "There's always a drainpipe. One of the few benefits of living in Scotland. There's always a load of rain water to get rid of."

"What?" asked Geri confused.

Martha started climbing the tall, lead pipe that reached all the way to the roof. It was cold and wet and made her hands sting, but the brackets were solid and she could easily reach from one to the next. She kept climbing until she reached the top. Geri was close behind, tyre wrench tucked into her waistband.

A cold wind whistled in Martha's ears. The distant lights of the city centre were dotted along the horizon like Christmas decorations.

"Okay, we're on the roof," said Geri. "Now what?"

"I don't know. I was hoping something would…"

Martha spotted the dim glow of lights coming from below towards the back of the roof, where it flattened out a bit. They carefully tiptoed over and found a filthy skylight. Wiping away the grime, the sisters could see straight down into the back of the shop. The voices were louder here even through the glass. Shadows walked across the floor, out of view from the skylight.

Martha ran her hands along the edge of the oblong window. She found a small catch and loosened it. Easing it open, the deep, smooth tones of Mal Edwards wafted up to meet them.

He was shouting and swearing, every second word a curse. He barely stopped for breath before continuing on his foul-mouthed rant. Geri hovered beside Martha trying to get a better view.

"Careful," she whispered. "I don't have a proper grip on this thing."

"Yeah I'm leaving, whether you like it or not," Mal was on his phone, his face so red that they could see his scalp beneath his hair. "Because things have changed. I've got to go, I'm getting the flight at ten. And if you're not here in the next ten minutes, then I'm leaving without you," he said, pausing for the reply. Then, "I don't care what you're doing. That's the deal. You either like it or lump it, sweetheart. I'm waiting ten minutes and then I'm off."

"Who's he talking to?" whispered Geri.

"I don't know," said Martha., straining to hear. "Although I suspect that it's—"

The edge of the skylight slipped from Martha's fingers. As it did so, the world seemed to slow down, almost to a stop. She saw the pane of glass dropping towards its ledge and she the terrible consequences of her slip flashed through her mind. But rather than simply letting it drop, she made the second mistake of trying to grab it again.

She lunged forward, losing her balance. The skylight crashed down hard on its frame, the glass shattering instantly so there was nothing to stop Martha from falling. She tumbled through the hole in the window. Geri reached for her, but too late, and she was dragged through the window behind her sister.

At least gravity was mercifully quick, the drop not too large, and a very surprised Mal Edwards was there to break their fall. The three of them wound up in a heap on the floor, nobody really sure what was going on.

Martha felt an uncomfortable pain shooting up her left leg. She tried to move but it was impossible. Among the tangle of limbs, hands and shattered glass, she was certain something was wrong.

"Geri," she shouted. "Helen."

Something squirmed and wriggled free from underneath her. A long, dark shadow made everything darker and she looked up to see Mal standing over her. He reached down with a giant paw and pulled her up by the hair.

Martha let out a shriek of pain as she tried to put weight on her leg. She was tossed away from Mal and clattered into the wall. Geri was next for the same treatment, hurtling into her sister.

"Martha," she said breathlessly. "You're hurt."

"I'm fine," Martha winced. "I'm fine."

"Well, well, well, three for the price of one," laughed Mal. "Even better than I could have hoped."

He seemed to dominate the tiny back room, filling it with his broad chest and square jaw. A trickle of blood ran down his forehead from a cut beneath his hairline. But he didn't seem to care. He stared at the two sisters with sharp, hawk-like eyes, pupils little more than dots.

"You know I've just about had enough of you three. Which is really saying something as I don't even know you."

"Charming," snorted Geri, trying to prop up Martha. "I bet you say that to all the girls."

"Where's Helen?" Martha asked, shutting her sister up.

"Ah, right, you must be the oldest one," scoffed Mal. "You'll be the one I talk to then, as opposed to the children."

"Where is she?" she demanded. "Tell me."

"I'll take you to her, shall I?" he smirked.

Mal reached into the pocket of his sweats. He pulled out a small, gleaming revolver and cocked it back.

"Move," he shouted, pointing it at the sister.

"Oh right, yeah, you're going to shoot us," Geri sniffed. "Like you're actually going to shoot us, right here, right now."

"You think I won't do it?" Mal's eyes flashed a wild, angry madness. "I can do anything, I'm the one with the gun."

Without hesitation, or aim, he loosened off a shot. The bang was loud enough to temporarily deafen Martha and Geri. They both screamed as the bullet ricocheted off the wall above their heads.

"There. Happy?" he said. "Now move."

Mal twitched the gun and pointed to the door that led into the main area of the shop. Geri helped Martha and they hobbled their way into the darkness. Mal was close behind. He flipped on the lights of the salon and suddenly everything became bright.

For just a second, Martha couldn't see anything. Then, as her eyes adjusted, she was overcome with emotion. Helen sat across from her, tied to one of the salon chairs, a dirty sock stuffed in her mouth.

"Helen," Geri cried, racing over to her.

Martha hurried as fast as she could and hugged both of her sisters to her as best she could.

"What a touching family reunion," he said sarcastically. "Seriously I'm moved."

"I'll move you," Martha hissed, turning on him. "Kidnapping an innocent woman and then shooting at her sisters? Who the hell do you think you are?"

"Shut. Up," he said.

"Or what?" Geri fired back. "You don't have the guts to do anything. You're all talk, just like your mate Gordon Coulthard. You're all the same you guys. You think you can wave your gun around, try to intimidate us, pretend you were going to shoot us and then what? You won't do anything. You're pathetic."

Martha felt Helen shuddering in her seat. She was rocking back and forth, trying to get her attention. Geri reached down and pulled the sock from her sister's mouth.

"Don't Geri," she said, gulping for air.

"Don't what?" Martha asked.

"Don't antagonize him," she hissed.

"And why not Helen?" Geri said, her confidence returning with every passing second. "I know what these guys are like. They're just bullies. Scared little boys, who wouldn't know real guts if it came and slapped them on their manicured faces."

She marched all the way up to him so she was almost touching his chest with her pointed little nose. He stared down at her like she was a doll, maniacal eyes transfixed on the petite little woman with the big mouth and fast tongue.

"You should listen to your sister," growled Mal, exposing his bright white teeth.

"Oh yeah?" said Geri, standing defiantly on her tiptoes. "And why's that Mr Bigshot?"

"Because he killed Gordon Coulthard," Helen shouted. "And he'll kill you if you keep going."

Thirty

THE ADRENALINE WAS coursing through Martha's body. The shock of what was happening, the pain from her leg, the realisation that they had figured out Gordon's killer, but he was now standing over them all with a gun—it all combined to fill her with the electric charge of adrenaline that coursed through her veins. It wasn't good for her, she knew that. But it was the only thing keeping her going.

"You killed Gordon?" Geri was the first to speak. "He was your best friend? Why?"

"Oh, I'm sorry," Mal grinned. "Is this the part where I tell you my dastardly deeds and the police come in just in the nick of time? I may be new to this whole incompetent murderer game, ladies. But even I won't fall for that."

He raised his gun, taking aim at Geri who was the closest to him.

"He was jealous of him, of course," Helen blurted.

All eyes fell on her, still tied to one of the salon chairs. Mal hesitated, his arm shaking as he kept the pistol directed at Geri's head.

"Weren't you?" she pressed. "You were jealous of the fact he was better than you, that he had more friends, prettier mistresses, everything. You were jealous of the fact he was getting promotion after promotion, and you were left counting the beans with all the other plebs."

Mal grimaced. For a moment Martha thought he was going to pull the trigger. Then he let out a powerful, bellowing roar of frustration. He stomped across the salon floor, tapping the handle of his gun against his forehead.

"God! How do you three do it?" he said, half-laughing. "How do you get under people's skin like this? It's a talent, I applaud you. You should be lawyers."

"We don't need your applause," said Martha bitterly.

"Well, what do you need?" he asked. "I feel I should grant you all a dying wish. That seems rather poetic, doesn't it?"

"We need you to tell us the truth about what happened," said Geri. "Why did you kill him Mal? What could you possibly have had to gain from murdering your best mate?"

"That's what you want to know?" Mal chewed the question over. He stared at the space between them, as if searching for the right answer from a million different options. When he was satisfied with the one he had, he shrugged.

"Money," he said, laughing fully this time.

"Money?" Martha asked. "But you're already wealthy Mal? You've got more money than you'd ever be able to spend. That car out there, parked in the street."

"A bad idea by the way, especially in this area," quipped Geri.

"I told him that too," added Helen.

"It's worth more than this whole part of the city, I'll bet. Certainly more than any of us will ever have. Why kill him for money, Mal?"

Martha wanted an answer, she wanted to know. How could something as frivolous as money lead a man to kill his best friend?

"You don't know what he was like," said Mal, his shoulders slumping. "This isn't a sob story I'm telling you, I stand by my convictions. I killed him because I wanted his money, his power. Simple as that. You didn't know him, none of you did. Even that moaning, sour-faced wife of his didn't know him. Nobody knew him like I did. I grew up with him, lived every moment, high and low, with him. We were like brothers."

"Brothers don't kill each other," said Geri flatly.

"Cain and Abel did," said Helen, just as plainly.

"That's not my point," Geri darted back.

"Are they always like this?" said Mal, nodding at Martha. Martha raised her eyebrows in affirmation. *Yes, they are.*

"You were jealous then? Like Helen said," she said, bringing them all back on track. "You were jealous of the fact he was getting on in life and you were flagging behind, living in his shadow all the time. I heard what you told her—that he wasn't the brightest, that you had to bail him out time and time again. That must have been frustrating, I imagine."

"Frustrating?" his anger returned, face scarlet. "Do you have any idea what it's like to play second fiddle to an absolute idiot? To laugh and smile and keep on somebody's good side, because you know they're too stupid to realise you're the only one helping them? To bow and curtsey, to wipe their arse, tell them how wonderful they are—all because you know one day they're going to be one of the most powerful men in the country, and they'll take you with them? Do you know how that feels?"

He had stormed over to Martha and was breathing heavily on her. It took all of her energy, all of her courage, to stand up to him. He was so close she could see the veins bulging in his forehead.

"No, I don't know how that feels," she said, trying to sound confident. "But I know that nothing in this world would make me do what you did Mal. Nothing."

He hovered over her. She thought he might punch her, or worse still, shoot her between the eyes. But he threw his hands up and stomped back towards the middle of the room.

"When did you do it?" asked Geri.

"What?" he snapped.

"When did you kill him? I mean we were there, at the flat, we saw his body. It looked pretty fresh to me. He couldn't have been dead for very long."

"Wait a minute," said Helen. "Wait a minute. Something has been bugging me. This place, it's Estelle's right? She was there, fighting with Tracey, out in the street outside Gordon's building. Why then? Why not some other time? Why not…"

"It was a distraction," said Geri, turning to Mal. "A distraction while you went upstairs and bashed Coulthard around the head."

"Then you set him in the bath to make it look he'd drowned," said Martha. "Only the police didn't see it that way, did they Mal? They didn't buy the fact that Gordon had suffered a terrible injury to his head, worse than anything he could ever get on the rugby pitch. Something so devastating that it had to be deliberately inflicted, deliberately done to kill him."

Mal looked pleased with himself. He shrugged again, gun waving around like a magic wand.

"But that means," said Helen. "That means that Estelle was also in on all of this."

"Did somebody say my name?"

The young, blonde salon owner strode in through the front door. When she saw who was waiting for her inside, she dropped the keys and staggered back a little in her six-inch heels. She almost tripped over her suitcase until she regained her footing.

"What the hell are these three doing here?" she screamed at Mal.

"Well, my sweet," he replied. "These three have it all figured out, don't you ladies?"

"They know?" Estelle looked dumbfounded.

"Yes," said Geri. "It's all over, Estelle."

"For you three," Mal said, turning the gun back on them. "Yes, I'm afraid it is."

Mal looked over his shoulder at Estelle, who was still goldfishing as her brain tried to process what was happening.

"I told you to be here half an hour ago," Mal snarled. "We should have been at the airport by now."

"I'm sorry babe, I had to put my face on," she tried to reason.

"Babe?" asked Geri with a smirk. "Did she just call you 'babe', Mal? You two aren't... not only did you kill your best friend, but you've taken his fiancée as well?"

Mal and Estelle exchanged a glance, a hint of guilt replaced immediately by defiance from her, smugness from him.

"No way man," said Geri. "No *way*! Estelle, you and Mal? But you were engaged to Gordon Coulthard!"

"Who was already married by the way," chirped Helen.

"This is unbelievable. Really, it is. You two are having a secret affair, behind Gordon's back, while you're also having a relationship with Gordon behind Tracey's back. It's like some sordid, horrible, untrustworthy onion."

"Yeah, it is," said Helen. "But it stinks a lot more."

Mal looked angry. Estelle looked confused. Geri shook her head and Helen was *still* tied to the salon chair. If things hadn't been so serious, Martha probably would have found the situation farcical. Only this wasn't a farce. This was very, very real. And they were very much in danger.

"So let me see if I've got this right," she said. "Just humour me for a second Mal. You two are together, right, that much is clear. You've set this whole thing up to rip off Gordon Coulthard?"

"What do you mean rip off?" asked Estelle. "What' does rip off mean?"

"Oh come on," Geri laughed. "You can't be serious? You're joking right? *Please* tell me you're joking."

She stared back at the Parker sisters, face like it was etched in stone.

"It means a con, babe, a con," said Mal, patience running thin.

"Ah right, why did you not just say that then?" she rasped. "Aye, we were conning Gordon, that's right."

"Shut up Estelle."

"Why? They know everything now anyway, what difference does it make? You're going to shoot them anyway, aren't you, babe?"

She took to the centre of the floor like it was an audition. Even now, in this dingy little salon with only the five of them there, Martha could tell she was loving the attention. She puckered her lips, catching sight of herself in one of the mirrors.

"We weren't meant to kill him," she said, with all the casual care of someone buying a new car. "We were just going to take his money."

"But how?" asked Helen. "He was married."

"I know that," said Estelle. "But he was going to divorce Tracey and marry me. He told me so. He even got me this ring."

She showed off the huge rock that dominated her left hand. Geri couldn't stifle a whistle of approval.

"What?" she said to the others. "Can't I appreciate extravagantly ornate and expensively ugly diamonds once in a while?"

"The plan was I would get married to him as soon as his divorce came through. Then I'd do the same. Get half the money, his reputation would be in the gutter and Mal and I would be on easy street."

"Simple," said Mal, stroking his stubble. "Or at least it should have been."

"That would have taken years though?" said Helen. "Why bother going to all of this effort just to ruin him?"

"Twenty -seven years," said Mal.

The atmosphere in the room chilled even more. The tall, broad shouldered banker seemed to radiate an angry bitterness.

"Twenty-seven years I have been in the shadow of Gordon Coulthard. Twenty-seven years of his narcissism, his whinging, his brown-nosing and his treachery. Twenty-seven years I've waited for the chance to ruin him. What was another year, two tops? Nothing."

"So why did you kill him?" asked Martha. "He's still married to Tracey, or was when he died. You two don't get a penny now, you're nothing to him. It's all in her bank account, or at least it will be when she's cleared of his murder."

"He had to go and poke through my business didn't he," said Estelle. "He used to get so paranoid, think I was talking to other men."

"You *do* talk to other men," said Mal angrily.

"Aye, I know, but not like *that*," she said, again missing the gravity of the situation. "I mean, what's a bit of harmless flirting here and there? Eh girls?"

The thought of being anything like Estelle made each of the Parker sisters shudder in unison.

"He found out about me and Mal. And he went tonto. Started throwing stuff about, threatened to cut me off. So I told Mal and he came up with the idea to bump him off and make it look like Tracey had done it. He had put me in his will, see? So with her out the picture, it could come to me. To us. Pretty clever, eh?"

"Yeah," said Martha. "Dastardly."

She dropped her gaze to the floor. Her head was aching almost as much as her leg. She propped herself up against Helen's chair.

"You know something," she said, her voice low. "This is a real mess. I mean, in our line of work, we're used to some pretty shady dealings, people doing stupid things for lust, for revenge, that sort of thing. But you two, you two really are on another level. The idea that you'd be willing to kill another person, to take a life, no matter how obnoxious or awful that person was. That's absolutely abhorrent. That you wouldn't even take the blame just makes it worse. Whatever you two decide to do with the three of us, I hope it hangs heavy on your consciences forever. Because I know that if I were in your shoes—it would never leave me."

Mal drew his gun up towards Martha. Even Estelle could sense that he was being serious now, that he had the will and the intent. He slowly walked over to her and pressed the barrel against her temple. He smirked at her, like a lion about to devour its prey.

"You know something," he said. "You learn to leave your conscience at the door on day one as a banker. Besides, when you've killed the person dearest to you, everyone else is just collateral. It gets easier and easier as you go along."

Martha closed her eyes and waited for the bang. But Geri's voice got in there first.

"Did you get that Pope?" she shouted.

"Loud and clear," came the voice of the policewoman. "Put down your weapon, sir."

Mal spun around quickly. Geri stood by the door, her phone held up in front of her. On the screen was DS Pope, smiling in her sickly, lopsided way.

"That's as good a confession as I've heard in a long while," she said. "Just as well I've recorded it so I can watch it over and over again."

"Geri," Martha exclaimed. "You didn't?"

"I certainly did," beamed the youngest Parker sister. "See? I'm not just a pretty face. Although I am that too. Looks like you did fall for it, after all, eh Mal?"

"Go get him boys," Pope called.

Blue lights suddenly filled the salon. Footsteps came thundering from outside as Geri pulled the door open.

"You little bitch," Mal screamed.

As the armed police came bounding into the tiny salon, the banker rounded. He opened fire, trying to shoot Geri. Martha was quicker to react and kicked him in the shin with her good leg, taking the weight on her broken one. She immediately collapsed in a heap, riddled with pain, as the police surrounded Mal.

For a brief second the whole salon was lit up with muzzle flashes. Three heavy thuds sent Mal reeling backwards—not fatal shots, but enough to disarm him. The armed cops swooped on him as one called for a medic. Martha crawled away as the mayhem ensued.

Geri hurried over to her and they cowered beside Helen. The three Parker sisters watched as the police got their man. And the case was closed.

Thirty-One

"WELL, IT'S BROKEN alright," said the doctor, who was far too chirpy for this time of night. "Looks like you're going to be in a cast for a couple of weeks Mrs Parker."

"It's Ms Parker," said Martha. "Parker is my maiden... oh forget it."

The medic laughed a little, although he didn't really know what he was laughing at. He clicked his pen closed and smiled.

"You might want to ask Santa to bring you a scratching rod of some description. Casts can get pretty itchy, especially around the back of your knee and the top of your foot. You'll want to get something that can get a good clawing action, really get in there."

"Thank you doctor, that's... reassuring to know."

"Just part of the service," he saluted. "I'll get the nurse to come get you prepped and I'll leave a prescription for some super, duper painkillers you can pick up when you get out of here. Although judging by what's happening outside, what with all the police in here, that might be some time yet. I've never seen it so busy, it's like Call of Duty in here."

"Line of Duty," said Martha.

"Excuse me?"

"Line of Duty is the TV show with the police officers. You said Call of Duty."

The doctor's wide smile stretched even further across his face as he realised his mistake. Then he started to howl with laughter, head lolling back. Martha guessed he'd either not had enough sleep or he was slightly bonkers. He pointed his pen at her as he went to leave the cubicle.

"I'll need to keep my eye on you Mrs Parker, you're a sharp one," he said, drawing the curtain behind him.

More than can be said for you, Martha thought. Sitting alone, she realised that it was the first time she had been on her own in ages. Things had certainly taken a strange turn on this case. They were so used to sneaking after cheating partners, but this had become altogether more frightening.

What had started out as little more than a hobby, had become a safe enough business, and had now turned into something much more serious. She had a husband and two grown up kids to think of after all. She couldn't really be running around being shot at all the time? Let alone putting her sisters in the kind of danger she had.

It troubled Martha as she sat alone in her cubicle. The answer was, obviously, to close up the business. Treat this as a one-off, a lucky escape, and try to move on. Yes. That was it. That's what she'd do.

But then she thought about the consequences for Tracey. What would have happened if Parker Investigations *hadn't* interfered? An innocent woman would probably have been jailed for life—all over a crime she didn't commit. Tracey Coulthard was an enormous pain in the backside and she'd made Martha's life pretty miserable. But she was innocent regardless. Justice had at least been served this way.

"He's a barrel of laughs isn't he?"

Pope slithered her way into the cubicle, nodding back at the doctor. Martha wasn't exactly happy to see her, but her attitude towards Pope had softened somewhat since she'd come to their rescue at the salon.

She stood at the end of the bed and started looking through the charts. Martha had to clear her throat to distract her.

"You know those are confidential," she said.

"Yeah," said Pope. "I guess I'm a bit of a Nosey Parker, too."

She let out a nasally, whiney laugh, which turned into a snort. "Get it?" she chortled, returning the notes to the hook.

Martha rolled her eyes. It wasn't the first time she'd heard that, and it wouldn't be the last. Leaning on the end of the bed, Pope clicked her tongue.

"Martha, Martha, Martha, what are we going to do with you?"

"I don't expect you to do anything with me Detective Sergeant," said Martha. "I'm just another innocent civilian, unworthy of your attentions."

The policewoman smiled. She was like a reptile at the end of Martha's bed—a lizard trussed up in a cheap suit and bad haircut.

"I don't know whether I should thank you or caution you, Martha," she said. "I don't think I've ever come across a member of the public who's been able to draw the very best and worst out of me the way you do. And that is really saying something. Believe me."

"Should I feel honoured? Somehow, it doesn't feel like a compliment."

"I wouldn't go so far as to call it a compliment," Pope said, rounding the bed and pulling up a seat. "But, thanks to you and your sisters, I've got a man sitting in the cells just now awaiting conviction for killing his best friend. And some dopey bimbo in for accessory to murder. So my bosses are pretty pleased with me. In one fell swoop you've managed to exonerate Tracey Parker, remove any blame from her doorstep, not to mention yourself—and hand me the real killer on a plate. I'm almost impressed."

There was what Martha could only describe as a warmth from Pope. It seemed to bring her out of her shell a little, make her a bit more human.

"The official line, however, is that you and your sisters were completely out of line," she added. "That the police force can't have vigilantes going around causing the kinds of trouble you lot did."

"Ah. There it is," Martha laughed. "You know for a moment there I actually thought you'd come to say thanks. But no, the DS Pope I've grown to mistrust these past few days is back."

"Cute," Pope said. "I just thought I should tell you face-to-face, save you having to come down the station."

She moved to get up. Martha stopped her.

"You mean that's it?" she asked. "You don't need anything else from me? I'm free to go?"

"You were *always* free to go Martha. I knew you didn't kill Gordon Coulthard. But I wasn't so sure about his missus," said the DS. "She looks to me like she'd be perfectly capable of beating someone round the head with a hammer. Or a designer handbag, whatever that lot prefer."

Martha couldn't argue with her. Instead she simply nodded. Pope wrinkled her nose as she headed for the curtain.

"You'll need to give statements of course, you and your sisters, but I'm sure one of the bobbies here can handle even that simple task," she said. "When that's done, I'll make sure you've got nothing else to answer for."

"Thank you Pope... I mean... I don't think I ever learned your first name?" said Martha.

"No, you didn't," said the cop with a smile.

"Does it get easier?" Martha asked, stopping her short.

"Does what get easier?"

"This, the whole crime and criminals, villains and killers. Does it get easier with time, the more that you see I mean? Mal Edwards and Estelle. I just… I just couldn't understand how callous and cold they could be. It was his best friend and they killed him for money. Even when I asked them why, they didn't seem to care. It was like… like they were completely detached."

Pope shrugged her shoulders. She tilted her head to one side and pursed her lips.

"I don't know," she said. "I've been doing this job for what feels like forever. I guess there comes a point where you just see the bad guy, not what they've done. Like I said though, you caught him, you caught both of them. And you only ended up with a broken tibia. That's not bad going Martha. Not bad going at all. Try to make sure that's *all* the damage that you get from this. Understand?"

She tapped her temple three times then took her leave. Martha didn't get the chance to thank her. She was back amongst her own company as Pope's words settled in her mind. The scale of what she and the others had done would take a while to sink in. But that was good advice from the policewoman. She had to make sure she wasn't scarred for life by what had happened. She had to stay strong.

"Being shot at is worse than being kidnapped."

"Eh, no, I don't think so."

Geri and Helen argued their way into Martha's cubicle. Their bickering voices were more comforting to her than she would have thought possible. And she smiled as they parked themselves on either side of her bed.

"Martha, settle the bet here," said Geri. "Tell Sherlock Holmes over there that being shot at by a maniac with a gun is a *lot* worse than being kidnapped."

"You can't ask it like that—that's a leading question," Helen darted back. "You have to put the two options to the witness with as much neutrality as possible. So they can make up their own minds."

"Whatever," Geri smirked. "How are you feeling, Mart? You going to have to give up on your hopes of being a professional footballer?"

Martha looked down at her leg. It looked odd, all bruised and fastened up in a makeshift splint.

"I'm afraid so, Geri," she sighed. "I'll just have to think of something else less dangerous to do. Like running a private detective agency."

They all laughed at that. Martha felt like a valve had been turned, that the tension and worry that had plagued them throughout the whole case had been released. In that small, singular moment, the sisters had been released of their duty.

"How are you both feeling?" she asked them.

"Can't complain," said Geri shrugging. "I won't be going to get my hair done professionally for a little while though. I've heard of PTSD from war zones but beauty salons is a new one on me."

"What about you?" Martha asked Helen.

She shrugged. She started to play with a particularly long curl that had dropped past her shoulder. Martha's heart ached as she stared at her sister. She went to touch her hand but Helen took it first.

"Geri told me about what you said," Helen started. "That you said it was your fault that Mal kidnapped me in his flash motor."

"Helen I—"

"No, shut up, just for a second Martha," she grinned. "Geri told me that you were blaming yourself for putting me in such a dangerous position, that you shouldn't have let me go into that penthouse on my own. Well, quite frankly, that's a load of rubbish."

Martha could feel the tears starting to sting behind her nose. She held on to Helen as tightly as her aching muscles would let her.

"I wanted to go in there, it was my idea," said Helen. "I knew the risks, I knew what I was letting myself in for. And whether you like it or not, I'm a grown woman who can make her own decisions and stand on her own two, usually sandal clad, feet. I'm all grown up Martha and I can take responsibility for myself when I have to. That doesn't mean I don't want you or the Sarcasm Kid over there going away anytime soon. But I wanted you to know that I don't blame you, not one bit, for what happened. And that I love you, both of you, very, very much."

She let go of Martha's hand and sat back in the hard, plastic chair beside the bed. Folding her arms neatly across her chest, she sighed.

"Now that's out of my system," she said. "You can tell Geri that being kidnapped is worse."

They all laughed again and enjoyed each other's company. It was Christmas after all.

Thirty-Two

THE SNOW FELL gently from the bruised, unhappy sky. It landed on the old stone sills and edges of the gravestones with a careful, polite silence. The whole place was quiet, tranquil. Everything had been coated in the pure brilliant blanket of the fresh snow the night before. The cemetery looked picturesque, ideal for a macabre Christmas card.

The soft sound of a single voice drifted down from a high hill towards the back of the graveyard. There weren't many people at the service, just close family. Tracey Coulthard stood looking down into the hole where her husband's coffin now lay. She was glad she was wearing sunglasses, Martha noticed, though how much of that was to mask her grief and how much to hide her impassive distance was less clear.

Beside her Gordon's parents were doing their best to keep themselves together. Their only son had been cut down in the prime of his life. All of the wonderful things he had promised them in the future were little more than what ifs? At least now he could be at peace, laid to rest in the same plot as his grandparents. Maybe one day they could find the solace they deserved. Though Martha doubted that very much.

The minister said his final words and bowed his head. The mourners all stood silently for a moment before they started to retreat to their cars. Tracey waited until everyone else was gone before she moved. She had smiled and pretended to be polite for too long. At least now she wouldn't have to keep up the act.

Martha was careful not to fall down the hole and wind up beside Gordon Coulthard's coffin. She angled her crutches and hopped around the grave's edge until she was beside Tracey. She wasn't sure what she should say. Maybe there wasn't a right or wrong answer to that question.

"I don't think I ever thanked you, did I?" said the soon-to-be former Mrs Coulthard.

Martha had to swallow her surprise.

"No, no I don't think you did," she said. "Not that it matters of course. You were a client, we were your employees. It was business, as you liked to remind me."

Tracey nodded in silent agreement. Her complexion was grey, even with her makeup on. She seemed fragile and tiny, a little speck dressed entirely in black.

"You did the right thing," she said. "You did the right thing in confirming my worst fears."

"I hear that a lot," said Martha.

"I knew he was cheating on me. I don't think that was what I wanted to know. I think I wanted the details, the dirty little secrets that he kept hidden from me for all of our relationship, all of our marriage. Is that wrong of me?"

"No," she said. "No it's not wrong Tracey. Nobody deserves to be lied to. Especially not by a loved one. It's sort of in the rules that you should be truthful and honest with each other, no matter what. And that's supposed to be the easy part. If you love each other then it just comes naturally."

"Does it come naturally for you?"

Martha picked up the slightest tint of jagged bitterness from Tracey. She was careful how she answered her.

"I'm lucky, Tracey," she said slowly. "I've got a husband who I've known most of my life and two grown up kids who can look after themselves. That and my sisters are always there to lend a helping hand when it's needed."

"Ah yes, chaos and calamity," the widow looked over towards Geri and Helen standing by the cars. "What you're saying is you have a support network, people you can trust."

"Yeah, I suppose so, if you want to put it like that. The people I trust are the most important ones to me. I don't think it's a coincidence that's the case."

The engines of the cars started up. They sounded odd amongst the serenity of the graveyard. Martha was about to go when Tracey took her by the arm.

"Will you walk with me to the main entrance, Parker?" she said.

"Okay," said Martha.

They started down the winding path that led from the graveside. The cars all pulled past them, slowly making their way out of the cemetery as the gravediggers began filling in the hole. Tracey stopped and looked back at her husband's final resting place.

"I'll never come back here," she said, her mouth curled into a frown. "That bastard has had his fair share of me over the years. He can rot in the ground for eternity now. Let the worms have him."

They started off again. Martha wasn't sure why she had been chosen to comfort Tracey. Of all the people in the world, it didn't seem right. Yet here they were.

"You've been through a lot," she said. "Maybe you should take some time to let everything settle before you make any big decisions."

"I've had my whole adult life to let things settle. If I wait any longer I'll be in the ground beside him."

"If you like Tracey, I'm only trying to help. In the past few weeks you've found out your husband was cheating on you, fought with his mistress, been told he had proposed to her, found him dead, been accused of his murder and then completely cleared of everything, and then found out that his best friend and his fiancée had actually plotted the whole thing to stop you getting his estate. I don't think I'd be in a position to make any big life choices if I were in your shoes."

"You would never be in my shoes," Tracey sneered. "These cost two thousand pounds."

She flashed the red sole of her stilettos. Martha chuckled.

"Even at half the price, you're right. And I'm only wearing one," she said, wriggling her foot in her cast. "That's how far from your league I am, Tracey."

The joke drew a grunt of approval from the widow.

"Have you thought about what you will do now?" Martha asked. "I mean, are you staying in that big house all on your own?"

"I'm not alone. I have May," she answered curtly. "But no, actually, I haven't thought about it. I've been putting it off. It all seems like far too much hard work at the moment. If I stay there, everyone expects me to be the grieving, but wronged, wife, Parker. It wouldn't sit well in the tabloids if I showed anything like any actual human emotion or fortitude. We all have characters to play."

"Are the press still bothering you?"

"Bothering *with* me, yes," said Tracey, sucking cold air through her veneers. "It's all about profile, isn't it? I was at the centre of a big story. I pleaded my case to the wider media on the steps of a police station. These blood suckers won't let me disappear off into the night that easily. But it suits me I suppose. I'm getting offers from talent agents and TV shows trying to tell my side of the story. They're offering a fortune of course. But it's only money. That's what they say, isn't it, Parker? It's only money."

"I suppose so."

Martha surprised herself. She thought that Tracey's utter contempt for anyone with a pound less than her would have been making her angry. Perhaps she had grown used to it by now. Or maybe she believed that it was all an act from the young woman who had clearly been damaged by this whole affair.

They walked on through the cemetery, following the gravel paths that weaved their way across the fields like the veins of a giant body. A tall, moss covered archway led to the main road that ran alongside the graveyard. Cars sped by, seemingly unaware of that supposed resting place just a stone's throw over the wall.

Two cars were parked up close to the arch. Helen and Geri sat arguing in one of them, the windows misted up from their heated breaths. The other was a long, sleek sports motor that looked far too expensive to ever be sat in a cemetery.

A man got out of the driver's seat when he saw them approach. He was dark skinned and wore sunglasses similar to Tracey's. He was tall and muscular, a stony face pasted across his head perched on top of his square shoulders.

"My new bodyguard, Fredrico," she said. "He protects me, among other things."

"Ah, I see," said Martha, keeping her thoughts to herself.

"Much like my late husband, Parker, I doubt I shall ever see you again."

"Oh I don't know. It's a pretty small world and getting smaller by the minute."

"Yes, if you like," said the widow. "I can't say that I was disappointed in your work. The three of you are actually very good at what you do. I mean, you caught a murderer after all. That's not something that I imagine the average idiot could do. Maybe it's something you should all consider for the future."

She flounced away on her expensive heels, swanning over to the car. Fredrico opened the back door for her and she paused before getting in. Tipping her sunglasses forward, she looked back across at Martha with her cold, steely gaze.

"Oh, by the way. I was being interviewed by one of the big TV news shows, you know, a pre-record, one that they'll put out when everyone's watching."

"Sounds nice," said Martha. "Good work if you can find it."

"It wasn't nice, the reporter was a skank. Anyway, they asked about how I found out Gordon was cheating. So I told them all about you and Tweedledum and Tweedledee. I *insisted* that your good work reached the national audience. I said I wouldn't agree to it going out unless you were all kept in it. All the credit, your sleuthing skills, everything. I was adamant."

"But... why Tracey?" asked Martha, not quite sure what was happening.

"Because I'd hate to see you go out of business, Parker. You're good at your job. And besides, there are countless other lying cheats out there that deserve to be caught by you three. Ciao."

With that she climbed into the luxury car and was whisked off in a roar of horsepower and burning rubber. Martha stood dumbfounded for a moment. Only when Helen and Geri called over to her from the car did she crank back into action.

"You alright Mart?" asked Geri.

"Yeah, I think so," she said, hopping over to her sisters. "It's just Tracey Coulthard, you know what she's like."

"Don't we just," said Helen.

"All too bloody well," said Geri.

"Yeah. She was acting kind of strange there."

"Well she has just buried her husband," said Helen, philosophising.

"But she thanked me, thanked *us* even for doing a good job."

"Bloody hell," said Geri. "She must be in shock if she's actually bothering to offer anything other than abuse."

"There was something else."

Helen and Geri looked at each other. Then they turned to Martha.

"What something else?" asked Geri.

"I don't like the sound of that," said Helen.

Martha had to try and recompose herself. When she drew her breath, she smiled.

"Ladies… I have a feeling we're about to get a whole lot busier."

ACKNOWLEDGEMENTS

As is normally the case with acknowledgements, it's impossible to thank everyone who has contributed and helped to the writing of this book and its characters. If I had my way there would be a whole VOLUME dedicated to the support, warmth and general good feeling that I always seem to get with my writing. But that's not going to happen, no matter how much I wish upon a star.

To that end I would like to highlight the following people, without whom you would not be enjoying the adventures of three plucky sisters who get into all kinds of scrapes and shenanigans.

The first is my publisher Red Dog Press – specifically Sean Coleman. From our very first exchange, he has been nothing short of phenomenal when it comes to supporting my writing and my vision. I couldn't ask for a more generous and genuinely lovely person to help share my dream of being a writer with. He, along with the whole Red Dog kennel have truly welcomed me to their unique, disgustingly talented fold. And I've been made to feel very much at home from the off.

Another special thanks to Red Dog's Meggy Roussel. Morning, noon or night she's always there to answer my questions, knock on journalists' doors and generally champion my work whenever and wherever it's needed.

I'd also like to thank my mother-in-law. No, this isn't the start of some 1970s bad joke. Margaret has been a vehement supporter of my writing from year zero. She also sparked the idea that would eventually become Banking on Murder. Without her, none of this might have ever been possible. So I'll be reminded that I owe her one until the end of time.

And finally, before I get something in my eye, I'd like to thank the wonderful writing and publishing community. Writing is often described as a very lonely business, but I've found since I became an author that there's a vibrant, funny, generous and loving community out there who are always willing to help with anything. To call myself a writer is one of the proudest achievements of my life – it is an honour to do so. But I can't and don't do it alone. So this is as huge a thank you as can be imagined.

— JDW

Made in United States
North Haven, CT
23 October 2022

25827343R00178